Gary Crew has been published internationally since 1986, gathering many national and international writing awards. Dr Crew is Associate Professor (Creative Writing) at the University of the Sunshine Coast, Queensland. He lives on a property overlooking Lake Baroon in the Sunshine Coast Hinterland township of Maleny. He freely admits to an obsession with Jack Russell Terriers. His first novel for adults was *The Children's Writer* (2009).

THE ARCHITECTURE OF SONG

GARY CREW

Fourth Estate
An imprint of HarperCollins*Publishers*
First published in Australia in 2012
by HarperCollins*Publishers* Australia Pty Limited
ABN 36 009 913 517
harpercollins.com.au

HarperCollins*Publishers*
Level 13, 201 Elizabeth Street, Sydney NSW 2000, Australia
31 View Road, Glenfield, Auckland 0627, New Zealand
A 53, Sector 57, Noida, UP, India
77–85 Fulham Palace Road, London, W6 8JB, United Kingdom
2 Bloor Street East, 20th floor, Toronto, Ontario M4W 1A8, Canada
10 East 53rd Street, New York NY 10022, USA

National Library of Australia Cataloguing-in-Publication data:

ISBN 978 0 7322 8587 6

Cover design by Jane Waterhouse, HarperCollins Design Studio
Cover images: A marquetry and parquetry-inlaid upright piano, 1881 (ormolu-
mounted mahogany, satinwood & fruitwood) by French School (19th century).
Private collection / Photo © Christie's Images / The Bridgeman Art Library.
All other images by shutterstock.com
Typeset in 12/17pt Historical Felltype by Kirby Jones

In memory of an upright piano, a mother,
and a boy who sang.

Contents

THE PIANO — 1

THE TENT — 5

THE HOUSE — 69

THE LIBRARY — 131

THE TEMPLE — 175

THE NECROPOLIS — 227

THE SANDSTONE SPRING — 257

THE PIANO

O N THE EVENING OF his twenty-first birthday Rosa hoisted Augustus onto a stool beside the piano so that he might be seen to better advantage while he sang. Being just thirty-seven inches tall, as he was swept upwards he caught a glance — somewhat askew, since he was so unceremoniously whooshed — of that liminal space between the keyboard and the floor. This space had formed the architecture of his childhood: the underside of the keyboard his ceiling, the piano-legs pillars, the whole a shadowy vault where he might crouch unseen in the boom of the strings, observing the miracle of his mother's feet as she crushed the papery soles of her black velvet slippers against the pedals.

But like all childhood architecture, that space had been lost. And though Augustus mourned, wondering what might have been, his mother did not mourn at all. Not since the day when Mrs Trump, having learnt from her physician that her son was a dwarf ('A midget?' she gagged, incredulous, into her hankie. 'A damned midget?'), handed him over to the circus passing through town. Which allowed her to return to her piano, striking the ivories with even greater *appassionato*, as her new-found freedom allowed.

THE TENT

AUGUSTUS NOW ENTERED ANOTHER space, striped with tigerish light, scented with the potpourri of elephant dung and sawdust, beneath the slatted benches of the big top. Here it was that, upon hearing his peculiar song, Rosa first discovered him squatting on his grubby heels warbling like a nightingale. Being wise to the opportunity of freaks, the girl stooped to haul him out.

'Ooo-er,' she gasped, goggle-eyed. 'What are you?'

'I am not a *What*,' he declared (being a precocious talker), 'I am a *He*. And I can sing.'

'Really?' Rosa snickered. 'So can the fat lady when she's on the sherry.'

Dumbfounded, Augustus shut his mouth. In that moment Rosa reached down, gripped his elbows and hoisted him onto the bench that he had been lurking under (thus establishing a lifetime precedent) to take a really good look.

'Ooo-er!' she declared, seeing him in his entirety.

The creature before her was a sideshow in himself, guaranteed to draw a crowd whether he could sing, dance or walk the wire.

'You're a queer one, you are. Look at your arms! Look at

your legs! They're like straws. Like drinking straws sticking out of a pumpkin.'

Augustus looked down at himself, wondering. 'What?' he said. 'I've had these arms and legs nearly five years and they haven't broken off yet. And you can't blame me for this romper suit. The pants might look like pumpkins, being orange and round and puffy, but that's what I was wearing when she handed me over. And the moustache lady hasn't changed me.'

'Ooo-er,' Rosa said, spinning him about. 'How old are you?'

'I already told you. I am four, going on five. How old are *you*?'

'Thirteen,' Rosa grunted and spun him around again, suddenly conscious of the size of his waist, how her fingertips touched, encircling him. 'All right,' she said, 'so who gave you to Moira?'

'Eh?'

'Moira. The bearded lady. The moustache lady. Who gave you to her? And why?'

'My mother,' he said, bold and clear. 'She teaches the *pianoforte*. She says my voice is liquid silver. My pitch is perfect. She says only Melba could compete.'

What is this thing? Rosa wondered. Having lived all her life beneath the big top and seen so much that was freakish and queer, she could not comprehend what stood before her: dressed as he was in pumpkin pants, a sweet little blouse and those tiny black shoes (were they off a doll?), with limbs as frail as straws. He was, nevertheless, perfectly proportioned, unlike the other little people she knew: Big Atlas in the red and black wagon had a head the size of a melon and a body the size of a toad. No. This little thing was a proper mannikin: his face pleasant (even pretty); his eyes pale grey (the colour of the trapeze artiste's silky pants); his yellow hair slicked back (with Hairy Moira's spit?); his ears flat; his little teeth white and even; his mouth a rosebud.

'*Nellie* Melba?' she demanded. 'That's stupid.'

'Why?' he asked, caring little. And he dreamily turned his eyes up to take in the enormity of the marquee, that mighty pyramid of space yawning above him. No longer the dim, secret ceiling of the piano keyboard, but an architecture of light.

'Because I seen her,' Rosa informed him. 'And I heard her too. She came here to sing for a war rally.'

'A *war* rally?'

'There *has* been a war, you know.'

Augustus did not know, being ignorant of the ways of the world.

'She stood out there,' Rosa said, indicating the vast expanse of centre ring, 'in her black dress with her big bosoms and her guts pulled in with a corset. Whalebone, Moira reckoned. Pearls, she was wearing, wrapped round her neck but hanging down her back, not over her front. Down her back and over her big bum ...' and the girl turned and stuck out her own backside to demonstrate.

So Augustus gave his attention to her. Not because, at four years, he had any particular interest in a girl's anatomy, but because in his own childish way he had already judged her bum to be pretty big (especially in that uncharitably shrunken red dress), and because her bulk (which was considerable, particularly her mass of frizzed, carroty hair) blocked his view of the sawdusty shaft of sunlight striking down from the hole where a pole pierced the canvas. And since his view was interrupted, he thought he might as well sing to prove his point.

'So what did she sing?' he asked.

'Some silly muck,' the girl sneered. 'Home Sweet Bloody Home, or something.'

'Hmm,' he sighed. 'Then I will show you what she might have sung…'

Throwing back his pretty throat and casting his eyes towards that hole in the air, he opened his mouth, again revealing his perfect little teeth, to sing Puccini:

One fine day you'll find me,
A thread of smoke arising on the sea
In the far horizon
And then the ship appearing,
Then the trim white vessel glides into the harbour …

As a circus girl with no knowledge of opera, Rosa slammed a freckled hand over his mouth.

He gasped, spitting. 'What? You can't say that was no good.'

'Yeah, yeah,' she grunted, stamping her tired boots. 'Yeah, yeah. You can sing. Not as good as that Melba, but. She could out-roar the lions. The elephants even. But yeah, you can sing. Only, you never answered one question that I asked.'

'What? I sang…'

'Why your mother gave you away.'

Now while Augustus could sing like Melba, he was hardly more than an infant, so this question hurt. She of the pianoforte and the velvet slippers was still, after all, his mother. And the thought came to him that he missed her. 'I don't know,' he snivelled, wiping his eyes with the back of his hand. 'I sang as best I could. I tried to make her happy. I really did.'

'There, there,' Rosa cooed, kneeling before him to play the mother herself. 'There, there. She might have needed to go shopping.'

'For two days?' the boy wailed. 'She left me with that Moira two days ago and I haven't seen her since.'

'Did she now?' Rosa mused. 'And where would a piano teacher meet Hairy Moira, pray tell?'

'At the hotel.'

'The hotel?'

'The pub,' he blushed. 'The Fortitude Valley pub. Round the back. Where she picks up her gin.'

'No!' Rosa gasped. 'And her teaching the piano.'

'"Gin's my poison", I heard her tell Mrs Hardwick.'

Envisaging the said Mrs Hardwick wearing elbow-length gloves, a black cloche hat and rouged to the eyeballs, Rosa declined to bite. 'And Hairy Moira was there?' she asked. 'Round the back of the pub?'

'Yes. With another person. I don't know if it was a man or a woman because he — or she — was hairy too. Wearing pants and a woolly jumper and a beret.'

'Ah ...' Rosa nodded. 'That would be French Betty. She's Moira's special friend. Betty's not one of us, you know. Not a sideshow person. She lives in the real world, like. She's working as a storeman, you know.'

'So French Betty is a man?'

'Oh no. Though she might as well be,' and Rosa gave Augustus a sly wink, which meant nought to him. 'The word storeman has nothing to do with what you might call her *sex*. At the moment she's stacking crates of grog, but she sometimes does other stuff.'

'Um,' he said, 'well, they were talking to me, Moira and French Betty, while my mother was collecting her order. Moira was making me laugh, curling her moustache, and that Betty, she was egging her on, laughing too. When Mother was done and came out with a man loaded up with her stuff, she said, "Oh, so you have made some friends?" And when I said that I had, they started talking so I wandered off. I know that money changed hands because I saw my mother digging into her purse and then she called me over and said that these nice people would take me to the circus. I thought that sounded pretty good so I climbed into this handcart Moira had and she pushed me through the Valley, talking and laughing all the time, until we said goodbye to Betty at another pub and we came to this park where I saw the circus and she took me to her wagon and made me a sandwich. She was very polite, and ... Oh!' he declared, 'speaking of manners, I do beg your pardon. What is your name?'

'Rosa Colleano,' she said. 'I am the sister of the Tumbling Colleanos, who are acrobats. What's yours?'

'Augustus Trump,' he said, smudging his cheeks, now grubby with tears. 'And do you do acrobat things like cartwheels and handstands?'

'No,' she said, turning away a trifle wistfully, though this may have been no more than pretence intended to endear. 'I have the wrong body.'

'Really?' he said.

How dumb was this kid? Any dick could see that she was as fat as a pig. She looked him up and down, as if for the first time. 'Hmm,' she said, wondering.

He looked out over centre ring, ignorant of her attention.

'So, would you like to be an acrobat?' she asked for the sole purpose of keeping him talking.

'Oh no,' he giggled. 'If I did that, I would probably not have the energy to sing. Can you sing, Rosa?'

Rosa boasted very few skills regarded as being valuable to young ladies of the day. She could read, thanks to the perseverance of Hairy Moira (who had once been a rosary away from taking the veil), but she could neither sew, draw, dance nor sing. And at this particular moment, nor could she imagine what she was good for, other than making plans for this little beauty. This little blond treasure who had sung his way into her life.

So she said, 'No, Augustus, I can't sing. Although I could find ways for you to sing for a crowd. I could do that. But first, tell me, why *did* your mother give you to Moira? I am busting to know. Goodness, if you were mine, I would love you forever ...' And she clasped her hands behind her back to stop herself hugging him to death.

Although the young Augustus never did articulate why his mother had given him away or sold him (did she?), Rosa nevertheless began the long and intricate machinations of how she might bring this protégé (as she very quickly considered the boy to be), to the eyes and ears of the world.

First she consulted Moira, since she was the person to whom the child had been given. 'Moira,' Rosa said as she loitered outside the hirsute one's wagon. 'Moira, what do you know about that child's mother?' And she slipped a meaningful glance in Augustus's direction.

'Hmmm ...' Moira began, inspecting what might have been a rip in her checked flannel shirt. 'I dunno.'

'Moira ...' Rosa warned, 'you and French Betty talked to her. And, I am told, you took money from her. So tell me what you know, or else ...'

Moira was a lumberjack of a woman. Although her beard was Elizabethan (not unlike Sir Walter Raleigh's) and rather debonair, she was disconcertingly pleased to display the shaggy mass of matted fur that sprouted from the open neck of her shirt. For all of Moira's swagger, it was an issue of consequence to be threatened by Rosa Colleano. Even among hardened circus folk — Hairy Moira included — the red-headed Colleano kid was feared. So if Rosa said, 'Or else ...' one should be afraid, as was the case when the India Rubber Man mocked Rosa's ample backside, or Skinny Eddie laughed at her crazy hair, or the corpse of that chimp (poor Hogarth) was discovered nestled in Zena the Ape Woman's bustier when she declined Rosa's demands for a bite of that marshmallow rabbit the previous Easter.

So Moira took a furtive look to see if the midget was occupied — he was, examining the wheels of her wagon — then she hummed and hawed for a minute before muttering, 'Ten quid, she give us. To mind him for a week.'

'Ten quid!' Rosa spat. 'She gave you ten quid?'

Moira twitched one hairy lip, indicating that the girl should move away from the wagon, out of earshot. 'He could hardly eat ten quid's worth of anything,' she hissed. 'Not in six months. Look at him. He's a weed. He's likely to be dead in a day or two. And if he ain't, Betty and me will leave him behind the Valley pub where we got him. She'll be back for more booze, that mother of his, I guarantee. She's a *real* drinker, she is. Should see what she hauled away that day. Cartons full. Fill a keg, I reckon ...'

'What about his clothes?' Rosa wanted to know — not because she cared, but because she wanted to be seen to care. To be thought responsible. From the beginning. From the very outset. So at some future time, if she were asked, in a court maybe, or even casual conversation, she could remind people that Augustus was hers and always had been. 'He can't wear that lot much longer. Horrible, they are. Grubby. And I got nothing that would fit him. Poor kid.' And putting on what she thought was a caring face, she sniffed loudly, to make an impression.

Seeing this tête-à-tête, and having the wit to figure that it was about him, Augustus sidled over. 'What?' he said.

'We were saying,' Moira hastened to explain, 'that you'll need a change of clothes.'

'Why would I need a change of clothes?' he wanted to know. 'I will be home soon, won't I?'

Moira looked to Rosa, who had always been quick. 'And where is home exactly?' the girl asked.

'The big white house,' Augustus answered off pat.

'Hmm ...' the girl replied. 'And you could take us there?'

Augustus blanched.

'I mean,' she persisted, 'to that address?'

'No,' he admitted, the tears welling.

Glances were exchanged.

'Most likely your mother will come here,' Rosa suggested to cover his ignorance. 'In the meantime, I'll flog a singlet from my brothers and get you some clean pants from Little Donny. He's bigger than you — taller and fatter round the middle — but I've got some belts in my wagon. Come on ...'

'And you think my mum will come?' Augustus called.

'Course she will. She knows you're at the circus, doesn't she? If not today, then tomorrow. She can't go letting you have too much of a good time, eh?'

Convinced of her authority, Augustus toddled after her.

Little Donny was a dwarf who would evolve (under the Darwinian influence of Disney) into Grumpy, of the Snow White species, although in his present incarnation he was no more than a depressed and sadly sentimental little man. With a preference for bright clothes (particularly his scarlet coats), Donny wore a drooping bow in his long grey beard, the colour changing daily. Being stout and in his sixties, he walked with the rolling gait of an aged sailor, the silver buckles on his ancient black boots always aglitter. He lived in a squat tent of his own design featuring a different striped canvas on each of its four sides: one being red and white, one yellow and white, one green and white, one blue and white. The roof was a panoply of faded cobalt, the underside covered in stars of red and yellow fabric so clumsily stitched that some dangled and hung as if about to drop, rather than fall, as any self-respecting and romantic star might expect as its end. Sometimes, if he was sad, Donny would look up at these peeling constellations thinking, *Like yourselves, my star has faded too,* and give himself over to weeping and stroking the silky ears of his two Great Danes, Bonzer (who was tan) and Bozo (who was black), until he fell asleep wrapped in the comforting paws of his canine companions.

Although Rosa was not known for her compassion, she did have a soft spot for Donny, possibly because she had not yet achieved fulfilment herself. And since she was eager to introduce the bearded dwarf to Augustus (both being of a kind), she stooped to lift the flap of his tent, allowing the boy to peer inside. There Bonzer and Bozo squatted with Donny sitting cross-legged on a cushion between them, sucking on a hookah. He had long been attracted to the possibility that his current ignominious body was not permanent, as evidenced by the fantastical metamorphosis of the caterpillar in Wonderland.

'Ah,' he sighed, when Rosa entered. 'You have come to cheer me up.'

'Not really,' she said, shoving Augustus in ahead of her. 'I've come to introduce you to a new friend of mine.'

Donny spotted the aberration standing before him and sat up, alert. 'What is this? A new attraction?'

'This is Augustus Trump,' Rosa announced, all smiles and falsehood. 'He has come to visit. His mother was kind enough to loan him to Moira and French Betty who she met at a pub — although that pair being what they are, he will be my responsibility.' (She added the latter with a degree of martyred pride.) 'But he's come without any spare clothes and I can't let him get around in these, can I?'

'He's not getting one of my coats,' the dwarf protested. 'They cost a fortune.'

'No, no.' Rosa feigned a laugh, barely hiding her disappointment. She would have loved to dress her treasure in one of those red coats, the better to bring out the roses in his cheeks, but dared not suggest. 'I can find him a singlet, but it's trousers he wants, to get him out of these awful baby things.'

'Ah, now I see,' Donny grunted, staring. 'He's one of us.'

'Eh?' Augustus piped.

'You're a ...' Here Donny stumbled. Despising his own puny physique as he did, he was loath to tell another that he suffered the same misfortune, especially when that other might not have arrived at that understanding for himself. 'You're ...' he looked to Rosa for inspiration. 'You're outstanding!', the statement concluded with an emphatic nod.

'Yes,' Augustus agreed, and added disconcertingly, 'but how did you know that I could sing?'

Silence hung in the air until Rosa suggested with a wink, 'Perhaps you heard Augustus singing in the big top, just half an hour ago? Isn't that right, Donny?'

'Indeed,' the confused Donny lied. 'Indeed ...'

Augustus beamed. 'I will sing for you now if you want. That is what I do. Fill a space with my voice.'

'Is he any good?' the dwarf whispered aside.

'He is better than good,' Rosa said. 'Together, we will be great.'

Little Donny flinched, catching the hint of threat in Rosa's tone. But he persisted, out of pity. 'And what would you sing?' he asked, expectantly setting his hookah aside.

'Whatever you like,' came the reply.

'I am not one for fanfare,' Donny admitted, nestling into his pillow. 'Sing me something soothing. Something to make me happy. Here, Rosa, lean against Bonzer. He makes an excellent armchair.'

The girl did as she was asked and, seeing his audience settled, Augustus stepped forward. He spread his tiny legs, planted his tiny feet, and throwing back his pretty head, fixed his soft eyes on that canopy of cobalt above. This was not done to pose or to posture. As he had said, it was done with the desire to fill the space with his voice, the innocent spirit of himself, since he understood nothing else. And so he sang, the eerie blue light falling pale on his upturned face:

I dreamt I dwelt in marble halls
With vassals and serfs at my side,
And of all those assembled within in those walls,
That I was their hope and pride.

But I also dreamt which charmed me most
That you loved me still the same,
That you loved me still the same,
That you loved me, you loved me, still the same.

'That was my mother's song,' Little Donny wept. 'How could he know that?'

Rosa shrugged, saying nothing.

Hairy Moira's wagon was much nicer than Rosa's; more like one a gypsy would live in: yellow and blue with a red roof and green shutters and golden scrolls and finials and a pair of white wooden doves (their beaks touching in a kiss), above the indigo door.

Rosa's wagon was little more than a stubby box, weathered and drab and dribbly with bird droppings 'from the time we did a week on the Scarborough Esplanade', as she informed Augustus when he asked.

'The ceiling is lower than Moira's too,' he said, staring up at the fly spots on the pressed metal. Rosa grunted, chucking the pile of clothing scabbed from Little Donny onto her narrow bunk. 'This reminds me of the space beneath my mother's piano,' the boy continued. 'While I like high ceilings to extend my voice — and Moira's ceiling was higher — I actually prefer low ones ... They add a certain resonance.'

'You don't say,' Rosa snarled. 'And how old are you really?'

'I am four years old,' Augustus shot back. 'I will be five in a month. I already told you that. Why do you keep asking me?'

Rosa held up a pair of Donny's discarded trousers and shrugged. 'Because you talk like you're fifty, not five. And what about those songs you sing? They're grown-up songs. Old people's songs. Not little kids' songs. Why's that?'

'Why's what? Why do I talk like I'm fifty or why do I sing grown-up songs?'

'Either. Surprise me.' Her only concern was to get him out of those rompers.

'Well,' he said, inspecting the posters of her acrobatic brothers lining the walls, 'the answer is most likely the same. My mother's house is always filled with adults who sing adult songs — opera mostly, though not always — and talk adult talk. I have no brothers or sisters and rarely meet other children. My mother considers them vulgar and they usually cry when they meet me, which is a pity, I suppose.'

Rosa cared little, and sat, sorting the clothes.

'Nobody takes me to kindergarten,' Augustus rattled on. 'My mother says she has no time and I don't know anything about my father. I don't even know if I have seen him, although I have always hoped that he might be a sea captain. A big, broad man in a white uniform did come a few times. He always stood close behind my mother at the piano, leaning down to kiss her neck, his gold-braided cap tucked under his arm. I hoped that he was my father but nobody said so, though I wanted him to be. I sometimes think that I would like to be him, or even ...' he paused, comparing himself to the images of full-grown men lining the wall, 'or even make myself into him ...'

'You what?' Rosa demanded.

'Nothing,' he giggled.

'Didn't you just say that you could make yourself into him? Eh?'

'I was being silly,' he hedged. 'I was remembering how I learnt the Puccini that I sang for you. My mother sang it for him.'

'Who?'

'Some man in a white uniform. Nobody, really ...' and, eager to change the subject, he said, 'My mother is an outstanding soprano, you know, but never could make a career of it. "Not fit for the stage, she isn't", as somebody once said when she had left the room,' and he brought his hand to his mouth several times, to simulate drinking.

'Is that right?'

'Yes.'

'But she sings for you, eh?'

'Not really. She just sings.'

'But not for you?'

'Hardly ever for me, but I hear. I sit beneath the keyboard.'

'Oh?'

'She doesn't like me to be seen, my mother.'

'Oh?'

'Never has. So that's how I learn, sitting there, unnoticed ...' He gave this statement some thought, finally adding, 'Not that it matters, either way, since that is the space I prefer, being intimate, you understand. Unless I want to project my voice, which I do sometimes, to prove that I can, that I'm alive — for her — as I did for you in the big top. As a result of such experiences — confined or otherwise — I am convinced that it is the nature of the space about me — the architecture, you might say — that obliges me to extend myself. To grow, so to speak.'

'Augustus,' she said, taking his hand, 'your intelligence and personal insight amaze me. And you speak so well — and sing so well, too — but irrespective of how smart you are, and how well you express yourself, or where you perform — the architecture, I mean —you're the size of a doll. Do you understand that?'

'I lived many lives beneath that piano,' he said. 'I heard ten thousand stories in that space. There I was privileged to observe, to gather — and not only gather, to concentrate within myself — so much that is usually denied a child of my age. As a result, I have, you might say, already *grown*.'

He had silenced her, but determined not to lose her advantage, she slipped from the bunk to kneel before him. 'We will never speak of size again,' she whispered, squeezing his tiny hands.

'I would like that,' he said. 'But we will, hopefully, speak of those greater spaces that my voice will fill.'

'We will,' she agreed, eager to convince. 'And how your voice will caress such spaces. Pervade such spaces. *Enhance* such spaces. Now there's a grand word!'

'I might even *create* such spaces,' he suggested, 'if my voice was pure enough ...'

'Yeah sure,' she grunted, and considering him to have lapsed into that grotesque masculine ego so common among her brothers, she got to her feet, declaring, 'but if you're going to get anywhere, the first thing we have to do is get you out of those awful pants. Where the hell did your mother turn them up?'

Finding clothes to fit her diminutive charge consumed Rosa's energies for some time. 'What will I do?' she moaned as she sat having a beer with Moira and Donny. 'They don't make male dolls, so there's no dolls' clothes to fit him.'

'You could always ask Needly Phyllis,' Moira suggested, adding a frothy frieze to her moustache. 'She can make anything.'

'Needly Phyllis? That skinny cow? I've hated her ever since she made that fluffy white tutu my brothers expected me to wear in their act.'

'It's not Needly's fault that you looked like a meringue. You're not exactly Tinker Bell, you know,' Donny assured her. Moira guffawed, slopping her hops.

'Ha bloody ha,' Rosa spat. 'What have you two got to laugh about? You're both freaks.' So saying, she took a generous swig herself.

'Oh!' Moira shrieked. 'Oh! At least we get paid to look queer, *Ginger*!'

Given that the circus was full of odd bods, not a great deal was said about Rosa's fuzzy red hair, although the terms 'Flame Brain' and 'Bushfire' had all had their day until Rosa rigorously stamped them out.

'Listen, love,' Donny soothed, reaching out to pat the girl's ample knee, 'nasty piece of work that she is, with our screwed-up bodies we all need Needly sooner or later. Who do you think makes those red coats that I like? Trouble is, she charges like a wounded bull.'

Little Donny spoke the truth. Needly Phyllis was the official costume-maker for the circus — who else but a crazy would want the job? — and knowing she had the weird rag trade sewn up, she exploited her clients to the hilt. So thin that she cast no shadow, Needly was aptly named for her scrawny physique, the particularity of her stitchcraft and her sharp tongue. She would never be invited over for a pot, although word had it that she enjoyed a drop of claret on the sly. Very dry.

'You know ...' Moira said, taking another swig on the gravity of the information she was about to share, 'you know, even after Stan Platten's chimp Hogarth got done in,' (Rosa attempted a sympathetic face) 'that Needly dame still sent Stan the bill for the little darlin's new show outfit. And Hogie never even got to wear it. How awful is that?'

'Top hat and tails, it was,' Donny confirmed. 'In black satin. Stan paid up too. Nice bloke, that Stan.'

'Shame about Hogie, eh?' Rosa purred, rolling the empty schooner between her palms. 'What happened to the outfit?'

'Dunno,' Moira shrugged. 'You'd have to ask Needly. Or Stan.'

Funny thing, Rosa thought, wandering off. I knock off the ape, and it leaves me a legacy.

Having worked at the circus for twenty years, Stan Platten was a sort of permanent roustabout, insofar as anything about the place was permanent. In his mid-thirties, of average height, Stan wore khaki overalls, parted his straight, brown hair on the left and used a drop of brilliantine to slick it down. His face was lean, his smile open, his false teeth glaringly evident. He did not drink or smoke or spit.

A jack of all trades who helped hoist the big top, repaired the generator when it went on the blink, serviced the fire extinguishers and made sure the dunny cans were emptied at the end of the day, Stan Platten was so nice, so reliable, he might have worked as a milkman. But Stan felt most at home with the circus, especially among the monkeys, of whom he was the unofficial keeper.

Rosa had always hated Hogie. She hated the fact that, after finishing its act with its owner, Zena the Ape Woman (born Bertha Bath in Ulladulla), the much-feted chimp invariably perched ringside and proceeded to make a disgusting display of itself in full view of the big payers in Gallery A. Not that the crowd minded. Delightfully scandalised, they oohed and aahed, looking away (and back again), until reliable Stan came to retrieve the little brute, wagging an admonishing finger in its grinning face. Zena stood to one side, looking suitably coy. But once Stan had Hogie out of the tent, it was Zena who took the chimp back to its cage and rewarded it with a banana. That's the part that stuck in Rosa's neck: the beast was encouraged to be revolting.

But it was not until the previous Easter when selfish Zena had denied the girl a bite of her marshmallow rabbit that Rosa decided enough was enough. Ignorant of Stan's feelings (being virtually oblivious of his existence), Rosa waited for the opportunity then opened Hogarth's cage, enticing the eager animal with a banana. Once Hogie began stuffing himself, she whipped a blade from her pocket and did the deed then stuffed his oozing body into Zena's costume, found discarded in her lean-to. No one was any the wiser.

Oh, the hullabaloo when the deed was discovered.

Oh, the disgust exhibited by Zena.

Oh, the change in Stan Platten.

No longer was his hair brilliantined and straight parted. No longer were the monkey cages cleaned. No longer did the generator reassure with its ceaseless chugalugging. And the dunny cans overflowed something awful.

Only then was Stan's love realised.

Only then was it made known (Zena feeling obliged to own up), that Stan had been after a chimp of his own for years. And for the past twelve months he'd been buying Hogarth from her (week by tireless week, shilling by hard-earned shilling), and the very day the debt was paid (that he finally owned his treasure and life's delight), some bastard did the ape in.

Only then did Needly Phyllis go to Stan in his sorrow and penury demanding reimbursement for what he owed on the chimp's black satin tails, personally commissioned. And the top hat wheedled out of an undertaker in Ipswich.

'Five quid, in all,' Needly demanded, 'and I want it next Mundy.'

Stan paid, getting an advance on six weeks' wages.

Though his loss had been months before, when the Colleano girl came to him, wanting to sit and talk outside his lonely wagon, Stan was grateful for the company.

'I'm Rosa,' she said, all smiles.

'Stan,' he said.

'Rosa Colleano.'

'I know,' he said. 'How could I miss that hair?'

She shot him a green-eyed look, wondering.

'Lovely,' he said. 'Coppery. Wiry, like monkey hair.'

'Oh?'

'My favourite,' he grinned. 'Since I was a kid.'

'You like monkeys?' she asked, playing the dumb card, as killers often do.

'Like monkeys?' he snorted. 'I love 'em! Hogarth was mine, you know.'

'Hogie?' she giggled. 'That naughty chimp. He's yours?'

'*Was* mine. Paid for him too. But he's dead, you know. Done in. Somethin' awful it was.'

'I'm sorry,' she lied. 'I didn't know.'

Stan shrugged, one brace of his overalls falling from his shoulder. 'We all gotta die sooner or later. Just that he went too soon.'

'Oh?' she grunted, concealing her blood-guilty hands beneath her fat thighs.

'Left him to bleed to death, the bastard did. Wouldn't do it to a dog, I wouldn't. I had plans for him. Livin' here with me.' He cast his head back at the wagon behind. 'Had a costume made for him, I did. Nice little dress suit. Real happy, he woulda been. And famous. All he did was make people laugh. Never hurt a fly …'

Talking to this bloke is a big mistake, Rosa thought. I should have gone straight to Needly. She would have got the costume for me. Damn. 'Awful,' she said, and shook her head.

'Anyway,' Stan said, slapping his knees, 'you don't want to hear some stupid old bugger whingein'. So what you been up to? Practisin' your acrobatics, have you? Your brothers are terrific, I reckon.'

Ignoring his final statement, and desperate to turn the conversation to her advantage, Rosa said, 'Actually, I've been occupied with a new friend. Would you like to meet him?'

'He a monkey?' Stan attempted a laugh.

'No,' she said. 'Better.'

'Couldn't be.'

'Will you wait a minute? Here? I can get him. You won't be disappointed, I promise.'

'I'll wait,' Stan sighed.

When the girl reappeared, Stan's interest was aroused immediately. Like everybody else, he had never seen anything like the thing she brought with her.

'I sing, you know,' Augustus said when the awkward introductions were over.

'Yeah?' Stan gaped.

'Certainly,' Augustus replied, cocky as hell. 'What would you like to hear?'

'Um,' Stan wondered, finger to mouth. 'Somethin' happy. I'm feeling down, you know.'

'Well, we can't have that, can we?' Augustus chirped. 'Rosa, can you help me onto this box?'

So Rosa whooshed Augustus up, as she would for years to come.

Now Stan took a better look. Before him stood the strangest little boy — a doll, was it? — blond, with lips like rosebuds, wearing a holey Chesty Bond singlet miles too big, a pair of enormous yellow trousers held up with a narrow red belt wrapped round and round, and all this on a body no more than twenty-eight inches high. But he was cute. Cute as any monkey. Cute as poor dead Hogie even. So Stan's heart warmed to him, whatever he was.

'I'll sing "The Happy Wanderer",' Augustus declared, planting his feet and lifting his eyes to a distant cloud. 'Ready?'

Stan nodded, entranced.

So Augustus sang:

I love to go a-wandering,
Along the mountain track,
And as I go, I love to sing,
My knapsack on my back.

Val-deri, val-dera,
Val-deri,
Val-der-ha-ha-ha-ha-ha
Val-deri, val-dera,
My knapsack on my back.

When he had sung all five verses, including their respective choruses, Augustus took a bow and declared, all smiles, 'Did you notice how I sang the final chorus an octave higher, for effect?'

Stan had not, but he clapped and grinned energetically. And while it had never been Rosa's intention to have her protégé infatuate the roustabout, Stan's obvious delight was a bonus, suggesting possibilities as yet unexploited.

'Mr Platten?' Rosa cooed. 'Stan?'

'Crikey,' he whispered as Augustus beamed triumphantly from his box. 'Crikey!' And before Rosa knew what he was doing, Stan leapt up to grab the boy, hugging him to his chest.

'Stan?' Rosa repeated.

'Yeah?' he said, turning to her, misty-eyed.

'Augustus will be living with me. He has no family. I am going to be his manager.' This heady notion had just occurred to her, but instantly made sense. Mercifully, Augustus did not hear that he was so recently orphaned. His trousers having begun to slip, he was too busy yanking them up.

'Yeah?' Stan gawped. He had been a boy scout, his anthem "The Happy Wanderer". How did this phenomenon know that?

'I was wondering,' Rosa said, pushing her luck, 'if you would be, well … his godfather, kind of …?'

Images of Hogarth flashed through Stan's brain. Contrary to what he let on to sympathisers, sincere as they were, he knew there would never be another to match the chimp but here, in this boy thing, Hogie might live again. 'I could help look after the kid if you want,' he mumbled, overcome.

'Look at him,' Rosa blurted. 'Abandoned, friendless, yet so gifted. It's clothes that he needs. Something to perform in. But where would we find them?'

'There's that dress suit I had made for Hogarth, my chimp. Very smart, it is. Hogie never wore it. This little chap could have that.'

'Really?' Rosa gasped, all the while thinking, Get it, you fool. Give it to me.

Stan went into his wagon, returning with both the suit and hat. It wasn't a perfect fit, but when Augustus was done up and posed on his box all lah-de-dah, he looked a smash.

'What will you do with him?' Stan asked. 'He's a beauty.'

'Not sure yet,' Rosa confessed.

'Don't forget my mother,' Augustus reminded her. 'She'll be here soon.'

Rosa turned her back to him, shaking her frizz and mouthing to Stan, 'Sad. Very sad.'

Poor dumb Augustus.

Alert to the absence of a mother in the boy's life, Rosa began to make arrangements for Augustus's future. There were certain clearly defined stages planned for this process: modifications to her wagon, a cautious introduction of the child to her brothers and the circus folk, then finally, when she had the home front settled, making his talent known to the world.

Rosa had little trouble getting Stan to make the necessary sleeping arrangements for Augustus in her wagon. An extra bed (a fruit box?), solved the sleeping problem and the addition of a curtain to provide a degree of privacy, not that Augustus expressed any concern about such delicacies.

Then came the meeting with Rosa's brothers, the famous Tumbling Colleanos, who were about as nasty as any Mafiosi the island of Sicily ever produced. Carlo, Claudio and Cristiano had long since booted Rosa out of their wagon to make way for their card games and booze. Independent as she was, Rosa didn't care, but when it came to securing financial help to back Augustus's brilliant career, she needed their patronage. Demeaning though it was to admit, the girl had no income, surviving on handouts from her brothers and the good graces of Donny and Moira.

So she dressed Augustus in his finest — the suit minus the top hat — and on the first available Sunday morning, when she knew the brothers would be lounging in the sun sipping coffee, she took him over.

'Rosa,' they shouted, all feigned affection and good cheer. 'Little sister. You come to cook the breakfast for us, yes?'

The girl approached with caution, shoving Augustus in front of her. 'No,' she replied, 'I have come with a proposition. Business, you know.'

'Business?' Carlo laughed. 'Business? What you know about business? You learn bake the bread. You learn the cooking, then we talk business.'

'I wanted to show you Augustus,' she said. 'He is my business from now on. And perhaps yours, if you care to invest.'

The three Colleanos stared. They were much alike: thick black hair swept back from their foreheads to tumble in waves behind their ears, olive skinned, dark eyed, fleshy featured with hairy chests and dressed only in leotards, they exhibited themselves for all to admire, though their little sister was long since disenchanted. Carlo, the eldest, and Claudio, the second, were two tough peas in a pod, but Cristo (as the youngest was called) was a 'mummy's boy', and easier to con.

'So, you find other midget?' Carlo sneered. 'You chuck Grumpy Donny for this one?'

'Maybe I eat this one for dinner, with the gravy, eh?' Claudio laughed.

'Your brains are in your balls,' Rosa spat. 'This is Augustus. He's a great performer. A singer. He could make us all rich.'

'He sing nice?' Cristo asked, inspecting the goods.

'I make him squawk, eh?' Carlo chuckled, wringing his hands as if throttling a chicken.

'He sings like an angel,' Rosa said, drawing the boy to her.

'What he sing?' Cristo asked.

Assured as ever, the boy stepped up. 'You like Caruso?' he asked, looking from one to the other. When they stared, stupefied, he said, 'Then I'll sing *Rigoletto*, yes?' And raising his head to overlook their ignorance, he proceeded to tell them who he was:

> *La donna è mobile*
> *Qual piuma al vento,*
> *Muta d'accento — e di pensiero.*
> *Sempre un amabile,*
> *Leggiadro viso*
> *In pianto o in riso — è menzognero.*
>
> *La donna è mobile*
> *Qual piuma al vento,*
> *Muta d'accento — e di pensiero.*
> *E di pensier!*
> *E di pensier!*

'He sing "Woman is Fickle". How he know, eh? He *bambino*,' Carlo asked.

Rosa covered Augustus's ears. 'He knows all right,' she assured them. 'His mother sold him for gin.'

'I buy him for crate of beer,' Claudio offered, mistaking the mood.

But Cristo heard, and hearing, understood. 'The man, he fickle too,' he sighed, and his brothers turned to him, suspicious. 'Rosa,' he said, louder, for the sake of the others, 'you sell boy to us, yes?'

'No, Cristo,' she said. 'I'm not selling him. I'm his manager. But I need money to set him up. I was wondering if you would help?'

Claudio snorted, turning back to his coffee. Carlo chuckled, 'You fickle too, little sister. You got the temper. We know. Claudio and me no deal with women, except ...' and he turned to Carlo, winking.

'Rosa,' Cristo said, leading her away, 'what help you want? Tell Cristo.'

'I want Augustus to sing in the big top. I asked Stan Platten to build him a little stage, on wheels you know, that can be pulled centre ring by a pony. What I need is a booking in the circus calendar. A slot where Augustus can be advertised. I need money for that. Posters, advertisements, you know.'

'How much?' he asked, wary.

'A hundred quid.'

'A hundred quid? We no got that money. You maybe work for that, okay?'

'Doing what?'

'We offer you spot in our act, you say no. You shoot through.'

Rosa laughed. 'You dressed me in a tutu and asked me to hold the bloody hoop that you dived through. How stupid was that?'

Cristo shrugged. This was true. She wasn't stage material.

Her fat embarrassed; her red hair looked crazy, even to them. They were glad when she quit their act.

'I tell you,' Cristo whispered, ensuring that his back was to his brothers, 'I ask my friend Bertie. Sometime he say yes, if I ask nice.' But he did not promise, nor did he smile. Bertie Sullivan could be fickle too, being the Boss's son.

Stan Platten was never happier than when he was in the company of Augustus, and the thought of building a stage for him gave his life purpose.

'Augie,' he called as the boy hung about his wagon, 'come and have a yarn with me.'

Augustus was delighted to oblige.

'I have met the Tumbling Colleanos,' he began, taking a seat on an upturned bucket.

'They're tough,' Stan warned. 'The circus is a tough place. Look what happened to my darlin'.'

'But Cristo seemed all right,' the boy said. 'He took Rosa to one side and spoke to her, promising that he would put in a word for me with the manager's son. That way I might be given the opportunity to perform.'

'Then I better get stuck into makin' that stage for you,' Stan said, being ignorant of any other reason that Cristo and Bertie might have to talk. 'So tell me, what did you have in mind?'

'I think the stage should be mobile,' Augustus said, 'and designed to reflect the theme of my performance.'

'Yeah?' Stan encouraged, having no idea what this mouthful meant.

'Is it true that there's been a war?' Augustus asked.

'So they say,' Stan replied, disconcerted.

'And that was between …?'

Given that Stan had been preoccupied with Hogie for the past five or six years, he answered, 'Between us and them,' and flicked his head back, leading Augustus to believe that the enemy had been entrenched somewhere between his bucket and Stan's wagon.

'And we won?'

'Yeah …'

'And would "we" be British?'

'Yeah …'

'Then I know what I will sing,' Augustus declared, triumphant.

'What?' Stan wondered, being none the wiser.

Augustus shook his head. 'That I can't say, not having discussed it with my manager.'

'With Rosa?' Stan asked, seeing a light at the end of this intellectual murk.

'Yes, but there's one more thing …'

'Yeah?'

'Could my stage look like a chariot?'

Stan sighed, finally relieved. 'It could,' he assured the boy, and having attended Sunday School before the worship of apes displaced all other gods, an image of the Egyptians chasing the Israelites into the Red Sea flashed before him.

'Then that is what I want.'

'How about I make a drawing?' Stan asked, 'and next time you're around I'll show it to you?'

'Excellent,' Augustus declared, slipping from his bucket to the ground. 'You are a good man, Stan Platten.'

Stan's dentures flashed in the sun.

* * *

While Rosa had seen to it that Augustus was fed, thanks to the long-suffering charity of Moira and Donny, she knew that sooner or later she would have to introduce the boy to the larger circus community who gathered in the mess tent. Given that people were afraid of her (though she had been on her best behaviour since Augustus arrived), and not knowing whose favours she might need, she was worried that the dislike felt for her might be transferred to the boy. After all, one kick in the guts from some circus yobbo would kill him.

The truth was, every time she went to the mess tent the combined power of the folk was turned against her. By some extraordinary conspiratorial collectivity, the moment she appeared, her red hair afire in the light of the uplifted tent flap, the crowd united to push and shove until she found herself at the tail end of the food queue, to be told by Slops the cook, 'Stew's orf' — though there was always a slab of bread and dripping to compensate, all salty and lip licking, which she devoured in the company of Buddha, the hippo, down behind the dunnies.

Given that Cristo might fail, Rosa wondered, having sought out the hippo's company, what can I do to ease Augustus in? How can I set him up without drawing attention to myself?

But she could think of nothing, and lapsed into that self-indulgent moodiness first perfected when the Colleanos chucked her out of their wagon some years before.

Why does everyone hate me? Nobody even knows what I did to that dirty little ape, and even if they suspected, they

37

couldn't prove it. Besides, it wasn't anything they wouldn't do themselves. Or wanted to do anyway. If they had the guts.

'Just wait until they cop an eyeful of the kid,' she muttered, chucking a goolie at the oozy Buddha wallowing in its pool. 'That'll make them jealous, that will. That'll make them *really* jealous. Because one day they'll see that I'm his manager. That he's mine, and they're just freaks ...'

So she paced, whinging and whining until an idea filtered through her brain: to do just that — to let them cop an eyeful of Augustus, all of a sudden. To let him *be there*, all of him, *all at once*, minus her — well, for a minute anyway — until he worked his magic. Until he had them in his pocket (so to speak), until they *saw* what a treasure he was, *heard* what a treasure he was ... 'He'll be the saviour of the circus, that's what!' she spat as the hippo wallowed. 'Then they'll thank me for lifting the game on their tired old acts —their puny Big Atlas and their drippy Rubber Man. Yeah. But how, eh? How?'

A glutinous bubble burst in the hippo's left nostril.

'Buddha!' Rosa shrieked, 'That's the answer. To have him pop out. To put him inside something and just like that, have him pop out! What an idea.'

The animal rolled glum eyes, doubtful.

'But inside what? What could he jump out of? I'd need to put him in beforehand and shoot through. Something that won't suffocate him. But what?'

And a thought came to her, There is that brass spittoon just inside the tent flap. I only saw old man Sullivan golly in it once. If I could put the kid in that ...

So she skipped away — a rare occurrence; not to be

repeated — her shabby boots kicking up dust, as the hippo sank, resigned, into its rancid pool.

'We need to talk,' she said when she found Augustus loitering outside her wagon. Whooshing him inside, she plonked him down on her bunk.

He sat up, crossed his legs at the ankle, his tiny shoes so pretty, resting the flat of a hand on each knee. 'What?' he said, all bright-eyed and expectant.

'We've got to have a natter about how you're going to meet the rest of the circus people,' she said, standing in front of him, arms crossed. 'You have to get out there and sing. We need the money now that your mother's abandoned you.'

'Eh?'

'Never mind,' she clucked. 'I don't have a mother either. There's no point in whining when you're an orphan.'

'But my mother's alive. And probably my father too. He's a sea captain. I reckon I've seen him. Tall, handsome, in a white uniform, holding a cap with gold braid.'

'Yeah, yeah,' she fussed, brushing back his golden hair. 'We've all got sob stories, eh.'

'What?

'Sob stories.'

'What's yours?'

'Ah,' she sighed, looking away in an attempt to appear wistful. 'My brothers took me from my mother years ago.'

'Why?'

'Because they wanted to see the world and be famous and she was a toothless peasant who wore a scarf and they hated her.'

'Well, that explains about her, but why did they take you?'

'Because they were arrogant enough to believe that since I was a girl I'd cook and sew for them when I grew up.'

'And?'

'And nothing. That's all you need to know. It's time I talked to you about what we're here to discuss.'

'So we're going to talk about my singing?'

'We are. And how I'm going to manage you.'

'Sure. But before you do, tell me, will I ever see my mother again? Or that sea captain in the white uniform?'

Rosa didn't much care, but seeing an opportunity, she said, 'Ah, that is a question only a *real* manager could answer.'

'Eh?'

'Only a real manager. A *personal* manager. Which I will be for you.'

'You'll help me find my father?'

'I'll make you a famous singer.'

'And then my father might find me?'

'He might hear of you.'

'And my mother too?'

'If you do what I tell you, since I'm your manager.'

'I will!' he cried, slipping from the bunk and clapping his tiny hands.

Rosa scowled. 'Well then,' she declared, 'the first thing we need to do is introduce you to the circus folk when they have dinner in the mess tent. Now, to do that ...'

'I want to eat with Moira,' he protested, 'or with Donny and Bonzer and Bozo. They're my friends. They ...'

'Shut up! Just shut up!'

His shoulders dropped, his chin dropped, his lip dropped, tears fell mightily.

Rosa could not lose a moment. To give in and hug him would mean defeat. She must rise above him, trample him, dominate him. She had seen such power exercised over horses, the ponies when they were trained. They must be broken. They must be taught who was boss. Like those revolting dogs that hopped in circles (the infamous canine conga), lashed by Edna, their bowler-hatted trainer, spruce in black leather.

'Stop snivelling!' Rosa roared. 'I can't manage a sniveller!'

'I wasn't snivelling,' he recovered. 'I was crying. There's a difference.'

'Augustus,' she said, maintaining her scowl, 'listen to me. Great singers don't cry. Nor do they snivel — unless the script calls for it. You understand?'

'Why?' he said, wiping his nose with the back of his hand.

'Because no matter what, the show must go on.'

Rosa was an avid reader of *Circus Tatler*. Someone among the folk — probably Wanda the Wire Walker, who was that way inclined — had left a copy in the ladies' lavs. Rosa loved the rag; it taught her so much about Business Contracts and Being Ambitious and Star Ego and other Management News, especially how the Show Must Go On.

But Augustus laughed. He planted his tiny feet and threw back his head and laughed. 'Rosa,' he gasped, 'that's so corny. That is so corny.'

Again, she determined to be strong. To give nothing. To reveal no weakness. She said off the cuff, 'Your snivelling was worse.'

'I don't like being yelled at,' he said. 'Performing artists are sensitive, you know.'

'So are managers,' she got in. 'Now, shut up and listen. I want you to make an appearance at dinner in the mess tent tonight. Yeah, yeah, you can still eat with Moira and Donny after. Donny told me he's having Chinese.' This was a lie. She had yet to inform Donny what he was having for dinner. If the debut was a success they could all have Chinese; if not, it was bread and dripping, alone with Buddha. Bugger Little Donny and the Chinese.

'Okay, so I'll have Chinese with Donny and Moira. But what do you mean by "an appearance"? Didn't your brother Cristo say he was going to set up something for me with that Bertie Sullivan?'

'Maybe,' she conceded. 'But when you've known the Colleanos as long as I have, I wouldn't trust any of them.'

'You're a Colleano.'

'Yeah ...,' she baulked, 'but I'm a girl.'

'Eh?'

'Forget it. Do you want to?'

'What?

'Make an appearance.'

'You mean to sing?'

'Of course to sing, stupid! For the circus crowd. While they have their dinner.'

'Love to. And will you introduce me?'

She had to come up with a reason why she couldn't. So she said, 'No, I want your appearance to be a surprise. I don't want to get in your way. This has to be all about you. After all, nobody has seen you, let alone heard you. Except for Donny, who doesn't count.'

'Won't he be there? Or Moira?'

'I just told you. They'll be getting the Chinese ready.'

'Oh.'

'So, what sort of song will you sing?'

'I'm not sure. Something will come to me. It always does. There's a song for every situation, you know.'

'Did you learn a lot of songs?'

'About two a week for every year I spent squatting under that piano.'

'A lot then.'

'They're all in my head, and when the time comes to project my voice into a space, the right song comes to me,' — he snapped his fingers — 'a song that suits the architecture, I always say. That completes me …' Seeing that she had no idea what he was talking about, he added, 'And my audience, of course.'

'Okay …' she said hesitantly, 'so do you know a song to suit a mess tent?'

'Eh?'

'A song about the pleasure of eating.'

'I don't hardly eat anything.'

'Hmm,' she sighed, glancing at her gut. 'I only have a bit of bread and dripping myself and look at the size of me.'

'We agreed that we would never talk about size,' he reminded her.

'Well think of a song, stupid!'

'Rosa, please don't speak to me like that. And I already said that something will come to me. But since you're going to manage me, you might as well know that you should never pressure an artist. Discussion is one thing; pressure another. You understand?'

Rosa chose not to reply.

Since the place was empty, Augustus made his way to the main arena, beneath the big top, to gather his thoughts. He liked to shuffle through the fresh sawdust spread over the surface ready for the night's performance, scented the aromas disturbed beneath his feet. This day he stood in the very centre of the ring, looking up at the faded blue of the canvas firmament above. My voice can reach that far, he thought. My song can fill this place — and those who inhabit it. Turning to shuffle away, he found himself confronted by the substance of the massive central pole, all sturdy and erect, a veritable Pillar of Hercules, and he reached out to touch it, his tiny hand pressing flat against its varnished surface. Like a leg of my mother's piano, he mused, holding up my world, and, ignorant of the irony, he wandered off in search of Rosa.

Mid-afternoon Rosa said, 'Augustus, I want you to have a rest while I set up for tonight. If I find that you have left this wagon, I will wring your neck. Do you hear me?'

'Yes,' he said.

Satisfied, she went to tell Little Donny what was for dinner.

'I already got sausages,' the dwarf complained. 'I sent Moira out special this morning.'

'I don't care,' Rosa snapped. 'I promised that boy Chinese and that's what he's getting.'

Having sorted out dinner (Chinese *would* be served), she made her way to the mess tent. She could hear Slops banging and cursing in the galley, otherwise the place was empty. There was the spittoon, squat and brassy, just inside the entry flap. Snatching it up, Rosa withdrew to the ladies' to rinse it out, her mouth puckered as a prune. Horrible as this pot is, she thought, it's big enough for him to squat, which he likes, but low enough for him to be seen as he stands to surprise them. She poured caustic soda filched from the makeshift laundry into the thing and gave it a swish. 'I better rinse this out good and proper,' she muttered, 'else if the golly doesn't kill him the lye will.' Anyway, she thought, he can't say I didn't try.

When Augustus woke to learn what he was to spring from, he was not so convinced. 'A spittoon? Rinsed in lye? What about my clothes? Why about my skin? What about my vocal chords? I'm not getting in that.'

'Augustus,' she said, adopting an authoritative tone, 'didn't your mother tell you that a little astringent is good for your vocal chords?'

'No,' he answered, 'she told me nothing. But I was under that piano long enough to understand an astringent is only used to clear the throat. And since I don't have a cold — not even a chill — I don't have any phlegm blocking me up.'

'Not at the moment, stupid,' she snapped. 'But you *are* about to hide in a spittoon. Think about it.'

Smart as he was, her caustic logic got the better of him.

When Augustus had been dressed in Needly's suit (the high hat pressed flat beneath his arm), he allowed Rosa to lower him into the spittoon without further complaint. Here the boy squatted (his vocal chords stripped clear as a bell) while the girl returned the vessel to its spot inside the tent.

'Sit still and shut up,' she hissed. 'When you hear Slops yell "Tea's up!" you are to stand and sing. You're on your mettle remember. On your own. So you had better be good.'

'Sure,' he gagged. 'Anything to get me out of here.'

'Smart,' she whispered, 'very smart,' and was gone.

Augustus squatted, stiff and silent, determined to get none of the caustic slick on his suit, or any of the residual golly either, and presently he heard the mob entering the tent. As their words tumbled into the urn, despite the less than ideal space confining him, Augustus listened, taking their communications in: their fears, their woes; even their occasional joys. And so a song came. Their song. The song he would sing for them.

When Slops bawled 'Tea's up!', the boy knew the time had come.

Not standing as he had been told, not springing up to cheapen himself as any common artist might, but crooning only so his voice resounded (rich, thrilling) within that potted space, Augustus's song drifted out in languorous swirls — some say the odour of sandalwood filled the tent — to settle among the jostling crowd. And when they sensed it, there was a hush, a calm, a stillness — and those who stood were suddenly seated and those who spoke were suddenly silenced and those who laughed fell quiet as the grave.

'*Please* ...' Augustus crooned, '*please* ...'

And straightening, he rose.

First his hat, then his lovely face, his shoulders, his chest, his waist then his tiny hands (palms open, thrust forward), and turning as one, the folk saw him and caught that glorious voice.

Not in the Ireland of tenors, nor the Europe of countertenors, nor on the wind off the Prairie, nor upon the sigh of Bedouin sands had one heard such song. And the hearts of the people were replete.

'*Please*,' Augustus sang:

'Please give me a penny, Sir,
My mother dear is dead,
And oh, I am so hungry, Sir,
A penny, please, for bread.
All day I have been asking
But no one heeds my cry.
Will you not give me something
Or surely I must die.
Oh! Please give me a penny,
Sir, my mother dear is dead,
And oh! I am so hungry, Sir,
A penny, please, for bread.

The tent was silent. Some stood, some sat, some remained, suspended as it were in an airy space of their own making. Until the flap flew up and the redhead appeared. 'Was he any good?' Rosa bawled. 'Was he? Eh?'

Then the mob sighed: the pent-up exhalation came all in a gushy rush sweeping Rosa's fiery hair from her skull, flattening her faded frock against her ample body. 'Awww ...' the mob moaned. 'Awww ...'

So Rosa knew she had backed a winner, but Augustus demanded the performance as his own.

'Please?' he cried, reaching out. 'Please?'

The crowd gaped.

'I am Augustus Trump. And I sing.'

The crowd roared.

'And Rosa Colleano is my manager,' he cried.

The crowd fell silent.

'I am,' she declared. 'And I am here to tell you that this child — this four-year-old — wants to join our circus. Wants to perform under our big top. Wants to sing on our Saturday Night bill. What should I tell him?'

'Awww,' they sighed. 'Awww ...'

Out of the crowd strode Cigar Sullivan, the Boss, the Big Man himself. Cigar was the life blood of the circus: the manager, the financier, the Boss. His fleshy lips sucking the butt of a long-dead cheroot, Cigar was not to be messed with. No doubt a role model for his colourful son Bertie, Cigar wore a vest of scarlet wool over a black and white polka-dot shirt, braces in yellow, coat in blue, trousers in red, string tie in slick black buffalo, crocodile boots in patent — but no hat (never a hat, neither sombrero, nor fedora, nor beret) that might hide the carefully oiled gleam of his naked skull.

'Yeah!' Cigar roared. 'Sign that idgit up!'

Rosa was taken aback. The Big Man rarely ate with the crowd, preferring to belch in solitude at a table behind the pie stall, his proximity to food being essential. But there he was, Cigar Sullivan himself, bawling, 'Sign that idgit up!'

Rosa's ambitions had extended only as far as the approval of the crowd. Where was her copy of *Tatler* when she needed it? Where was that article on 'Doing Deals'? (Where was Moira? Even Little Donny?). *Where?*

'Mr Sullivan?' she said, advancing.

'I never heard nothing like that kid,' he growled. 'He's worth two a that misery Little Donny. How much you want?'

'Now, now,' Rosa wheedled, attempting to be coy, 'let's not be hasty.'

'Hasty? Hasty? The kid could write his own cheque.' And dismissing Rosa with a hairy hand, Cigar turned to Augustus. The boy stuck out of the urn like a flower in a vase —a top-hatted daisy, some said, later, over a beer, recalling his sunny smile. 'How much you reckon, kid? Come on, tell me.'

Augustus, of course (never having read *Tatler*), had no idea.

Rosa used both hands to sweep her hair up in a fiery crown. 'I will do the negotiating,' she declared, stepping between Cigar and the boy, her hair effectively blotting the child from sight. 'I am his manager, Mr Sullivan. If you would follow me to my wagon, we will talk,' and she led the Big Man away.

Bony hands lifted Augustus from the urn. The boy looked up to see Stan Platten grinning at him. 'You was really good,' the roustabout said. 'You made me proud. Hogie would have been too, the darlin'.'

'Thanks,' Augustus replied, being placed on a table top. 'I'm glad you liked it. But why would Rosa leave me? I did my best.'

'That's the circus, I reckon,' Stan mused. 'Tough place, the circus. Never mind, I brought someone who wants to meet you ...'

A face as thin as a splinter was thrust into his, long yellow teeth grinning. 'Phyllis,' the teeth said. 'I thought yer was good too. I made the suit that yer wearin' yer know. Fer the monkey.'

'Oh,' Augustus grunted. 'Thanks.'

'Luv,' she said, 'luv, 'cause yer so good, I was gunna say, if there's anythin' yer ever want made, free like, yer let me know. Nothin's too good fer yer, kid. Nothin'. Yer made me cry, yer did.'

'Oh,' Augustus said. 'You liked my song?'

'Liked? I loved it. That was my song, yer know. 'Ow did yer know that?'

'Just one of those things,' the gracious Augustus shrugged.

'Yer got that right. Me dad sung that ta me years ago. Just afore he died of the lockjaw. Stood on a nail, he did. Shame ... Yer got a father, have yer?'

'I believe he's in the navy,' the boy said, looking desperately for rescue. 'An officer. With gold braid on his cap.'

'Lovely,' she said. 'Just lovely. Like yerself, I reckon,' and she nipped his tiny cheek with her skinny fingers, hurting.

'Ow!' he jumped. 'Well, Stan, well, um ... I must go now. I'm having dinner with friends.'

'And we ain't yer friends?' Phyllis demanded, thrusting her face forward. 'Kid, I feel like I known yer fer years.'

'Sorry, Needly,' Augustus gulped. 'I really must go,' and jumping from the table, he exited through the open flap.

'*Needly?*' she squawked. 'He called me Needly!'

Stan said nothing.

Augustus did not go in search of Rosa, nor did he go back to Little Donny's for dinner. Feeling strangely depressed (had his performance really been okay? Or was his mood a result of the poisonous contents of that spittoon?), he found a spot near a willow beside a dribbly creek at the bottom of the park. Here he squatted, thinking.

What was to become of him? He was not sorry that his mother had given him away. If he had stayed in her world he would never have met Rosa and Stan, both of whom might help him. Rosa was hard and Stan dim, but together they could provide him with the chance to sing, to tell the world who he was. His mother would never have done that. If he thought of her and the big white house at all, he mostly remembered that special place where he had squatted (as he did now) beneath the piano. But he could not dwell on such matters, not since he heard that doctor declare him a midget, and never once had his mother protested, 'But he's my boy, and I love him all the same!'

Of course he knew that size didn't matter.

Of course he knew that his voice was his life.

Yet, he also knew that to grow — to recreate himself through the poetry of song — was his calling.

If he could do it.

If he could find the right place.

The right song.

And if his voice allowed.

Then he might grow.

Then he might become ...

Yet he was not entirely convinced.

Not quite, not utterly.

He was not there yet.

And if he stopped to wonder, to doubt, as he did now, he had to admit that he would give anything to be that man in the uniform; to have his big hands, to have his deep chest, to have his long legs, to have his power, his *manhood*.

To be, in a word, normal.

Why am I so condemned? he wondered. Why?

Sobbing, he got to his feet to stand beneath the willow. He had visited this melancholy place before; in his heart, his head.

I should sing, he thought, I should find a song, to relieve perhaps, and raising his eyes to look beyond those mournful leaves, to search the vast and careless sky, he sang:

> *On a tree by a river a little tom-tit*
> *Sang 'Willow, titwillow, titwillow!'*
> *And I said to him, 'Dicky-bird, why do you sit*
> *Singing "Willow, titwillow, titwillow"?'*
> *'Is it weakness of intellect, birdie?' I cried,*
> *'Or a rather tough worm in your little inside?'*
> *With a shake of his poor little head he replied,*
> *'Oh, willow, titwillow, titwillow!'*
>
> *He slapped at his chest as he sat on that bough,*
> *Singing 'Willow, titwillow, titwillow!'*
> *And a cold perspiration bespangled his brow,*
> *Oh, willow, titwillow, titwillow!*
> *He sobbed and he sighed, and a gurgle he gave,*
> *Then he plunged himself into the billowy wave,*
> *And an echo arose from that suicide's grave -*
> *'Oh willow, titwillow, titwillow!'*

So, he thought, at least I can admit my weaknesses, and willing himself to be taller — if only a little — he toddled off to enjoy his Chinese.

* * *

At sun-up, having completed her negotiations with Cigar Sullivan, Rosa strode away to inform her new charge of his good fortune.

Finding Augustus talking to Stan Platten outside the roustabout's wagon, she announced, 'I've done the deal. Cigar gave me seventy quid for your first performance, and if that goes okay, it's a hundred-a-week contract for twelve months, at just one performance per week. To rest your voice, I told him.'

'A hundred pounds?' Augustus gasped. 'That's a lot.'

The figure cited was a lie. Cigar had offered two hundred for the first show and two hundred a week if the crowd liked the kid — big money indeed, but Cigar was a big man — although as a result of her nocturnal meditations Rosa had come up with the lesser figure, the difference to be deposited in her panty drawer where — ignorant as he was — the chaste Augustus would never look.

'Stan,' she continued, taking no notice of her client, 'if I approve your design for this mobile stage, I'll give you five quid for materials and another five to make it. Take it or leave it.'

'That's all right!' the roustabout exclaimed. 'You want to see the drawings? I got them in my wagon.'

'Oh yes please!' Augustus cried. 'Get them now.'

Rosa stood, pensive, as Stan hurried away.

'There is one thing,' Augustus said while they waited. 'That is a very big tent, that big top. I really should have some musical accompaniment.'

'Musical what?'

'Someone playing a piano or some other instrument to give me a chord, to help me keep true to my notes. To provide my musical line. Like my mother playing for the people who sang for her.'

'What?'

'Well, so far I have only sung for you unaccompanied. In a *really* big space, like that tent, I might also need some other instrument accompanying me to help my voice carry and fill the whole space. Like a piano. Or something...'

'The circus doesn't have a piano, stupid.'

'What about something in brass?'

'Like?'

'Or maybe a sax?'

'Augustus,' she said, her lips lemony, 'this is a circus, not an opera house.'

'Well,' he said, with just a hint of disdain, 'you are my manager. And I would have thought that finding someone to play for me was part of your job.'

The idea of backhanding the brat crossed her mind, but she resisted. This was, after all, Day One of his contract and if she upset him, or worse, bruised him, things might turn sour on her. Besides, she had money to lose. 'Hmmm,' she said, 'let me think about this. I'll ask around. Okay?'

'Absolutely,' he agreed. 'I mean, no date has been set, has it?'

'I'll have to check,' she said, frowning as if she couldn't remember. Cigar *had* set a date, just two weeks off, but Rosa had no intention of divulging that information. 'Anyway, we've got time to make plans. And here's Stan now...'

The roustabout appeared with a few sheets of lined paper torn from a school exercise book. 'They're only rough,' he beamed, bending to spread them on the ground. 'And they're not to scale. It was the idea I was after really. I wanted you to see the idea.'

Augustus saw at once but Rosa, being taller, bent over with a grunt. 'What's this?' she exclaimed. 'A billy cart?'

Stan's face fell. 'No,' he said. 'It's a chariot. It's what Augie wanted.'

This was too much. 'Augie?' she gasped, hand to mouth. *'Augie?* My client's name is Augustus. He will be known by no other name. The boy has class, you understand.'

'Sorry,' Stan uttered, head down. 'I'm sorry, Rosa.'

'And what is this chariot *thing*? I asked for a mobile stage. Not a chariot!'

Sensitive to Stan's silence (the roustabout was not prepared to be abused again), Augustus stepped forward. 'I appreciate that, Rosa,' he said. 'But I also have a plan for this first performance. A grand plan.'

'Oh do you now?' she sneered. 'Do you? And what is my role in all of this? You stood there not five minutes ago lecturing me — ME! — on the role of the manager and now you're taking over yourself. Are you? ARE YOU?' Crush him, she thought. Crush him now. Show him who's boss.

Augustus couldn't have cared less. He had lived through many such performances chucked by his gin-fuelled mother, complete with sufficient ragings and arm flailings and posturings and scarlet-lipped wailings to make the Lammermoor look like a choir girl.

'No, Rosa,' he declared. 'I don't want your job. I'm an artist. A performer. A singer, not a manager. But that doesn't mean I can't have ideas of my own. Discussion, as I told you before, that's what I expect. Discussion, not drama. I left all that behind in my mother's salon. Pathetic, it was. So let's sit and talk, shall we? Stan?'

Stan did as he was told, meekly squatting by the outspread plans.

'Right,' Augustus said, planting his feet and folding his arms. 'Rosa, here is the situation. When Stan and I last spoke about this — my first real public appearance — I had an idea for a performance to suit not only the tent — the big top as a vast architectural space — but also the politics of the time; that is, a war has just ended, and I believe,' in vain he glanced at Stan for confirmation, 'our side was victorious. Given that's true, I have deliberately chosen a patriotic song. Making a choice prior to a performance is unusual, I know, since my songs generally come to me spontaneously, but in this case, where spectacle is vital, I need certain show-business accoutrements. And since staging is so important, I need the chariot that I have requested Stan to design, and the musical accompaniment, of course, as I have already outlined to you, Rosa. So that is the situation.'

Faced yet again with the power of the boy's words, the logic of his planning, the maturity of his thinking (how old *was* this kid?), Rosa stood dumb.

Stan merely gaped, lost in love.

'So?' Rosa managed.

'So I want my friend here to make me a chariot. Stan, would you say that the vehicle is small enough to be drawn by a pony? I can see myself standing in the thing, being pulled into centre ring as the beast prances before me.'

'Excuse me!' Rosa spat. 'Am I invisible?'

'I should say that you are both visible and audible,' Augustus purred. 'So I ask yet again, could we discuss this please? I do so hate scenes. My mother made scenes, which is the reason I spent the better part of my life beneath a piano. Rosa?'

'Right,' Rosa huffed. 'Okay. Right. So, would you mind telling me, as your manager, what song you chose?'

Awed, Stan looked from one to the other.

'A victory song,' Augustus said. 'To capture the crowd's need for the celebration of peace.'

'Which one?'

'I'm not prepared to say. After all, you still haven't told me whether or not I will be accompanied. Or on what instrument.'

The girl knew then that she had lost. 'This is a circus,' she roared, sufficient to ruffle the waters in Buddha's distant tank. 'A circus, I tell you. Not some Salvos Brass Band.'

'There is that calliope,' Stan muttered.

'What?'

Stan knew enough to be wary. 'A calliope,' he said. 'A pipe organ that works using steam.'

'What?'

'This circus has one. On wheels. Pulled by a horse. And Una, who can play it, is still here too. Working in the mess tent like I said. Okay?'

'I've never heard of this instrument,' Augustus piped up. 'Is it at all melodic?'

Stan shrugged. 'Dunno what you mean by "melodic", but Hogie sure liked it. Jumped up and down every time he heard it, he did. But he was just a baby then.'

'Perhaps I should meet this Una?' Augustus said, averting his eyes from Stan's welling tears.

'Pardon me? *Excuse me?*' Rosa demanded. 'Tell me that I'm not standing here, right? Answer me! Am I?'

'I've already acknowledged that I can both see and hear you.' Augustus spoke with infinite patience. 'I only said that I should meet my accompanist.'

'Ooo-er!' Rosa mocked. 'Well, ooo-er-*er*! I am so sorry to question your plans, Lord Muck, but will you be serving champagne and caviar? And will that poncy Bertie Sullivan be in attendance, dressed up to his poofy nines? Oh I do hope so, seeing that I am your manager!'

Augustus looked down at the drawings, adroitly leaving Rose to rage. 'And could a pony pull this?' he asked.

'You bet,' Stan agreed. 'That's the way I designed it.'

'Or ...' Augustus wondered aloud, 'a zebra?'

'A zebra?' Stan laughed. 'Why not? They're pretty easy to get along with. And you would stand back here,' he said, pointing, 'holding on to the reins with one hand and the bridge part up front with the other. Get it?'

'But I wanted to hold a sword ...'

'A sword?'

'Just a little wooden one. Only pretend ...'

'I'll make you one special,' Stan assured him.

'Great,' Augustus declared. 'You're a good man, Stan Platten. That Hogarth was one lucky monkey. And since Rosa has said she will fund its construction, I suggest you begin immediately. Now Rosa, shall we pay this Una a visit?'

Defeated, Rosa gaped.

Later, when describing his meeting with Una to Stan, Augustus resorted to images of food. The boy's reasoning —

incomprehensible to the roustabout — was that, as a baby, his mother had parked (or abandoned?) his perambulator outside the window of a German smallgoods store. Here the infant had been exposed to the delights of all things Deutsch for hour after glutinous hour, until Mrs Trump (in search of her hip flask) returned to find him sucking on a gobstopper of truly Wagnerian proportions. And so, years later, as he explained to the bemused Stan, when the boy approached the tripe-and-onion-slicing Una from behind, he was struck by the similarity between her bum and a pair of cheesy rounds of delectable *Marschkäse*. And when the woman turned at his touch, timorous as it was, he was overawed by the languorous Bockwurst lolling from her arms. Her fingers were finer, being mere Frankfurters.

But that mouth!

Without a tooth in her head, Una's lips were sliced liver, meaty slabs drooping, barely able to form a word.

Looking down on Augustus, she shook her head. First she touched her mouth, then her ears, indicating to him cheerily enough, he thought, that she could neither speak *nor* hear.

Standing beside the boy, Rosa spat, 'Thanks for telling us, Stan, ya dill.' Not that Stan heard. He was off fetching materials.

'Can't she speak either?' Augustus gasped.

'How would I know?' the ever helpful Rosa added, ignoring Una's wild-eyed gesticulations. 'I never saw the tart before. Hides out in the galley, I guess. Besides, you're the one who wants an accompanist. You work it out.' She's an ogress, the girl thought. Maybe I should put her on my payroll too. I could team her up with Buddha.

But Augustus was more tactful. Pulling out an imaginary piano stool, he pretended to sit while proceeding to open the lid of an equally imaginary piano. And having played momentarily on the imaginary keys, he indicated to Una that she should be the pianist and he, singing an imaginary song, her soloist. He then pulled an imaginary cord to blow an imaginary steam whistle, releasing an imaginary *whoo-hoo*! and for all her mute wisdom, Una understood. Or imagined that she did.

'Kaliiooppeee!' she blurted. 'Kaliiooppeee!'

'Yes!' Augustus crowed. 'Calliope. See Rosa, she *can* speak *and* she knows what it is.'

'Yeah,' the girl grunted, running her eyes over Una's massive gut. 'I bet she knows what strudel is too.'

'Now Una,' Augustus continued, 'I was wondering if that calliope was still in working order?'

The big woman nodded.

'And you could play it for me?'

Una nodded again, her chins atremble.

'Wonderful! Then I will have Stan haul it out. I suppose it will need a good clean-up. Especially if the elephants have been having their way with it.'

Una shrieked, the spit splattering.

'Oh,' Augustus muttered, stepping back to avoid drowning. 'So you like that idea then?'

'Yairs,' Una replied, bending low, her lips all but brushing his own. 'Yairs.'

'All right,' the boy assured her, turning away. 'You get on with your tripe and onions and we'll sort Stan out. We'll get back to you when the calliope is all shipshape and ready for rehearsal. Just think of the Empire!'

Una emitted a sound that may have been a gut-rumbling belch or a gut-bubbling 'Bye' and stood, waving, as the manager and her client retreated between the tents in search of Stan.

All was bustle and confusion over the next few days. Stan was distracted: to build the chariot or to repair the steam organ? Not that he minded either challenge — he would have done anything for Augie — but which was the priority? The calliope, he decided. His reasons were practical, as was his way. The singer needed to practise with his accompanist, not that Stan understood the term, and the calliope's brassy pipes, licked paper thin by over-fond elephants, needed work. The tin-pot boiler needed cleaning and firing. And, of course, an elephant was needed to pull the thing. Stan was rather fond of Aunty Dora, the seventy-five-year-old Indian; hardly a *white* elephant as she was touted (although maybe a tad grey and grizzly) and *a bit* short in the trunk, true, but who needed a trunk to haul a steam organ?

'So there's my reasons for doing up the calliope first,' Stan announced to the sour-faced Rosa. 'Anyway, I'll still need a few days to work on the chariot but I don't reckon Augustus will be wanting any advice about how to stand up in that. Will he?'

'Why ask me?' Rosa sniffed. 'My client seems to have taken this performance out of my hands. Have fun with Una. You're welcome to her.' And off she went, her nose in the air.

When Augustus came around to Stan's van of a morning, hoping to get an invite to see the roustabout's progress, he was met by a firm rebuke.

'No,' Stan said, holding up a stern finger. 'Not until I'm finished. I want it to be a surprise. Besides, if that old boiler blows up while I'm priming it, you'll get your head blown off. And then where will I be? I already lost Hogie and I don't want to lose you. You're my mate, okay?'

While he was very pleased to be considered Stan's mate and delighted to be aligned with the legendary Hogarth, Augustus was far from happy. He so wanted to see this marvellous steam instrument that his chin dropped and his lip trembled and the tears began to well.

'Crying won't help,' Stan warned. 'Cause if you do, I'll start bawling too and that will hold up the work even longer. And you wouldn't want that, eh?'

'No,' Augustus admitted. 'But it will be ready, won't it? You wouldn't let me down, would you?'

'Let you down?' Stan gulped. 'Never!'

But when the child had gone, the roustabout crept back into his van. 'Let you down?' he blubbered. 'Never. Not after Hogie. Never…'

Stan was true to his word. When the night of the performance came, all was in readiness. Crowds flocked; hundreds, thousands queued, shoving, grunting. Everybody — every mum and every dad, every basin-cropped kid, every smarmy-bloused girl, every blue-singleted bloke who wanted a smarmy-bloused girl — everyone had heard of the *dwarf,* the *midget* that sang 'Better'n Our Nellie'. Or so Rosa's advertising posters spruiked. Financed by Cristo, these had been stuck on every park bench, in every shop window, behind the bar of every hotel from Brissie to Toowoomba. And who could doubt? None other than Hairy Moira and Pretty Betty had been given the task of pasting them up and when had that pair failed to pull a crowd?

Since it was to be such a Big Night, such a Peerless Presentation, such an Awesome Event, who other than Bertie Sullivan should be ringmaster and lead the grand parade? Who but Bertie Sullivan could mince (all giggling and aglow, all make-up and mascara) about the ring, twirling his twinkling baton, cocking his cheeky chin, flashing his pearly whites, batting his baby blues, fluttering the Union Jack in one hand and the Southern Cross in the other? Eureka!

The Grand Parade followed: the ponies first, their plumes fluttering, plucked live from the bums of an ostrich; the tigers, their cages rank; the acrobats, the Tumbling Colleanos, their hair oiled slick and flat, their tights tight; the fat lady, galumphing; the Skeleton-Man clanking; Little Donny, scowling atop a mobile mushroom, all spotty in red and white; and so on and so on, until finally, the crowd, possibly a bit sick of Bertie Sullivan ('His father's the Boss, hey ...') and eager to get what they had paid for, caught the suggestion of steam, a whiff of a wheeze, and to the delight of the mob, that matronly pachyderm Aunty Dora came lumbering, her elderly brow adorned in scarlet, her leathery throat festooned in yellow (who had found such violent marigolds?), her monstrous feet weighed down with silver, towing a red and gold coach (was it?), a castle that wailed (eh? what?): 'A calliope ...?' some wiseacre in the front stalls muttered.

'A kaliiooppeee!' the mob roared, stamping their eager boots. 'Oooh! Aaah! Kaliiooppeee! Kaliiooppeee! Oooh! Aaah!'

Cocooned inside sat Una, her body swathed in a sari of searing vermillion, her massive flab belting away at the hardwood keys. But (Oooh! Aaah!) the wheezing of steam, the whine of wind, the thumping and pumping of pipes, the roaring of ear drums! Awful the noise was: a sick tuba, a dying cow, an off-key castrato, a geriatric coloratura. But through it all (Oooh! Aaah!) how the audience thrilled to that circus of sound.

Deaf though she was, Una knew her stuff. When the calliope had once circled the ring, she straightened and, having kneaded her bulbous fingers — how the fearful keys quivered — she drew from those pipes a chord of such manifest *maestoso* the crowd gasped, their fidgeting stilled, their eyes turning, expectant, to the entry: the lifted canvas, the raised flap, the *Arch de Triomph*!

So Augustus appeared.

First his zebra (regal in purple), then his chariot (ashimmer in silver — though none could have known, save Stan who had made it — this was the tinsel lining of a thousand Ardath packets), and then, a triumph in a white linen toga and a garland of gold, came the *dwarf*, the *midget*, and stepping forward in his *vehiculum argentum* to brandish his tiny sword, Augustus parted his rosy lips for King and Country to sing:

Rule Britannia,
Britannia rules the waves.
Britons never, never, never shall be slaves.

Some well-intentioned matron had paid for half-a-dozen kids from the local charity school to see the show. Like the rest of the mob, most of these were only interested in the promise of glitz and glamour but one, Ollie Dogson by name, being blind, was there because he had what someone said was 'a way with words' and it was felt that he might 'get something out of hearing the midget sing'. So Ollie sat in the stalls, gawping this way and that, and up and down, and round and round, his lips set in that silly smile he hoped would communicate 'I'm having a good time', which he was, though he could see nothing. Still, he was more than happy to wait for something to happen, as he knew it would, because someone had told him.

Then Augustus began to sing.

And while the rest of the crowd was more interested in what might appear next, or that a pony shat on the fresh-spread sawdust, or a clown lost a shoe, or that 'them tigers stink', or some other circus hula-hula, on hearing the first note, blind Ollie sat bolt upright, his head snapping in that direction, his sightless eyes following the prancing path of the zebra, and as Augustus lifted his voice to fill the yawning space above, Ollie looked up, each note transforming, until where once had been an indigo haze he saw a firmament of stars: the very architecture of song.

'I can see,' he bawled. 'I can ...'

If anyone heard, none believed.

So the phenomenon was lost, the architecture once more mundane as the mob beneath, blind as they were to all that was wonderful, ignorant of the sublime, wanting only the beer and skittles, the 'MORE! MORE! MORE!' of the brash and crass, of the boom and tinkle, of the tinsel and tulle that every mob has always wanted, that every mob has ever equated with 'Having Fun' and a 'Corker Night Out'.

* * *

When Augustus stepped from his conveyance, exhausted, the crowd stood. Not to scream and cheer as Rosa had so ambitiously hoped, as Cigar Sullivan had so earnestly desired, but to turn, as one, and file out, tramping mud and dung as they headed towards their horses, their buggies, or the long walk home, convinced they had been duped. They could see a circus any holiday — or the football, which was better — but as some bloke whined, 'Them ads fer that singin' dwarf reckon he's a corker but he weren't, eh? Bit of a runt is all. Nuthin', eh?' And satisfied that the age of miracles had passed, they left.

Save for Ollie Dogson, all smiles, who, having heard, had seen.

'We're ruined,' Little Donny wailed. 'The mob couldn't care less about him. It's over.' And a vision of his future self, face-down in the tar pits of Disney, clouded his dismal gaze; for Donny he was, but Grumpy of the Seven Dwarfs he would become.

'I say that Rosa ruin us sooner or later,' Carlo, the oldest Colleano moaned. 'She no good. She never been any good.'

'And him,' the second Colleano whined, 'that midget, he no better. He push her to it, he did. He up hisself. He no reach the peoples, not like us boys, eh?'

'I didn't hear nothin' special, did youse?' Bertie Sullivan sneered. 'Not a showman's boot lace, he wasn't. Didn't rate a whistle. Not a hoot. My father already chucked him out. Freak. Fact they're all gone. Losers, all-a them. See how far they get without us. There's no show without us. Youse reckon?'

But Cristo declined to catch his eye, wondering, Maybe I miss something. Maybe I too busy making my brothers happy to hear? And downcast, he looked across the paddock, watching them leave: Rosa and Stan and young Augustus, making their melancholy way through the long grass, across the dribbly creek, down by the silent willow.

THE HOUSE

THEY WANDERED FOR YEARS, sleeping rough. Useless as he was, Augustus gave pleasure wherever he could, serenading many a hobo under many a street lamp, in many a shed, on many a country road, but he did not grow. At eleven years old (six years being the duration of their travels), he stood just thirty inches tall.

Stan picked up work as a labourer, never complaining, not with the kid to care for; not with his surrogate Hogie to love.

Rosa had her hair bobbed, selling the red hanks for profit. Most often she worked cleaning public facilities, which she hated, cursing the silly caps, the buttoned-up uniforms, the flat-footed boots.

'I feel like that stupid elephant. What was her name?'

'Aunty Dora,' Augustus chirped. 'I miss the circus.'

'The circus is over,' Rosa hissed.

She hated the mops, the slop buckets, the stink of stained urinals, the white-shirted bosses, but especially those kids who dropped stuff or dribbled stuff or spilt stuff or puked, then looked at her, bold and expectant, until she'd had enough, vowing she would rather starve than mop. And she nearly did, a circumstance that cost her that adolescent fat — farewell Buddha — as she matured into something of a vamp.

'You look real good,' Stan told her.

'Surprisingly attractive,' the ingenuous Augustus obliged.

At the end of six dreary years, Rosa's sexy body held their future.

As they set up camp one night in an Ipswich Park, broke as usual, a drunken miner approached their fire, face coal-black from the pit, eyes white and wide in surprise. Stan stood in defence of his charges, but it was Rosa who handled the situation. She'd been lying on the grass, dress hitched up, keeping cool. Seeing the drunk staring, his eyes huge, she got to her feet. With a cock of her pretty head she led him to the shrubbery. Nor was she seen again until the following night.

'I found work,' she said, appearing out of the dark. 'And a place to stay. For all of us. You pack up. I have to go. Miss la Vie's. Just down the way.' She gave a vague wave. 'There's a red light out the front.'

Miss la Vie's whorehouse was a rundown Queenslander. Low-set at the front, raised on ten-foot wooden stumps at the rear, the weatherboard house was surrounded by a verandah with french doors opening out. From these pulsed fleshy curtains as if inside were a living thing, and breathing.

The first morning, on waking in a shed down the back, Rosa told Augustus, her face pressed close, that the nature of her work at Miss la Vie's was to remain confidential for 'personal reasons'.

'What?' he asked.

'I'm saying, stupid,' she snarled, 'that what I do up in that house is none of your business.'

But while Rosa was doing whatever she did — and didn't seem too happy about — and when Stan left to find work, Augustus soon came to appreciate that this lecture on the mysteries of what went on 'upstairs' at Miss la Vie's did not extend to 'downstairs'. Enjoying confined spaces as he did, he soon learnt the pleasures of the crawl space between the verandah floor and the powdery black dirt beneath. He might play the Red Indian there (grubby knees and elbows creeping) until, flat on his stomach, he could peer directly into the ant lions' craterous dens to observe their massacres close up. And sometimes, moved by the myopic proximity of it all, he might hum something dark: *The Funeral March of the Marionette* being a claustrophobic favourite. But always *pesante*, as his mother so often instructed: 'It's *drear*, Dear, *drear*.'

Augustus learned of the origins of Miss la Vie's business from Mary Smokes, who he first discovered squatting in that very dirt. Mary was what Rosa called a 'gin', sometimes an 'abo'. Mary was as fascinated by this pallid dwarf as he was by her bony blackness. Encouraged by her ready acceptance of him, the boy found the courage to ask: 'What happens upstairs?' and most particularly, 'Why aren't I allowed to go there?' Ever willing to share, Mary informed him that upstairs at Miss la Vie's was a brothel ('A what?'), and that both Mary and Rosa were pros ('Pardon?'), and paid to have 'bloke's things' put inside them, but Mary, being an 'abo', was obliged to earn her living downstairs, in the dirt.

Several sessions were required to absorb all of this, Augustus sitting wide-eyed as Mary carried on, occasionally pausing to fill a cigarette paper, running the dribbly tip of her tongue along its edge then pressing it firm.

Through her smoky meanderings Mary told Augustus this land had been her people's and only when that White Boss Fred Watts came and took it to build this house was her mob moved on. But Bossy Watts, after building the place, big as it was, never lived to enjoy it. 'Died down the Sunset Mine, he did,' Mary informed him, wide-eyed. Rather than lose the house, Helen Watts (born Daphne Fooks, out Goondi way), his grieving widow, changed her name to Miss la Vie and took on a new career. Augustus was informed of this some time later by Blue Butterfly, a sad and solitary whore much given to melancholy histories. Mary Smokes didn't care for such tales, the melancholy history of her own people being more than enough.

'Ya live 'ere, mate?' she asked, rolling a smoke, the matches appearing out of some fold in her daggy floral. She had blacker spots on the back of her black hands. Moles maybe. Fat as the ticks on the bulls in that yard at Goodna the night they slept in a Moreton Bay fig. Flying foxes swarmed that night, munching and twittering in the boughs.

'We live down the back yard,' Augustus said. 'In the shed.'

'Ya wid Rosebud, eh?'

'Rosa, you mean?'

'Missa Vee call 'er Rosebud up there,' and she raised a thumb towards the floorboards.

'Oh?' he said.

'An' Stan, eh?'

'Yes,' he said. 'Stan shares the shed with us.'

'Stan oright, eh?'

'Yes. Stan's all right.'

'Bud not 'er, eh?'

'Sorry?'

'That Stan, he orright, bud she ain't, eh?'

'Rosa?'

Mary scratched herself. 'That Stan, he wannin' nothin', eh?'

'No,' Augustus conceded, having no idea.

Mary Smokes nodded, in agreement, apparently, her hairy chin scraping her leathery chest. 'Bud 'er ...' And she gave the boy a canny wink.

'Rosa is good to me,' Augustus said, so there could be no doubt.

'Yair,' Mary said. 'Yair ...'

After a longer than usual session with Mary one sultry afternoon, Augustus crawled out from under the house to loiter beneath the jacarandas by the roadside. He might have sung, to cheer himself, but could find no melody, nor anybody to sing to. Mary Smokes had no interest in his high-tone warbling; Stan had found work in some hell-hole mine and Rosa wouldn't listen, although she did take the time to tell him about 'the birds and the bees', and finally, when he insisted, all but putting Mary Smokes's words into her mouth, how she made a living.

'Yeah,' she growled, 'and you better be grateful 'cause I'm doin' it for you. Don't think I want them filthy blokes sweatin' and steamin' over me. You got that? I might work here, but I ain't no miner's tart. You got that?'

Difficult as this admission was to hear — more so to accept, especially if it was all his fault — Augustus maintained his faith in Rosa. After all, she was the one who had saved him when his mother so cruelly sold him off. Her and her black velvet slippers. And her grog. And what about that man he thought might be his father? That tall man in the white uniform with the gold braid on his cap who stood behind his mother at the piano — might he ever come for him? Might he ever accept some responsibility for him *One Fine Day*, as Puccini promised? Or maybe, the boy mused, staring into the purple depths of a jacaranda bloom, if I could find the right song and sing it to perfection, I might recreate him myself, perfection being the miracle that it is. Suddenly conscious of his pretension, he tossed the flower away.

One morning as he wandered in the stony yard, Augustus was astonished to hear a song come spilling from the verandah, the voice poignant, the vibrato evident but not affected. Is that a man or a woman singing? he wondered, and ignoring Rosa's orders, he clambered up the front steps to hear:

> *Plaisir d'amour ne dure qu'un moment,*
> *Chagrin d'amour dure toute la vie ...*

The front door being open, he crossed the verandah — one stride, two, three, he was so small — spreading his arms to steady himself between the door jambs. Samson, was he? Or Odysseus? Both had heard that siren song:

> *The joy of love is but a moment long,*
> *The pain of love endures your whole life long.*

The darkness of the hallway appeared impenetrable, but as he paused, knees trembling, heart fluttering, adjusting to this new reality — this maw of love — he saw that the walls were not black, but floor-to-ceiling red. He thought of blood, a red, oozing heart feeding those fleshy curtains, pulsing in and out, and he pressed his palm against his chest, suppressing his fear. Being no hero, no Odysseus, no Samson, and having neither the will nor the companions nor the wherewithal to restrain himself from that siren song — his dear little overalls having no belt — he felt himself succumb.

One foot after the other, softly, softly, he trod the red runner there. The walls were glossy, even slick. Is it blood? he wondered. Oozing … And he stopped to take stock, aware that if he were to grow he might do so through song, and here, at last, even in this awful place, an extraordinary voice was calling him, a certain poetry of promise. 'Go on,' he whispered. 'Go …'

He made out a door to his left. Another, opposite, both open. Both rooms empty. Being aired, he thought as he caught the smell. What is that? Stale tobacco? Spilt beer? But he knew it to be *sex*, as one *just knows*, and he went on, palming the wall.

Here were more open doors, more rooms. He put his head around to see a great bed, four-posted in brass, the scarlet cover pulled back like a scab, the sheets soiled bandages, the pillows rumpled. They must fight, he thought. Like at the front. Like in that war, and wrinkling his childish nose, he withdrew, since he knew nothing of that ordeal, not really, not like those lovers who had wrestled and gouged and torn and wept as they fought that fight: that frightful battle of love — although he did give a thought to Rosa and the sweaty miners, like she said, and wondered, Does she do it for me? Really? And guessed that she did, because nothing else made sense.

So he went on, fascinated to see. To hear. To know, if he could.

The corridor ended in a great red room stretching between the french doors opening on to the verandah either side. The walls were swathed in fabric, drooping and scalloped, but pink too, like those curtains, all veined and fleshy, and everywhere littered with lounges and loveseats and smokers' stands and rugs and carpets and cushions of satin and silk, and palms in brass pots and sepia photographs of the buxomed and breasted and dimple-thighed and cupid-bowed with curls crimped and girly yet for all their amplitude squeezed or pressed, like bovine tongue, into frames of cheap, flaking gilt.

In a corner, at an upright piano like his mother's, sat a person in a black bustier, thick blonde hair falling to cover the back lacing — though not all the way, since Augustus could see that the bottom was strung tight, the whale bone pulled in, the hour-glass waist narrow. The boy saw legs too, and black net stockings, and pallid thighs (a slab of hairy flesh just visible) tapering to a shoeless foot where the velvet slipper ought to be, pressuring the pedal, easing, pressuring, easing ... This was the singer, the one who lured him, the siren, the poet:

Plaisir d'amour ne dure qu'un moment,
Chagrin d'amour dure toute la vie ...

'Ma'am?' he said, tentatively, and when the singer turned, spinning the piano stool, 'Sir?'

* * *

'Morphodite?' Augustus wondered aloud. 'A morphodite?'

The morning after, he sat opposite Stan at a table in the shed down the back. They enjoyed their breakfast (toast and marmalade and Bushells tea from a brown china pot) before Stan left for the pit.

'Yeah,' Stan said, mothering the brown china pot. 'One turned up at the circus once. Lookin' for work as a freak. A sideshow, like.'

'A morphodite?'

'Yeah.'

'And?'

'Well, he reckoned he was.'

'He?'

'Could be a she. Dunno.'

'And?'

'So Bertie Sullivan took him behind a tent for a look-see. To check.'

'And?'

Stan hesitated. 'Reckoned he saw the works. Up here, down there ...' He touched his breast, his crotch, then turned away, embarrassed. 'Sorry, mate. But you wanted to know ...'

Augustus picked up his cup with both hands, his eyes narrowing above the brim. 'Why would anyone believe Bertie Sullivan?' he said. 'He sees dirt everywhere ...' Then, remembering his own grubby version of show-and-tell with Mary Smokes, he looked away.

Stan failed to notice. 'Anyway, man or woman, the morphodite didn't work out. Bertie's dad, old Cigar, said he

79

wasn't havin' no peep-show in his circus. So the freak left. Pity really. Had a nice dog, he did. Nice honey-coloured Pommellanian.'

'Pomeranian,' August corrected.

Stan shrugged. 'So what did he look like, this one you saw?' He needed something to think about down pit.

Augustus thought for a minute. Considering his own peculiar appearance, he hesitated to mock others. 'Interesting,' he offered, satisfied with the word. 'Like her voice. Interesting.'

'Her?'

'I'd say "her". Yes.'

'Garn …' Stan prodded.

'Well, she had a handsome face.'

'She?'

'Insofar as a woman can be termed handsome. I saw a handsome mezzo once. Statuesque. She had a very fine neck and shoulders,' and taking a sip of his tea, Augustus paused to wonder: 'What are those women called who hold up the portico of the Erechtheum in Athens? The ones carved out of marble? There were pictures of them in the encyclopaedia my mother stacked on the piano stool so I could reach the keys. Caryatids, was it? They were women and said to be handsome, weren't they?'

'Dunno,' Stan grunted.

'Hmm …' Augustus mused, warming to the memory. 'Of course her moustache was a drawback. If she was a woman, that is.'

Stan's head shot up. 'Hang on,' he said. 'Hairy Moira had a beard and she weren't no morphodite. You best be careful. Moira travels. And French Betty. Word gets around. I don't want any of their mates after us.' And he looked to the window, suddenly fearful.

'Sorry,' Augustus muttered. 'I wasn't thinking. Sorry. Rosa so wants me to forget the circus. To put that life behind me.'

'Forget the circus?' Stan grunted, pushing back his chair to look out. 'And Hogie? Is that what she means? Forget Hogie? I'd rather forget Rosa, that's who I'd rather forget. Besides, there's more freaks in that house up yonder than ever there was in those tents, under that big top. I think you're forgetting who you are ...'

'Stan, I'm sorry. Absalom's voice was so sensitive. I mean, I would never have gone in there, not into the house, especially since Rosa told me not to, if it hadn't been for her voice. I so miss singing. *Any* singing. I'm sorry Stan ...'

Stan moved behind him, hugging his frail shoulders. 'It's all right, mate,' he said, all sniffly and sad. 'I'm the one who should be sorry. We both need some lovin', eh? Now go on, I'm listening. Absalom, you say? Her name was Absalom?'

As Stan quite rightly surmised, both Hairy Moira and French Betty had long been acquainted with Absalom and his or her disputed gender. Travelling rural Queensland as they did, the girls first learned of the existence of the said morphodite while rolling kegs in any number of seedy pubs on the Darling Downs but she or he — born Ruby Pratt to Pastor Doug and his wife Dulcie out Dirranbandi way — had not come to their attention in the flesh until an ugly scene occurred at the Toowoomba Railway Station, Toowoomba being the 'Gateway to the Downs'.

Fanny Schmak, wife of Adolf Schmak, Station Master, first observed a person of dubious intent (the aforesaid Ruby

Pratt) apparently loitering on Platform One and later, upon closer scrutiny from beneath a cubicle door, applying lipstick and fluffing her blonde tresses at a soot-streaked mirror in the ladies' lavs. Alerted by the masculine width of shoulder, girth of bicep and general hairiness of both hand and foot, since libertine Ruby wore neither gloves nor stockings, Fanny ordered the deviant out, obliging the flustered Ruby to make an awkward exit, lurching fortuitously into the arms of Hairy Moira and French Betty, who at that time were loitering on the very same platform, though canny enough to disguise their equally hirsute selves as ample-hipped dowagers, black-veiled and bombazined in full mourning.

(Tricksters, were they?)

So, amid many tears, and with much snot and snorting, Ruby introduced herself. And later, over tea and scones in the Pot Luck Café (assuredly *not* Toowoomba's finest), the solitary weeper explained the terrible circumstance of her adolescence: that at the age of thirteen, when still pretty as a picture and the light of Pastor Doug and Dulcie's lives, the undeniable evidence of her manhood had so suddenly appeared.

Momentarily lifting their veils, Moira and Betty exchanged glances.

'Well,' Moira suggested, 'apart from changing your moniker, I reckon you oughta get back to Master Schmak in the ticket office and buy yourself a one-way to Sydney. They take to people such as yourself much better down south.' Extracting a ten-pound note from her handbag, Moira pointed the unfortunate morphodite in the general direction of the station.

Being a sensible girl, Ruby took Moira's advice.

Huddled in a gritty corner of Third Class, she resolved to call herself Absalom, her father having made her aware of that Biblical character's flowing locks, but since she urgently needed a little of that cash to buy men's weeds, Moira's kind donation could only take her as far as Ipswich, so dewy-eyed Ruby never did make it to the flesh pots of Sydney, which led her (or him, was it?) to seek solace in Miss la Vie's Crimson Parlour. There, some years later, while expressing her woes in song, the diminutive Augustus Trump applied a tap to her shoulder.

'Ma'am?' he said, tentatively, and when the siren turned, spinning the piano stool, 'Sir?'

The moustachioed singer looked down. 'What,' it said, 'are you?'

'I am not a *What*,' Augustus declared, having grown tired of that question over eleven years. 'I am a *He*. Although I might ask you the same question.'

'Ah,' the singer sighed. 'And therein lies the agony ...'

Augustus was taken aback. 'The *agony*?' he repeated. 'Do you hurt?'

'Yes, I hurt. To be me, you understand. Not here,' — it touched its crotch — 'but *here* ...' It touched its breast.

'Your heart?' Augustus asked, wide-eyed. 'You have a weak heart?'

'Indeed,' the singer nodded. 'A *very* weak heart ... But I am rude. Too personal, too soon, as usual. Always the way with me. Always. And there you are, cute as a button in your little overalls. A gentleman, I can tell. I'm sorry, my name is Absalom. I'm what is known as a "Lady of the Night" — though since most boys around here do twelve-hour shifts down pit, I might also be called a "Lady of the Day". I'm versatile, you see.'

Augustus did not see, not entirely, but he was cunning enough to turn the subject to a topic he could appreciate. 'I am Augustus Trump,' he said, extending his hand. 'And I really like your voice. You have an awfully sensitive tone.'

'*Awful* or *full of awe*?' Absalom chuckled. He had long since quit his girly giggle — such a giveaway. 'Clarify, please!'

'It's interesting ...' Augustus said, considering the musical veracity of the term. 'Yes, *interesting* ...' and he decided to remember the word, in just such a context, should the occasion arise.

'Well, well,' Absalom replied, dropping his tone an octave, 'what a nice young man you are. And what is it that brings you to the notorious Miss la Vie? You don't look like a sex-starved miner to me ...' Glancing away, then suddenly back, he intoned, even more deeply, '*Are you*?'

Augustus giggled. 'I have been travelling with Rosa,' he explained. 'Rosebud, they call her here. She is what you might call my guardian, though she prefers the title "Manager".'

'Not red-headed Rosebud? Not that little firebrand who can charge what she likes? Not *that* Rosebud? She's your *pimp*?' His hand was at his chest, his cleavage heaving.

'No, no!' Augustus laughed. 'Rosa is my *manager*. I sing too, you know.'

Now Absalom's hand was on his moustache, nervously twirling one waxy blond tip. 'My father conducted a male choir — he was a minister of the church — and I wanted to sing with the boys. I swear that's why I turned into one — so be careful what you wish for, like they say ...'

'I wish that I would grow into a man,' Augustus offered. 'A proper man, like.'

Fingerless gloves slapped ruby-rouged cheeks. 'A *proper* man? Ha! Tell you what; you show me a proper man and I'll show you a miracle.'

'Perhaps that is what it might take,' Augustus said, reaching up to stroke the keys. 'Pretentious as it might sound, I sometimes think that if I could find the right song, and the right place to sing it, and do that right — sing it perfectly, you understand, every note pure poetry — then something good might happen to me: some change, some transformation. There could be such a moment, you know — that one pure note, approaching the sublime.'

'I never heard it,' Absalom scoffed. 'Nor sang it neither. If I had, maybe I wouldn't be in this lousy place. Sorry, mate, after what I been through, after what I seen, I don't believe in miracles ...'

Sensing Augustus's disillusionment, he suddenly declared, 'So you're a singer, eh? Fair dinkum? What do you sing? Come on. Tell me and I'll play.' So saying, he spun the piano stool to face the keys.

'Older people's songs mostly,' Augustus admitted, ever ready for an opportunity. 'Although I'm usually pretty good at finding something to suit an occasion. Considering what I heard you singing when I walked in, I reckon I know a song you'd like. I don't need you to play, by the way, I've been singing without accompaniment for years. Ready?'

As Absalom sat agape, Augustus planted his pretty feet to sing:

I leaned my back unto an oak,
I thought it was a trusty tree
But first it bowed, and syne it brak,
Sae my true love did lightly me.

But love be bonny,
A little time,
But when 'tis auld, it waxeth cauld
And fades away like morning dew …

When he had finished, the boy waited, but Absalom turned away, weeping.

'I'm sorry,' Augustus cried, reaching out. 'I am so sorry. Is the pain that bad?'

At this, Absalom drew him close between his stockinged knees. 'Your song reminded me of the angelic voices I heard when I was a girl, praying in my father's chapel. But that was another time, another place, another person, before this *curse* descended. Now I am nothing: I am the hole in the dyke; the crack in the floor; the fault in the earth's crust. Nothing! Men leer, women snicker. There is not one who doesn't think that I chose to be *this,* that I like being *this,* that I want to be *this.* Believe me, I do not. If there was some tincture, some cure, some miracle that might change me, that might make me other than what I am, I would drink from that phial, I would risk that fate, I would die to endure it. I would have any *body* but *this*! Yes, my little friend, in this whorehouse, this hellhole, I might laugh and play the girly fool, but if I could, I too would be a proper man.'

Augustus stood quite still. At first he thought this tirade was nothing more than melodrama, a mode of theatre he had seen in his mother's salon — overwrought and signifying nothing. Yet when he considered what was being said, despite the smears and smudges and sobs and slurps, the boy understood this Absalom to be a kindred soul who would, if he could, transform himself. And choosing to reflect privately upon this possibility, he prised his sobbing captor's fingers from his wrist and crept away.

A stand of eucalyptus survived at the bottom of Miss la Vie's yard, behind the shed. Hardly anybody went down that way other than Mary Smokes, occasionally, to wail over her lost land, or maybe her lost self — nobody cared either way — but somebody, probably the pretty Rosebud, Demure Flower of the House, had strung a length of rope between two struggling gums to hang washing. 'Away from the eyes of perverts,' as she informed Augustus, which he acknowledged with a nod.

Having gotten Stan off to work, the boy had left the shed to see Rosa at the line, reaching up to peg a blouse. She wore a pink and white spotted frock with a belt of the same material, and white canvas tennis shoes. Despite her protests and avowed hatred of the place (and all that went on there) she was, after all, Rosebud, Flower of the House.

'Rosa?' he called.

'What?' she grunted, a wooden peg in her mouth.

'Can I talk to you?'

'You can talk,' she said, 'but I won't promise to listen.'

'I saw Absalom yesterday,' he said, perching on an upturned bucket. 'We talked. I even sang a bit ...'

She glared, clenching her teeth on the peg. 'What?' she demanded. 'You *what?*'

'You heard me,' he said, inured to theatrics. 'I want to ask you about it.'

'You went into that house?' And without waiting for a reply, 'Didn't I tell you not to?'

Augustus shrugged. 'I didn't see anything except some unmade beds and a big red room.'

'You went right through to the Crimson Parlour?'

'There was nobody there, except Absalom at the piano.'

'Ha!' she laughed. 'Now you expect me to tell you what Absalom is, eh? Like, man or woman? Right?'

'No,' he said. 'I already asked and he told me himself.'

'So,' she said, reaching down into a wicker basket, searching for pegs, 'since you know everything, what do you need to ask me?'

'Rosa,' he said, 'I need to sing.'

'No-one's stopping you.'

'Rosa,' he said, getting her attention, 'I mean to *really* sing. Somewhere with a piano, and an audience. Like a proper singer. Like we said we'd do when you were my manager.'

'Times change,' she said, stretching up so as not to catch his eye.

'Rosa,' he said, tugging at her dress, 'I have to sing. I'm shrinking. I'm dying here.'

Stepping back from the clothesline, she gave him the once-over. 'Augustus,' she said, 'you're not dying and you sure ain't shrinking. For crying out loud, you're a dwarf.'

'And I want to be more than that. That's why I have to sing.'

She shook her head. 'What's all this about, eh? You want to run away, do you? Is that it? Well, I got news for you! You think that I want to be here? You think I like this place? You think I like what I do here?'

'No,' he said, 'I don't. And I appreciate that you do what you do to put bread on the table. And Stan too, but Rosa, I've got to live. I've got to grow. I've got to have a chance to make something of myself. You understand?'

'Augustus,' she said, her voice smouldering. 'This is a brothel. You want me to ask Miss la Vie if my friend the dwarf can sing in her Red Parlour?'

'Yes,' he said. 'I do.'

'Get lost,' she spat. 'Go on, get. You're crazy.'

'You know what?' he said, pushing his luck. 'I never even saw that Miss la Vie. Where does she live? And Absalom? And the other ladies?'

'So you want to pay her a visit?'

'I was just wondering ...'

'All right. If I tell you, will you shut up?'

'Maybe ...'

'There's two flats at the back of the house. Behind the Crimson Parlour. Private. Miss la Vie lives in one and Absalom lives in the other. He cleans her flat, she hides him from the world. The other girls live in the town. Satisfied?' She said this with her face buried in the billow of a freshly hung sheet, Miss la Vie insisting upon hygiene.

'And are they happy?' Augustus asked. The clip on the ear that followed was unexpected. He sprang back, hurt. 'Ow!' he declared, rubbing the offended part. 'You could have burst my eardrum. Then where would I be?'

'Couldn't be much worse off than where you are right now,' she sniggered. 'And what do you mean, "Are they happy"?

What do you think? They're whores. I'm a whore. Do I look happy?'

He thought of saying, You never did, but chose not to risk further injury. 'I was just wondering,' he began again, 'about singing up there. I wouldn't be doing it for money. Just to make a change, you know …'

'Ooo-er!' she mocked. 'Ooo-*flamin*'-er! Is this the weed I found at the circus, up to his armpits in sawdust? So you wouldn't be doing it for money, eh? Not like me! Not like that cheap tart Rosa. Not like the only person in the world who stood up for you when your mother sold you off. For how much? Remind me? Ten quid, was it? Well let me tell you something, Lucky Legs: first, you *only* work for money, *ever*; second, you already proved that what you got, no-one wants — remember that disaster in the Big Top — and third, you got me to thank for the little you *have* got. And believe me, from where I stand, you got very little. Okay?'

He felt the tears and blinked them back. She didn't mean it, he knew. She was just unhappy with her lot. And to avoid further hurt for both parties, he said, 'I'm sorry, Rosa. I didn't mean to upset you. It's just that now we've stopped travelling, and with both you and Stan at work, I've got nothing to look forward to.'

'So what do you expect me to do about it?' she said, wrestling with a drooping sheet. 'Find you a job? Huh? Like singing in a pub. How about that? You'd love that, I don't think.'

Augustus reached up, offering her fresh pegs. He knew now that he would have to work on this alone. Or with Stan, maybe, but never Rosa. So he said, 'I think I'll go and have a talk with Mary Smokes. She likes me. She'll listen.'

'Good idea,' she grunted. 'Real good.'

During this period of misery, when he longed to enter the house, to sing, and boldly so, yet lived in fear of the consequences, Augustus sometimes lingered on the verandah, savouring the melancholy of what he interpreted as a liminal space, being neither in nor out. Do lovers feel like this? he wondered, meditating on the many miseries of the unrequited in the songs so familiar to his mother's parlour. If they do, who would fall in love? And casting his eyes down to the weathered timbers beneath him, he contemplated the splinters there, long and lethal, dangerously sharp. I need to take care, he mused. For the ordinary man, one of those would prick deep, but for me, at my size, to be so pierced would be as a dagger to my heart. So he quit the verandah to wander beneath the jacarandas, between the whorehouse and the road, though the dangers of this space — likewise liminal — were masked by the velvet of fallen blooms.

Augustus first knocked on Miss la Vie's door just two days after his conversation with Rosa Colleano at the clothesline down the yard. Having long since grown out of Hogie's outfit, he wore a smart little dress suit that Stan had found in the window of a bridal store, on a tiny mannequin there. A model bridegroom, no doubt. Very nice it was too, complete with black bow tie and wing-collared shirt and grey satin cummerbund and patent leather pumps — not that he had much call to wear it, the last time being to sing for some drunks in a bandstand at Redbank, where no-one cared anyway. But on this occasion he wanted to look his best.

Creeping into the house late afternoon when the girls had gone home to rest in readiness for the night ahead, he padded down the hall, crossed the Crimson Parlour and noted, as Rosa had advised, the doors to the flats at the rear: one being Absalom's, the body of its snoring occupant partially visible upon a divan, the other (he hoped) belonging to the Madam.

Augustus knocked, arranging himself as if he was about to sing: feet planted, tie straight, chin up.

'Entrez,' a woman's voice called.

Alto, Augustus surmised, and opening the door, he stepped in. He was struck at once by a wall of light and, blinded, he drew back, covering his eyes. Finding the support of the door, he removed his hand and looked again. This was the rear of the house, the flat Rosa had spoken of, but it was not timber like the rest. Before him stretched a row of glazed casements, dazzling in the afternoon sun, the corners of each fixed with a lozenge of amethyst glass. He remembered a ring, secret in his mother's jewel box. There was a scent too. Roses? He remembered weighty blooms, black and heady, arranged in a crystal bowl on the card table beside his mother's piano. Yes, roses. When he looked about, adjusting, he saw perfume bottles dotted along the sill: tall and twisted and tortuously spun; likewise scattered creams and unguents, fat-potted and squat.

'Do make yourself comfortable,' the unseen alto cooed.

He understood then that she was behind a screen of embroidered roses in the corner, hiding among the petals there. Prepared to wait, he sank onto a pink-buttoned pouf, since that was all he could reach.

Miss la Vie appeared in a haze of musk, a Venus in rosy

silk. Seeing her there, he felt his first pubescent surge. Only then did he understand that to woo this Madam, this whore — improper as she was — he must first find a song, and singing, grow.

She stood imperious, her gown of pink silk spiralling upward from a shimmering pool spread wide upon the floor to wrap, close-fitting, about her creamy breasts. (Those fat potted creams.) Her yellow hair piled high, her brows dark-pencilled, fine and arched, her blue eyes cold, her cheeks rouged, her lips scarlet and moist, the skin of her throat aging yet taut. (Those squat-potted unguents.) One hand extended, long-gloved, amply ringed, to greet. And everywhere, all about, the cloying scent of roses.

'Augh!' she exclaimed upon seeing what he was. 'I was expecting …' but she did not say.

Augustus clambered from the pouf, gabbling, 'I am Augustus Trump. I share the shed down the back with Rosa. You call her Rosebud. And there's Stan, my mate,' and somehow he brushed the back of her hand with his lips.

'*Mon cher*,' she said, whether charmed or otherwise was impossible to tell considering the set of her mouth. 'You are in need of my services?'

Augustus suppressed a gulp. 'Madam,' he muttered and blushed, and since he could think of nothing more, he stood, stupid.

'I should be flattered,' she conceded, 'but there are laws. And besides, I am expecting another …' She inclined her head towards the door.

'I beg your pardon,' he said, recovering. 'I will be brief. I was wondering …'

'Go on,' she demanded. 'I am, as I said, expecting ...' and she made a move towards the door, presumably to check.

'I sing,' he blurted, foolishly.

'Sing?' She stopped. She turned. She looked down. 'You *sing?*'

Flagging, Augustus sank into the pouf. Why did I come here? he wondered. What should I say? So he flustered, his palms clammy, his eyes cast down. Never had he been in the presence of a person who so confused him. Who so attracted, yet repelled. Finally, he mumbled, 'I want to sing for you.'

'Ah,' she breathed, drawing herself up. 'Then it's Absalom you are after. He likes that sort of thing. At the piano, out in the Crimson Parlour ...' And she waved a hand towards the door.

Augustus clenched his tiny fists. 'Ma'am,' he said, making a stand. 'I have been living in the shed down the back for some weeks, and have already spoken to your friend Absalom. It is yourself I wish to sing for. Yourself, alone.'

'Sing? For me?' She was already planning a strategy to terminate. 'Songs mean nothing to me. None of my girls have time for songs.'

'Without song I could never grow,' he began. 'I could tell you ...' But it was too hard, and he faltered, and blushed, and fell silent.

Miss la Vie saw her chance. 'You are a boy,' she said. 'Too young. Too small. I am expecting another. A man ...' and ushering him out in a rosy mist, she closed the door.

Augustus stumbled into the Crimson Parlour. He heard Absalom's snores thundering from his flat, and looked to the piano. Vulnerable as he was, an image of the instrument in the big white house, with his mother seated there on that black leather stool, flooded his mind and crossing the room, he clambered up, stretching to touch the keys. But when he saw, he drew back. These ivories had yellowed, the ebony dulled. Nor was there music on the stand as there had always been at home: a sonata, a waltz, a song...

Overcome with yearning, he slipped to the floor to crawl beneath that keyboard, to enter that sanctuary, that womb, to hide there again, crouching, eyes closed in that shadowy vault — the very architecture of his childhood — listening for the song of the strings, longing (if fate would allow) to begin again, to leap out, reborn, voice *appassionato* — to hear his mother say: 'Augustus, my son, my man, sing for me ...' But looking up, expectant, he saw (did he?) only that tall man, that captain in white (a vision, was it?), his gold-braided cap under his arm, knocking at Miss la Vie's door, and her opening to him.

Augustus cursed aloud, railing against his fate, but in raging he saw a plaster rosette of cherubs surrounding the light on the ceiling, each naked *putto* rejoicing in song, yet not one as big as himself. He wondered what had just happened: Who was that whore to affect him so? His muse? His mother?

Stepping out, he walked the blood-red passage to the door, determining to sing, to grow. To be that man. To *become*.

Stan sat outside the shed. He drank Bushells tea from the brown china teapot that he liked.

'I went in there the other day,' Augustus said, looking up at the house.

'You told me.'

'Not the time I saw Absalom. The day before yesterday. In the afternoon, when you were at work. I saw that Miss la Vie.'

'Yeah?' Stan held his blue enamel mug halfway to his mouth.

Augustus shrugged. 'She was good looking, but ...'

'But what?'

'But hard.'

Stan grunted. 'She's a whore.'

'She wouldn't let me sing.'

'You was surprised?'

'Hmmm.'

The conversation lagged.

'You tellin' me what happened, or what?' Stan wanted to know.

Augustus told.

'So she was waitin' for some bloke?'

'I'd say.'

'You see him?'

'Don't know. When I was in that Crimson Parlour, by the piano there, I thought I saw a man in a white uniform. Like a sea captain. With gold braid on his cap.'

'A sea captain? In Ipswich? Garn ...'

'Hmmm,' the boy mused.

'Eh?'

'I have imagined him before.'

'You lost me, mate,' Stan admitted, not being taken with the idea of imagining men in uniform. 'Did you see a bloke or not?'

Augustus reflected on the events of that afternoon and, deciding that sensory experience was all (reality being irrelevant to the poetic spirit), he said. 'It was her windows that got me excited. The light coming in. You see there?' He pointed to the casements at the back of the house.

'You sayin' this captain came through the window?'

'No, no,' Augustus corrected. 'But the light coming in was beautiful. Blinding. Through those casements. Up there, see? Running along the back of the house. Behind them is the flat where she lives. She's on the left and Absalom's on the right. I imagined that the verandah went right round the house, but it doesn't. Or it did once, and it's been closed in by those casements to make the flats. Thing is, you can't tell from here, from the outside, because they're dull, but from inside, with the afternoon light shining through, they're dazzling and the corner bits that look black from down here, they're actually purple. Like amethysts, like jewels, and her flat looks like a fairy's cave. Enchanted. You follow?'

Mistaking his mate's silence for meditative appreciation, Augustus finally made his point. 'Stan,' he said, 'there's something I want to talk to you about. About Miss la Vie, up there. And what happened.'

'Yeah ...' Stan grunted, wary.

'I told you that she wouldn't listen to me sing ...'

'Yeah ...'

'Well, I was wondering, what would you do if a woman did that to you?'

'What?'

'That.'

'She wouldn't.'

'Why?'

'Because I can't sing.'

'No, no. I mean, what would you do if a woman denied you?'

'Dunno.'

'Stan,' Augustus insisted, 'Stan, Stan...' until the wretched man looked at him. 'What am I going to do? I mean, I really want to sing for her. I do, to show her I'm a man, but she's so, well... hard.'

'I never even seen her,' Stan parried. 'I seen the others when they come down...' he nodded towards the outdoor privy up the yard, 'but I never seen her.'

'Really?'

'They come down the dunny. You seen 'em, haven't ya?'

'Who is they?'

'Them tarts from up yonder. Maybe 'cause I work shifts it's only me who sees 'em, late at night like, when I sit out here by meself, but I do. 'Cept her.'

'Miss la Vie?'

'Yeah. The Madam.'

'Stan,' Augustus sighed.

'I reckon she thinks she's too good for any dunny down the back. I reckon she uses a chamber pot and that Mary Smokes empties it. I seen a china one out on the verandah early one mornin' when I come in, newspaper on top, keepin' off flies, and that Mary Smokes carryin' one down just a bit later.'

'Stan, you're obfuscating.'

Ignorant, Stan chose to sulk.

'Stan,' Augustus moaned, 'I was simply asking what a man does when a woman says no. That's all. I don't want to know about Miss la Vie's bowels...'

'Mate...' Stan began.

'Come on,' Augustus urged. 'I bet you know a lot about women, eh?'

'Mate,' Stan hedged, eyes cast down. 'Mate ...'

'Yes,' Augustus leaned forward, expectant. 'Go on ....'

'Augie,' Stan said, 'I need to tell you somethin'.'

'Yes?'

'I never got knocked back.'

'Never?'

'I couldn't. I never asked.'

Augustus sat up.

'Augie,' Stan said. 'You gotta know. I'm a virgin.'

Augustus said nothing, the concept of virginity having no meaning for him.

'Yep,' Stan sighed, reaching for the boy's hand. 'I never asked a woman and no woman ever asked me.'

Augustus sat.

Stan fiddled with the lid of the teapot. 'That's how come Hogie meant so much to me. I ain't got no-one now. 'Cept you.'

Silence.

'Stan,' Augustus said, 'I'm sorry. I think. I mean, that's bad, isn't it? Being a virgin when you're grown up?'

Stan fiddled again.

'Doesn't matter. You could still help me, couldn't you? Like you did before? Remember the chariot you made? You could give me an idea.'

'Mate,' Stan said, 'I'm a moron.'

So they sat, until out of the blue, Stan said, 'I got one idea. You see that mango tree, outside the casements there?'

Augustus nodded.

A smile lit Stan's skinny lips. 'Birds sing in trees, eh?'

'They do,' Augustus agreed.

'Well,' said Stan. 'The way I see it, that particular mango tree is real close to your fairy's window.'

Then Augustus saw.

As a result of his loitering beneath the jacarandas, Augustus developed an interest in trees. He thought especially of how a tree trunk, gnarled and knobbly as it was, could become a piano leg. He knew of an item in an encyclopaedia that told how Michelangelo had imagined his David within a block of stone. He figured that the makers of a piano leg shared that same skill: to both see and realise the unseen.

He also came to understand that each tree had its own architecture, since all were homes, harbouring life: grubs and beetles — both furry and hard — snakes — a python one time, draped languid in the mango — and lizards and moths and butterflies. And birds too, as Stan so rightly said.

He spent time among the gums down the back. These were not grand trees, not forest giants, as the cliché went; rather they were straggly and twisted and bent, their bark peeling, their leaves grey and brittle. Some days, if he turned quickly as if to catch them, he saw these trees as the bodies of the aged, crippled, their clothes in tatters; other days they were just trees, so insubstantial they cast no shadow.

He took a good look at the mango. He stood in its black shade, stroking its rough bark; fingering its leathery leaves, so tough they neither decomposed nor burnt like the heaped foliage of others. He also considered the new leaves: pink, translucent membranes, easily bruised. Most of all he wondered at the fruit: weighty gonads forming in the trunk (like that David, in the stone) to squeeze down the branches, bursting out at the ends in clumps.

'Them mango no good,' Mary Smokes informed him. 'That mongrel tree, that one. That kero mango. Bad, that one.' Augustus did not understand until he peeled back the skin, putting the orange, juice-oozing flesh to his lips, expecting the exotic but tasting only the bitter fluid Stan used in the lamp down the shed. Grimacing, he chucked the dribbling seed to the ground.

Jacarandas were different. He loved running his fingers over the rills and valleys of their grey bark, wondering that a surface so fine could nurture the clouds of misty blooms rising from the foliage. And when the flowers dropped, he would choose one to cup in his open palm, thinking of the depth in the purple throat there — was that the *stigma* or the *style?* — and how it had been made: Surely not by some fluke, not by some accident of biology, but a miracle, of God. So Augustus loitered beneath the jacarandas, thinking, That same God made Miss la Vie.

His time with the Blue Butterfly was short, brief as the life of the insect itself.

She sat in a cane chair beneath the red lantern by the front door, the blue fabric of her dress shot through with green. Seeing her arms dangling and her sleeves billowing, he thought immediately of a butterfly he and Mary Smokes had seen beneath the verandah. Some cruel wind had knocked the insect from among the jacaranda flowers and it crawled in the dirt, flapping its gorgeous wings, doomed. He might have crushed it, putting it out of its misery, but Mary Smokes placed her black and spotty hand over his, shaking her head.

'That one die,' she said. 'Die soon, eh. Don' need your help …'

So he left it.

Even when he stood beside her, the blue woman did not look up.

'I'm Augustus Trump,' he said.

She adjusted her eyeglasses, the lenses black and round.

He understood then that she was blind, though he never could remember if she was pretty. Or how old she might be. Or the colour of her hair. Although he did remember her blue-green wings and the huge black lenses of her insect eyes.

'I am sorry,' he said, stepping back. 'I didn't mean to frighten you. I didn't know.'

She said nothing.

'Are you waiting for someone?' he asked, not so much to busybody as to help.

'I work here,' she said, and he accepted.

'I live here with Rosebud,' he said. 'And Stan, my mate. In a shed down the back. I sing, you know.'

'Oh?' she said, addressing no-one in particular, least of all him, unless he was perched on the verandah rail, which he was not.

'It's said that I sing very well.'

'Oh?' she addressed a roof beam.

'I am thirty inches tall,' he said, since she could not have known.

'Oh?' she said, turning in his direction. 'You are that young? A boy soprano?'

'I can sing any part,' he said.

'Oh ...' she said, growing bored.

'And you?' he asked, determined. 'Do you like to sing?'

'What would I sing about?' she asked the sky.

'I'm sorry,' he said.

'Miss la Vie calls me the Blue Butterfly because, she says, the colour suits me.' She laughed a harsh laugh. 'I never saw a butterfly or the sky, not even the colour blue. I never saw anything.'

He made a sorry sound. Presently he said, 'Would you like me to sing for you?'

'No,' she said, adjusting her great round eyes. 'I am not one for songs.'

'Oh?' he said. 'Nor is Miss la Vie.'

'There is a reason for that,' she declared, animated.

'What?' he asked, eager to conspire.

'Because ...' she stretched, extending her blue-green wings, 'because Miss la Vie lost her first love.'

'Tell me,' Augustus begged.

'Hmmm, it's not really a story for a kid, but ... Bossy Watts was his name. He owned the Sunset Mine. He owned this land too, this house ... I never saw him, you understand, on account ...' she adjusted her eyeglasses, 'but I did know him. Once ... His voice ... His hands, soft for a miner ...'

Augustus squatted, absorbed.

'I remember ...' she sighed, then recollecting her audience, 'they were married for just one day. Him and Daphne Fooks — now Miss la Vie. One day, one night, then he went down without his bird ...'

'I'm sorry?'

'His bird. Miners take canaries down pit. In cages. If there's gas down there, poison gas, you understand, the bird dies. When it falls dead in the cage, the miner knows to get out before he dies himself.'

'Ah ...' Augustus thought of Stan.

'This particular day, the day after his wedding, with his new bride waiting at home — this was his home, I might add, this very house — Bossy wasn't paying attention. So when his bird dropped dead — I guess, not being there myself, having only heard — he didn't notice and when he lit a smoke — I guess — the place went up, Young Bossy with it, like that!' She clapped her hands, to demonstrate.

'Goodness!'

'That's why Miss la Vie is miserable. She lost her first love, you understand?'

'Love ...' Augustus sighed, eager to please.

Blue Butterfly laughed her harsh laugh. 'Although she *was* happy. Briefly. For one night. One moment, you might say. But later, much later, when she'd done with her mourning, she took us out, us girls, to a hotel, myself included, where they had a stage show, very lively. Some woman must have sung alone — I wished I could have seen her — her song was awful sad — the whole place falling quiet as the grave — and when she finished, Miss la Vie stood to applaud. Not that I saw her — although I know that she did — but I did hear her applaud. "Lovely," she called. "Just lovely."'

'And the song?' Augustus prompted.

'A love song. Very touching. Very sad.'

'Can you remember?'

'I might ...'

'Tell!' Augustus gushed.

'La Vie isn't the only one. I'm a woman too. But her with her ways ...'

Augustus sank back on his heels. There's bitterness here, he thought. There's envy. And he said, 'Perhaps I might know the song. Perhaps I could sing it for her. For you too, if you want.'

A silence fell as Blue Butterfly considered, possibly remembering, possibly trying to forget. She slapped her blue-green knees and laughed that laugh. 'You know,' she said, 'you men are all the same, always wanting a bit, eh? And for nothing. Well, you got me. You stirred me up. You sucked me in. Worse, you made me remember. My Bossy. My man. He was mine too, you understand. Once.' So saying, she folded her wings on her chest. 'Here it is,' she said, 'and it's all you'll get from me ...' And she sang one line to the unseen jacarandas.

'There's the branch I would sing from,' Augustus said, pointing into the mango. 'And there's her window, but the trunk, you see, is too thick, too smooth for me to climb.'

Stan scratched his chin. 'I see,' he said. 'What you need is a ladder.'

Augustus turned to make sure he wasn't joking; not being a *card*, as Stan could be, sometimes.

But he was not. 'Sometimes there's ladders under these high-set houses. Even a whorehouse needs keepin' up,' and he headed off to look.

'Wait,' Augustus called. 'I can't climb a ladder. Not an ordinary ladder. The rungs are too far apart.'

'Stupid,' Stan growled. 'Sorry, Augie. Stupid.'

They stood, gaping up.

'You got the song?' Stan asked, more to mark time than doubting.

'I've got the song all right,' Augustus assured him. 'That Blue Butterfly sang me a line and I knew it straight away. A music-hall song, but a pretty one. My mother had some showgirls over every so often. Voice lessons, you know. I got on all right with those girls. Pretty, but rough.'

'They was nice to you?'

'Sometimes they'd give me lollies.'

'I always liked them gobstoppers,' Stan confessed.

'Too big for my mouth,' Augustus admitted. 'Besides, they're bad for your teeth.'

'Hmmm,' Stan mused, having lost his own. 'You still got your baby teeth, right?'

Augustus nodded, baring them. 'I'm immature in many ways. Mary Smokes told me that.'

'Maybe,' Stan muttered. 'Maybe not ...' Virgin he may be, but he had a pretty good idea of what went on under houses, in the dirt.

'So?' the boy wondered. 'What can I do?'

Stan thought. 'I could make a ladder. I could nail the rungs onto the tree at spaces to suit. There's usually timber and nails and stuff under these houses. She had a man for a while, this Miss la Vie, didn't she?'

'Bossy Watts. This was his house. That's what Blue Butterfly told me.'

'Then there'll be somethin'. I'll have a look.' He set off up the yard.

'Stan,' Augustus called. 'Stan?'

'Over 'ere.' The man had vanished under the house, into the gloom.

Augustus hadn't been beneath this high section before. The space had a different mood from that low part beneath the verandah where he crawled with Mary Smokes. Back here was a forest of stumps, rising direct from the ground like those unbuttressed American Redwoods in that book his mother kept on the cane table in the conservatory at home. The floorboards above were dead flat and dull, but these stumps were lively, their knots and nobbles bursting like carbuncles from the slick black of the creosote. Between them hung cobwebbed branches, their tacky foliage swaying mournful in the draft.

Uniting the stumps along the side of the house, binding weatherboard and earth, were rows of battens, vertical strips of black-oiled timber. On impulse he reached out, pressing the flat of his tiny hand against that surface (as he had done beneath the big top, against that mighty pole), and in that moment, in that instant of knowing, it was no tent pole that stirred him, nor some book about distant redwoods on some distant table. Rather he heard his mother playing and the dark beneath her piano returned to him: those sleek, lacquered legs, the very pillars of his childhood, his poetic psyche. 'Ohh,' he sighed as the hurt flowed. 'Ohh ...'

'Have a look,' Stan called, bending, ignorant, way up where the floor was low, the dirt close, the dark musty and dank. 'There's spare boards up here,' and going up (since he moved with ease despite the close space), Augustus saw a cache of timber stored between the bearers and the floor.

'I reckon there's enough to make a ladder, eh? If I can find a hammer and saw and the odd nail ...'

'Where?' Augustus bleated, since the concept of construction (other than through song) was alien to him.

'I bet that Bossy bloke had a bench under here. There, see, by that corner stump? Down the bottom. On the left. Behind them battens. See?'

Augustus did see. The bench was made from timber slabs, inches thick, standing on legs as thick as a man's arm, though the boy was hardly tall enough to make sense of what was on top.

'Okay,' Stan said. 'What's he got here? Vice? Good,' — and he fiddled with the handle — 'Saw? Okay. Rusty but ...' Ignorant though he was, even Augustus could see that. 'Nails? You see any nails, mate? Aaah ...'

Augustus watched him reach up to unscrew a jam jar, its lid nailed to a floor joist above his head, and empty into his hand a pile of nails, letting them fall in a clatter onto the dusty bench. 'I reckon we got us a ladder in a mango tree!' Stan crowed. 'Let's get stuck into it.'

Fascinated, Augustus watched as Stan set each piece of timber in the vice, locked it there then sawed it through. Yellow sawdust piled in little hills, a sight new to him, and hearing a sound, likewise new, he looked up to see Stan fixed in concentration, humming. Not a song, not a melody, that more primal sound: the contentment of a man, making.

When the boards were cut into bits, Stan gathered them in his arms. He picked up the nails and reached for a black-headed hammer hanging off a nail on a board at the back, against the battens. When the hammer was removed, Augustus saw another, a painted version, indicating where it should hang; where Bossy Watts had left it, unknowing, before that fatal day.

They went out to the mango.

'Now, Mr Trump, sir,' Stan said, all tradesman like, 'I want you to show me how high off the ground you want the first rung, and we'll go from there.'

So Augustus did, Stan nailing the rung to the tree, and the ladder was built.

Augustus did not climb into the mango immediately. 'I would like to be by myself for a while,' he told Stan. 'I would like to have a little wander and collect my thoughts.'

'I'll make a cuppa,' Stan said. 'Let me know how you go, eh?'

'I will,' Augustus promised, and they parted: Stan to the shed and his brown teapot, Augustus to wander among the gums, talking to himself, bolstering his courage.

About three that afternoon Augustus began his climb, rung after shaky rung, creeping out along the branches until he found a solid fork where he could stand, straddling the gap, one foot on each branch, one hand raised to grasp a branch above, the other across his chest, calming his heart.

So he opened his mouth to sing:

Goodbye, little yellow bird,
I'd rather brave the cold
On a leafless tree, than a prisoner be
In a cage of gold.

There was no response.

Perhaps she isn't there, he thought. Or asleep.

So he sang again, pouring out his heart like the nightingale in the story. This time he saw movement. Though those amethyst panes remained closed, he saw a shadow move behind them and pressed his hand against his breast to sing again, his heart's blood draining.

The edge of a casement trembled, opening ever so slightly. A pink-gloved hand appeared in the gap, its many rings glinting, and a voice called, 'Bossy?'

'It's me, Augustus,' the boy replied, fully expecting the worst.

The gloved hand eased the casement ajar, coming to rest on the sill.

'Augustus?' the voice said.

'Yes,' he said, leaning forward. 'I have come to sing for you.'

'I thought that he was come back,' she answered. 'My Bossy.'

'No, no, it's me, Augustus. Shall I sing again?'

The hand was still, the voice silent. He held his breath, his own tiny hand trembling.

Then she answered; cold, distant, abrupt: 'Sunday is quiet. The Crimson Parlour, at noon,' and the casement closed.

Three times a day Augustus climbed the tree, ten times in all before Sunday noon. But sing as he might, no hand appeared, no voice responded.

On the fourth climb, or possibly the fifth, he saw movement beyond the casements: a blur of pink, a blur of blue, and voices. That is Miss la Vie and the Butterfly, he thought and he sat in the fork, silent, to listen.

'Where would you go?' the Madam asked, her voice acid. 'What else could a blind moll do, except lie on her back?'

Try as he might, he could not hear the Butterfly's reply.

The Madam spoke again: 'I kept you here out of pity. Yes, there's some will pay for you: the one who wants no one to see, because of his own ugliness or his own shame. So yes, for a liability, you serve a purpose ...'

Again, taunting: 'How could you know? How could you? Love, you say? He gave me all, he gave me life. How could you understand, you poor blind fool ...'

And again, cruel: 'You don't know. You don't even know what you look like. I have given you a roof over your head. I have named you ...'

Then against the window, her body obvious, Blue Butterfly replied, 'I can know. I do know. I never saw him, true, but he knew me. And what he told me, you could never understand. He was hardly cold when you turned to this whoring. He was hardly in his grave when you tarted up ... When you chose ... When you named ...'

Augustus could hear no more; the distance, the closed window, the broken lines, and he sank back into the leaves, afraid.

On the fifth climb, or possibly the seventh, he contemplated the house, fearful. How hard was this Miss la Vie? How cruel? Yet he was determined. He had sung only once. Perhaps a second time he would win her, perhaps a third time she would see him for what he was, what he would become: that man, he determined, that proper man.

* * *

Since news of the discovery of King Tut's tomb was relayed to him by Stan, who brought it from the pit — rumours of mummies and gold and curses and ancient wisdom beyond knowing — Augustus developed an interest in things Egyptian. And since he so often sat waiting in the mango tree looking down on the house, eager to sing, he observed that the galvanised iron roof rising uniformly from all four walls to climax at the apex was, in fact, a pyramid. Could it be true, he wondered, that those who live beneath such a structure are somehow empowered?

But when he asked, Absalom laughed and Rosa sneered. 'Lust isn't empowerment, ya dill, it's enslavement,' and fed up with his childishness, Rosa pushed him away.

What is there about the body that enslaves? he wondered. Which led him to think of bodies he had known. There was Stan and Una and Little Donny and Needly Phyllis and Hairy Moira and now the Blue Butterfly, hardly deities, any of them. Glancing down at his own puny form, he laughed. But when that rosy blush crossed the casements, he sat up and thought again. Miss la Vie is not beautiful, so to lust can't be about beauty. It's got to be something else ... But being eleven years old and immature, as Mary Smokes had observed, what exactly that 'something else' might be, he could not imagine.

Then Sunday came, and he perked up.

Augustus wore the bridegroom's suit to his presentation at noon. He told Stan what he was doing and guessed that Rosa knew, though she made no mention of it. Still, as he entered the Crimson Parlour from the hallway, he was struck by the turnout. Every chair, every couch, every love seat occupied, every tongue wagging, every hand holding a glass, every glass bubbling.

'Good afternoon, Augustus,' Absalom declared. 'I will let Miss la Vie know that you have arrived.'

The room fell silent, eyes goggling.

Undaunted, Augustus moved to the centre of the room. He looked around. Well, he thought, there is hardly an attractive body here. What have I got to worry about?

He saw that Mary Smokes was missing. This was no surprise. He saw Rosa seated on a divan and noted that she averted her eyes and he, likewise, vowed not to own her, as she would want. Still, she looked nice; the youngest by far, and the prettiest, wearing ruffled white voile, very feminine, such that even he was impressed. He saw the Blue Butterfly in a corner, her dark glasses huge, cocooned in a blue shawl, secret it would seem. This being the limit of the girls he knew, he chose to stand before a mountainous woman in red; her lips red, her skin red, her fingernails red, her shoes red, and over the silence he said to her, 'Good afternoon. My name is Augustus Trump. I was wondering, do you like the colour red?'

The moment he spoke, the room resumed its hubbub, the tongues their wagging, the glasses their clinking, the bubbles their popping, and the red woman said, 'It's what I do, darling. I'm a whore.'

'I'm a dwarf,' Augustus replied, indicating his body, 'but I'm not dressed for a freak show.'

'What else would you call this place?' she shrieked. 'A nunnery?' And she shrieked again, slopping her champagne.

'This is a house,' Augustus declared. 'As a building it can ask nothing more of you than what you make it to be.'

'Sure,' the woman said, beginning to take him seriously. 'Sure ... I'm called Red Hannah. Miss la Vie, the Madam, named us all. I'm pleased to meet you. It's not every day a gentleman with a brain engages me in conversation. But I got news for you, Master Augustus, house or no house, some of us don't have no choice. Look at yourself, with that body — I mean no offence, being built like a cow myself, this is only a question — did you make a choice?'

'I chose not to work as a sideshow freak, if that's what you mean.'

'Oooh, did you now? I like a man who knows his own mind. So you're earning a quid as a salesman, are you? Or maybe a copper? Or a soldier? Or are you on the game yourself? Come on, confess. Since you admit that you're a dwarf, and I can see that you are, how do you make a quid?'

Red Hannah had him, of course, and in desperation he shot a glance at Rosa, who made a lemony mouth and held it, waiting to hear his response.

'I sing,' he said. 'That's what I do.'

'Oooh,' said Red Hannah. 'And singing pays well?'

Augustus took care. 'For some,' he said.

'Oooh,' said Red Hannah. 'And you're one of them lucky ones?'

Augustus would have admitted, and steeled himself to do so, but as he drew breath, Rosa leaned forward, her glass on her knee, and said, 'I was wondering, Hannah, if we might begin again. As I recall, Augustus asked if you liked the colour red. Do you?'

Conscious of being warned (possibly threatened), and by Rosebud, Flower of the House, Red Hannah sank back in her chair. 'To tell the truth,' she said, 'no, I don't like the colour red. Especially when it lights the front of a house. For me, it's more of a uniform, like cops wear blue and soldiers khaki.'

'Nice,' Rosa said, choosing that moment to primp her white voile.

'Interesting,' Augustus offered, ignoring the feminine politics. 'But what came first? The choice of colour or the name?'

'Oooh,' Red Hannah declared, clapping her massive hands. 'You are sharp, aren't you? I could take to you, no trouble.'

Augustus blushed. This may have been a reflection of the red or, possibly, as other men had noted, the radiation of her body heat. Red Hannah was one mass of woman.

'Like I told you, I was named. We were all named, by her, the Madam. She hauled us in off the street, hey? She put a roof over our head.' She glanced up at the frollicking putti on the ceiling. 'And it's her house, ain't it?'

Augustus was beginning to understand. The pyramid, the empowerment — worse: the enslavement.

'But it's good to try something different sometimes, isn't it?' he suggested. 'Otherwise people might take you for granted. Might even boss you around?'

'She does,' Red Hannah sneered. '*She does* ... but shush, here she is. In her pink, as usual ...' And she shot a look at Rosa, to let her know.

The Madam struck a pose at the piano. Seeing her there, Augustus drew back, overcome. Removed from the dazzling light of her boudoir, that amethyst enchantment, she was changed. Though she wore that same silk gown, extending that same gloved hand, he saw the skin of her neck stretched taut as a mummy's, her face the mask of a rouged cadaver. Now I see, he thought. Now I understand. I was deluded. Yes, that is the basis of lust. Delusion ... And he knew her to be dead, embalmed as she was in the rosy shroud of pretence, her life forfeit to the past.

'Girls,' she cooed, 'I know it is the Sabbath, and how you feel about that, but ...' No laughter followed. She was despised, he realised. 'This little fellow ...' she pointed, vulgar, 'came to call the other afternoon. Whatever he wanted, foolish boy, I would not provide ...' a faded glove pressed her coy lips. 'But since he is so eager, as all boys are ...' she paused to snicker, 'I thought that I would give him the chance to show us what he's got,' and being a whore, she winked broadly.

Affectation was one thing, patronisation another; but her cruelty astonished him. She had called him here to ridicule. Fool that he was, he had hoped that she might appear as a woman who appreciated that he could sing, who believed he could make a difference to her loveless life. Delusion, he understood. All delusion ...

Augustus stepped forward. 'Madam,' he said, 'before I introduce myself to your guests, I have something to say. While you obviously relish the naming of names — labelling your employees as one might brand a cow — for me to be referred to as a boy is hardly an insult. I am, after all, just eleven years old. And while your remark, "show us what he's got", was intended to demean, since I am a dwarf you could not diminish me further. For all of that, you will not make me into a freak whose body people pay to gape at, or, in your own particular case, to probe and grope. I am an artist, Madam, I sing. And in so doing, I both construct myself and those who hear me. Absalom, please, see that this person is seated. I fear that she is faint.'

Having watched Absalom lower her, trembling (creaking?), to the piano stool, Augustus took his place beneath the plaster-white cherubs and, lifting his head, announced, 'My name is Augustus Trump. And I sing.' So he did:

Goodbye, little yellow bird,
I'd rather brave the cold
On a leafless tree, than a prisoner be
In a cage of gold.

Whore though she may be, he sang for her, finally. Properly, too, at a piano; and so Augustus constructed himself: not to become taller, nor broader, nor uniformed in white, nor braided in gold, but wiser, and he was glad.

As a result of Augustus's singular display of virility (The man in that dwarf, was it? the Madam later wondered, panting, there in that amethyst light, Or his song? Surely ...), Miss la Vie experienced something of a romantic lapse, a yearning to indulge, even wallow, in all things relating to melancholia, lost love and what might have been. As a result she grew enamoured of the desire to learn more of the cruel fate of others, and where better to begin than in those cheap, weepy novels so eagerly devoured by her silly girls who really should have known better — as should she. Nevertheless, indulging the spirit of the broken-hearted, Miss la Vie appealed to Rosebud, whose cautious sensibility she much admired (the term 'frigidity' being, as yet, *avant la lettre*).

'Rosebud,' she said, 'on your next visit to Cribb and Foote, those self-proclaimed universal providers who own that emporium in Brisbane Street, I was wondering if you could purchase me a novel.'

'By what title?' Rosebud wisely asked.

'A romance. A love story, if you don't mind.'

'It's not for yourself then?' the droll Rosebud inquired.

'It's to have by me,' Miss la Vie sighed, 'should I find the need,' and in an attempt at the enigmatic she cast a lingering look towards her casements and the drooping mangos beyond. Had she seen him there, that Lilliputian lover? Nay, heard him? Ah …

But Cribb and Foote sold no love stories, Ipswich not being famous for romance, and, eager to please, the innovative Rosebud paused to borrow one from the West Moreton School of Arts Travelling Library, whose horsedrawn wagon she had fortuitously spotted tethered to a lamppost outside a tearoom in Brisbane Street.

Which is where Barkus Hardacre first laid eyes on her.

English, mousy, twenty-nine, a lean five foot ten, given to wearing circular spectacles with tortoiseshell frames — an affectation, his eyesight being perfect — Barkus was unmarried. As a librarian, he saw many women who were eligible, and dreamed of their being his, but none was good enough. Having attained perfection in what mattered — sobriety of dress, cleanliness, hygiene, an ordered mind, an impeccable catalogue — Barkus expected a similar perfection in the woman he selected as his wife. So when nineteen-year-old Rosa Colleano tapped him on the shoulder, he was immediately aroused.

Wearing that pink-and-white spotted frock with a belt of the same material and white stockings (the straightness of her seams an orthopaedic triumph), matched with a pair of white leather brogues, Rosa presented as the epitome of style. And having intended to buy a book, she had, for the first time, plaited her auburn hair, pinning the thick braids on top of her head to frame her face in a halo of bronze — as she had seen librarians do when she borrowed books on King Tut, and poetry, which he liked, for Augustus. Librarians always look smart, she thought, though rarely attractive.

'May I be of assistance?' Barkus asked, a trifle too eagerly.

'I am companion to a widow of some means,' Rosa informed him. 'I am looking for a novel to read to her. A romance, perhaps.'

Barkus's heart beat faster. 'I was just closing up,' he explained, indicating the half-raised running board on his horsedrawn wagon. 'It's almost five and I must have the Travelling Library back at Central by five-thirty. But how can I refuse a widow's need?' And lowering the step, he offered his hand.

Rosa Colleano was no fool. Not only had she learned a great deal about men from her brothers, her employment at Miss la Vie's had added to her experience of that weaker sex.

'Ah,' she sighed when Barkus offered, 'you have such strong fingers,' a comment that caused the librarian to blush to the roots of his brilliantined hair and possibly, as was Rosa's intention, encouraged him to latch the wagon door behind her. 'You would be surprised,' he said, reaching up to B for Bronte, 'at the energy expended in filing catalogue cards. No doubt that is the reason for the strength of my digits,' and handing her *Jane Eyre*, he considered how nimbly he might untie her brogues.

'It's close in here,' the canny Rosa observed, deftly re-opening the door. 'Now tell me a little about this Jane Eyre. Is she an interesting person?'

'She's an orphan,' Barkus mumbled, the wind knocked out of his sails, 'then becomes a school mistress, then …'

'I've heard enough,' Rosa declared. 'My mistress is a woman of the world. Don't you have anything more romantic?'

Barkus dithered. 'Had I known,' he said, 'I would have recommended *East Lynne*, a novel which has proved very popular with those in search of love. And,' he added, glancing back, 'those who seek to escape.'

'Really?' Rosa beamed.

Encouraged, the wretched Barkus provided a synopsis, neglecting none of Lady Carlyle's anguish following her doomed elopement with Sir Francis Levison (the cad), and consequent loss of husband, children, wealth, home, retainers, all … At which Barkus almost wept, and might have, had not Rosa reached up to touch his cheek with the tip of her handkerchief.

'*East Lynne*,' he moaned, 'touches my very core …'

'Quite,' Rosa remarked, not wanting to excite him too much. 'But having heard your glowing review, I'm certain that my employer will agree. Could you stamp the card for me please?'

'With pleasure,' Barkus declared, his prospects renewed. 'You have one week to return it. To myself, I trust.'

* * *

The ill-advised elopement of *East Lynne*'s remorseful heroine did nothing to dampen Rosa's desire to quit her demeaning employment in Miss la Vie's house. Lady Carlyle's romantic fling, doomed as it was, may in fact have been further encouragement for the girl to seduce the excitable Barkus Hardacre in order to gain a similar outcome — without remorse, naturally, Rosa having no time for such indulgence. It could be said therefore that from the moment Rosa returned the novel to Barkus outside that very same tearoom in Brisbane Street, neither luck, chance, nor fortune's wheel had any more to do with her future; every step being planned, every flirtation schemed, every dropped handkerchief perfectly placed in her determination to be free.

'I simply can't tell you what this book meant to my employer,' she gushed as she handed the novel over. 'Madam cried and cried. Quite wore herself out with tears, she did.'

'I am so glad,' Barkus responded, then realising his gaffe, he corrected, 'that she enjoyed it, I mean. Not that she was reduced to tears. I do beg your pardon.'

'Tush,' Rosa giggled, a girly antic she found very difficult to accomplish. 'Please don't apologise. I found myself likewise affected. The novel is very moving, demonstrating the awful risk a young woman takes when she surrenders her heart. Tell me, is it likely that young men are so stricken?'

'I know so few young men,' Barkus hastened to inform her (being eager to let her know that not all male librarians, himself particularly, were of the Wildean persuasion). Glancing down at his virile fingers, he added, 'But I would say that a few of us are so affected, yes. Those who are sensitive, you understand.'

'Oh,' Rosa simpered, 'don't tell me that some wicked woman has broken your heart already?'

'Several have passed my way,' he smiled, knowingly.

'Really?' Not wanting to appear too eager, Rosa surveyed the shelves. 'So,' she cast carelessly over her shoulder, 'there have been many women in your life?'

Inept though he was, Barkus now realised that he had laid it on too thick. To agree positioned him as a Don Juan; to deny would undercut his amorous boasts, making him nothing more than a boor. So he chose the romantic option. 'I am bound to confess,' he said with a shake of the head, 'my lovers exist only in the pages of novels and the little wisdom that I have, in matters of the heart, you understand, is book-learnt entirely.' And plucking up the courage to meet her eyes, he said, 'I am, you see, in need of an experienced teacher. A real lover. In the flesh.'

'Flower of the House' she might have been, but Rosa Colleano had always longed to escape Miss la Vie's employ. How she hated the men. How she hated the lies they told their wives. How she hated her own tacit complicity in such lies. How she hated their need for sex, being incapable of negotiating even that most basic animal act without resorting to payment. How she hated herself for accepting that payment. How she hated the sex itself: the crude beginnings, the sordid exposure of flesh, the repugnance of the kiss, the mechanical duration (the grunting), the unseemliness of the conclusion — 'You seen me braces? Me socks?'

Yes, the sex paid for food. Yes, the sex paid for clothes. Yes, the sex put a roof over her head and yes, while she had otherwise let Augustus down, the sex spared the boy the hardships of the road; yet the house was still a brothel and she longed to escape.

But how to accomplish this? Rosa was a circus waif; literate, although otherwise vocationally ignorant, unemployable, except for the most menial, the most demeaning: cleaning bins, flushing urinals, emptying bed pans — until Barkus Hardacre, the librarian. So opportunely attempted to seduce her. And what a long seduction Rosa allowed him ...

Got him! Rosa rejoiced, And all the better that he has a horse and wagon ... and, inclining her pretty head, she said, 'Sir, you are forward. We are not yet introduced.'

'I do beg your pardon,' Barkus gushed. 'I have *your* name from the library card you completed last week. I am Barkus Hardacre, a single gentleman, and manager of the Moreton Shire Travelling Library that we stand in. I do apologise,' and he made an attempt at a bow.

Interesting, thought Rosa, her prospects so suddenly expanded. 'The Moreton Shire, you say? That is impressive. And extensive too, I suppose?' — the later question carried the greater weight for one on the cusp of escape.

'Oh, very extensive,' the smitten fool agreed. 'Covering hundreds of square miles. The inexperienced could easily get lost.'

Even better, she thought. 'And you live in this wagon?' she wondered aloud, glancing beyond the shelves and catalogues to assess the interior.

'It is most commodious,' he boasted. 'The sides open out, you see, to allow me to display the books if there is a need.

And there are sleeping quarters, should I travel. Which I do, of course. I am only in the city temporarily. Assisting the librarians with staffing problems.'

'I am impressed,' Rosa admitted. 'And you manage all this alone?'

'Not by choice ...'

Rosa hesitated, then committed. 'Barkus ...' she said, and brushed his cheek with the back of her hand.

'Miss Rosa,' he said, catching her fingers in his. 'I have already apologised to you for my apparent rudeness. I apologise again. I tend to run on when it comes to matters of the heart. I confess to being an incurable romantic.' He pressed her fingers to his lips, ever so gently so as not to bruise. She did not resist, all the while thinking, I can manage this clown. I have put up with worse, and with much less hope of reward.

'I was wondering,' he said, 'if I were to close for half an hour, if would you have tea with me? There are some very pleasant tearooms at hand. Would you?'

'Please ...' she sighed, allowing him to lead.

Some weeks later, on a dozy Saturday afternoon, Rosa came down to the shed, calling Augustus's name. Since Rosa supplied him with books on all things Egyptian that she borrowed from a travelling library — mystery of mysteries — the boy was lying on his bunk reading, a skill he had taught himself, his language skills being precocious.

'Yes, Rosa?' he answered.

The girl stood in the doorway, her hair dishevelled, her eyes teary. Augustus had never seen her like this.

'You have to come up to the house,' she said. 'Something has happened,' and though he hurried after her, up the side, by the battens, she would say no more.

When they reached the front yard he saw a black, plumed horse pawing the road and a black coach drawn up beneath the jacarandas. A hearse, he knew.

'Who is dead?' he demanded. 'Is it Stan? Is it? Down pit? Down pit without a bird? I told him. I told him,' but tears or no tears Rosa was Rosa, and grabbing his wrist she yanked him up the front stairs.

'No, it's not Stan,' she spat. 'Now stop your mewling or I'll clip you. This is a funeral so act your age.'

'But who is dead?' he wanted to know, squirming. 'Who?'

Immediately he reached the front door, he knew. At the end of the hall, in the Crimson Parlour, was the Butterfly, laid out upon a cloth of blue.

'They found her down the old Sunset Mine,' Rosa whispered, shoving him. 'Threw herself down, she did. Same shaft where that Bossy Watts died. Miss la Vie's man.'

Appreciating this fatal logic, Augustus entered the parlour, saying not a word.

The girls had assembled, weeping; Absalom in blue taffeta to suit; but there was no sign of the Madam, and no Mary Smokes.

Augustus moved to the corpse. Whoever presented the corpse had done so with sensitivity. The dark glasses were nowhere to be seen (lost down the mine perhaps?), the blind eyes closed she appeared to sleep, her head on a blue cushion, a blue cloth draped over and about to hang down beside. (Her wings?) Something caught his eye: she lay on the work bench he had seen under the house. There had to be another table to put her on, he thought. And who would have the strength to carry that workbench upstairs? And why? He saw Stan hiding behind the girls, head down, looking sheepish beside Red Hannah. They know something, he decided. And have acted.

Absalom led him away, behind the piano. 'My father being a pastor,' he explained, 'I have already said a few words. Although I was wondering, before she is taken, would you sing?'

'Of course,' Augustus agreed, 'but where is Miss la Vie?'

'Gone,' came the reply. 'Shot through. The Blue Butterfly left a note for me to read to the house. She done herself in, hey, down a mineshaft. Reckoned her and that Bossy Watts were lovers. Reckoned they kept it secret. All in the note, it was — her confession, like — but when the Madam heard, she up and left. Down the hallway and out. No tears, no abuse. Not a word. Gone, just like that. And still done up in that pink dress. With nothing ...'

'Say no more,' Augustus whispered, and having invited Red Hannah to whoosh him onto the piano stool, he planted his feet to sing:

Plaisir d'amour ne dure qu'un moment,
Chagrin d'amour dure toute la vie.

So pure was his voice, so true, clouds of purple blooms stirred among the jacarandas, drifting up the front stairs, across the verandah, that liminal space, to float the length of the hallway and enter the Crimson Parlour, arcing upwards to circle the plaster cherubs upon the ceiling, and having circled, what had begun as blooms were changed; a thousand blue-green butterflies, all taffeta-winged, swooped down, then spiralled up, shunning those fleshy curtains to discover the French Doors and vanish into the blue. All invisible but to Absalom alone, who saw — who knew — and none other, not even Augustus himself.

I am changed, Absalom groaned. I am changed by song. By poetry ... though he said nothing, choosing to wait.

The next day two hawkers — men, were they, or trousered women? — appeared at the door, their suits drab-black as a pastor's.

'We have had the funeral,' Absalom informed them. 'The Butterfly was buried yesterday.'

'Oh, no,' one chuckled—an especially hairy brute reeking of booze. 'We are sales persons. Would you be interested in some tea towels?'

Absalom was surprised. Hawkers in morning suits, and fresh from the pub? Selling tea towels? Irish linen at that. Sensing a con, he took a better look.

The second was hairy too, though more aromatic. Smelling, oddly enough, of eau de cologne.

'I think not,' Absalom decided. 'The ladies here prefer gin to tea. But thank you all the same,' yet as he stepped back to shut the door, he caught sight of a shamrock embroidered in a corner of the linen and a distant memory flooded over him.

'Never!' he roared. 'Not the Pot Luck Café!' and in a moment was wrapped, weeping, in the bear-like embrace of Hairy Moira, French Betty having dropped the merchandise down the stairs.

What stories were told, through the day and the night (tricksters, as they were), and next morning, amid love and laughter, all three set out in that yellow-and-blue caravan with a red roof and green shutters and golden scrolls and finials and a pair of white wooden doves, their beaks touching in a kiss, above the indigo door.

Augustus read of the early death of Tutankhamen and marvelled that a dynasty could crumble so fast, but the fall of Miss la Vie's whorehouse proved faster.

When the Madam vanished (who knew where?), Red Hannah took over, but smart as she was, she was not tough enough to manage the place and quit, giving up the life to take work in the railway workshops, a place where she was often seen lifting sleepers and lengths of track and, from time to time, according to rumour, certain of the smaller locomotives.

But she was happy in her royal blue overalls.

So Rosa had a go. No longer Rosebud, demure Flower of the House, but a woman on a mission, a businesswoman, eager for cash — though not at the expense of her body.

'I'll do no more of that,' she informed Augustus. 'I've seen enough body parts to last me a lifetime; big and small, black and white — and the occasional yellow — so I'm making a quid and getting out. From now on, it's the life of the mind for me.'

And true to her word, in a year or two (perhaps more, perhaps less, who knew?), having engineered the arrival of the West Moreton Travelling Library out the front of the house, its glue-factory nag round-shouldered and drooping, she embraced the driver, a foolish young librarian by the name of Barkus Hardacre, so craftily conned, and hailing her companions to join her, they left.

Stan and Augustus were delighted, revelling in the prospect of the adventure, but as Augustus turned, wanting one last look at the house, he saw Mary Smokes sitting on the front steps, waving him back.

"Ere,' she yelled. 'Got somethin',' and she held out her hand.

'That's sawdust,' Augustus observed, mystified. 'From Stan sawing my ladder.'

'Nah,' she said with a grin. 'From borers, down there, under da v'randa. This house rotten, eh?'

And delighting in the poetry, Augustus kissed her lips.

THE LIBRARY

Opposed as she was to the exploitation of her body, Rosa had no qualms about getting all she wanted from the smitten Barkus Hardacre, vowing that she would use every coy and callous wile to keep him forever in that state of wild ecstasy and mad pursuit — which he might have wised up to had he chanced upon a Grecian urn — until she had learnt all she could of the life of the mind, this library business, after which, unravished bride as she determined to remain, she would give him the boot.

Having once ensnared him — and the use of his commodious wagon — all that time ago, she had watched and waited as Miss la Vie's house fell.

First the suicide of the Blue Butterfly (tragic, though convenient); then the curious exposure of the Madam (who would have thought she had a heart?), and her remarkable disappearance; then that Red Hannah chucking it in to work in the railyard (better off lugging locos, she was).

So Rosa had come to manage the house in its final days. And since she was the boss, she didn't need to get dirty (the others could do that), all of which allowed her to croon as the love-struck Hardacre pulled away from the place, 'Oh Barkus, you are so smart. Would you, will you, teach me the joys of cataloguing?' and giving his gluey nag the giddy-up, the smitten fool did.

They clip-clopped the country for six weeks, Rosa and the willing Barkus up front, she taking notes on her tight-pressed knees, Stan and Augustus at the back, legs dangling (Stan's, at least) as the tin billy clattered and the red dust rose.

On clear nights the boys slept under the stars, Augustus staring up while Stan snored. The boy (was he still?) would have liked to ask, 'Stan, do you believe in God?' because he often wondered if he did himself, considering the beauty that surrounded him, or arched over him, or spread beneath him, to which he was closer, tiny as he was, often spotting stuff in the dust, the dirt, like flowers. He especially liked white daisies, particularly those papery ones with yellow centres, and ants and beetles, although the beetles with hard black wings (the carapace, was it?) he did not like because of the *crack* they made if trodden on, and the fact that the black ones grabbed his finger and clung if he poked, but he liked the blue-green iridescent ones that were a bit like the colour of that butterfly he saw under the house with Mary Smokes that time, and Blue Butterfly herself, of course, though dead now, and in the proper long dark. But these stars: Surely, he thought, some Creator, some Super Being, some God made them. And a sudden memory came over him of those other firmaments: the cobalt blue of the canvas roof in Little Donny's daggy tent and the peeling stars, and he sighed, wondering, has Little Donny's star fallen? And that earlier firmament: the underside of his mother's keyboard, and darkness there. And fearing he would cry because it was all too beautiful, all too awful, he tried to calm himself, to will himself to be quiet, but could not.

How he wished that Stan would wake up so he could sing for him, if only to ease his spirit.

And the thought occurred to him, I don't know any spiritual songs, any religious lyrics, anything like what might be called hymns. Such songs were never sung at his mother's (although believers must have come, must have been there somewhere, must even have been moved to sing, yet silenced, suffocated by her presence or asphyxiated in the vapours of her grog, which was possible, the gin always cheap.

As he wondered, staring, the thought came to him that singing was a spiritual act in itself, which must be, he assumed, why he harboured the hope that he might make that perfect note, and having made it, *struck* it, grow; that he would create that note out of himself, his own tiny body, and through his own voice reconstruct himself. Re-create himself, as it were, as some other Creator—Some other Being—had made the night.

But once asleep, Stan never stirred, so Augustus was obliged to keep his spiritual self to himself, which was probably all to the good, Stan being who he was and a bit rough round the edges.

One morning as they wandered behind the library wagon, Augustus said to Stan, 'Stan, I was looking at the stars the other night, thinking, and I wondered, do you believe in God?' He waited, since he knew that Stan would have to consider this.

'Mate,' Stan said eventually, slowly, pondering, 'mate, I believe in love.'

'No, no,' Augustus protested. 'I said, God, not love. Do you believe there is a God? You know, who made the stars?'

'Mate,' Stan replied, 'I answered that.'

Augustus frowned.

'What?'

'I said that I believed in love, okay?'

'Stan,' Augustus said, 'that's not what I asked.'

Stan stopped, looking down. 'It is,' he said.

'Sorry?'

'I'm saying,' Stan sighed, heaving on, 'that since there's love, there must be a God. See?'

'Not really,' Augustus muttered, sorry he had got into this.

'There ain't nothing like love,' Stan said, addressing no-one in particular. 'Mate, the love I had for Hogie, well, that was something.' he paused, framing ideas into words. 'Then you came along and I knew. I had nothing like that before. Nothing that good, that special. So yeah, I believe.'

'But,' Augustus wondered, 'there must have been someone else ...'

'Let's just walk,' Stan replied.

So they did.

That is how they lived for six weeks (was is only six?), loving the serenity: the bush, the stars, the talk, (the times of no-talk) as they ambled side by side or perched on the wagon's back, taking it all in, until one afternoon while Barkus was off talking to a teacher, or a preacher, or some other person in need of the succour of literature, Rosa joined the boys for a cuppa.

'Stan,' she said, sitting on a log in front of the boiling billy, 'Augustus, the time has come for me to call a halt.'

'Where? Here?' Augustus stared about. 'We're in the middle of the bush. There's nothing here but gum trees.'

'I seen wattle,' Stan added, helpfully.

'No! No!' Rosa declared, getting to her feet. 'The time's come for me to break it off with Barkus.'

They looked at her, astonished.

'I've got what I wanted.'

'Which was?' Augustus demanded.

Stan poked the fire.

'We travelled and he taught me,' she said.

'Eh?'

'I know stuff now. Library stuff. Like how a catalogue works. How to organise one. How to develop one. I can live the life of the mind.'

'Eh?'

'What I'm saying is, I don't need him anymore.'

'I thought you liked him.'

'Well I don't.'

'I'm goin' for a pee,' Stan offered, striding off.

'But he's nice. He's not dirty like those miners. And he doesn't pay you, does he?' He looked at her intently, his meaning clear.

'No, Augustus, he doesn't pay me because there is nothing to pay me for. I am not his whore. You need to understand that.'

'Oh.' Augustus would need to tell Stan, who suffered under the same misapprehension.

'Are you sure that's clear?' Rosa demanded. 'I don't want you thinking … Those days are over, you understand?'

'Yes.'

'You're sure?'

'Yes.'

'Positive?'

'Yes, yes, yes!'

'Good.'

'But he likes you. I can tell. And he feeds us.'

'So?'

'So how can you dump him?'

'Augustus,' she sighed. 'How he feels has got nothing to do with me. He wanted me, he didn't get me. That's it. Finito. The end.'

'That's pretty tough, isn't it?'

'Yes, Augustus, it is tough. But that's life. Think about yourself. Your own situation. You're a dwarf. A smart dwarf, a talented dwarf, but a dwarf, all the same. When did life do you any favours?'

'I can sing.'

'I already said that you were talented. Go on, tell me how good life has been to you.' He gripped the teapot tighter. 'I found Stan. And you have looked after me.'

She shook her head. 'Okay, okay, I'm glad to hear that you appreciate me. Us. But don't you ever think that you have to do something to get out of this mess? Like find a job. You know, do something for *yourself*?'

'Rosa, I haven't even been to school.'

'Don't look at me,' she snorted. 'I'm not your mother.'

'You could still take me.'

'I don't think so. I've put up with Hardacre so I could get

a decent job. I'm not going to chuck all that in to cut lunches and walk you to school like some miner's wife.'

'So what can I do? Go back to the circus and be a freak, like Little Donny? Is that what you mean? Augustus, the Singing Freak. Didn't we already try that?'

'Sometimes I could strangle you,' she wailed. 'I really could. You're just too sharp for your own good. Okay. Okay. Let's talk about me. No matter what you want to do, or what Barkus wants to do for me, or to me, I want my own life. That's why I took this pony ride. To learn from him. Get it? And I did. So now ...'

'So you used him.'

'Huh?'

'You used him. You let him think that you would be with him. Or something. And you never were going to be. Ever. Not from the start.'

'You got that right, kid. You sure got that right. But let me sort you out on something: you think Stan is with you because he likes you? Huh? Do you? Don't be a dill. He's with you because that monkey copped it. Because that Hogie died. That why he's with you. Because he's got nobody else. Get it?'

Augustus took this on the chin. He had long wondered, and was prepared to accept. 'Maybe,' he declared and, suddenly brightening, 'but that doesn't explain why Stan just told me that he loved me. And he did. And I believe him. So who cares what you say? I'd rather believe Stan.'

Rosa laughed. 'You're right again. But only insofar as the "Who cares?" bit. I mean, why are we having this stupid conversation, anyway? I don't need your approval to do what I'm going to do. So like you say, "Who cares?"'

'You might one day, Rosa,' he muttered. 'Here, let me pour your tea before it gets cold. And tell me — since I know that your mind is made up — what are you going to do? More importantly, what are you going to do with us? Leave us here to starve?'

'Don't be stupid. Why would I leave you to starve after I just spent years letting disgusting men maul me so that I could look after you? Smart as you are, Augustus, you can also be stupid. And hurtful.'

'I'm sorry,' he began, 'but you did say awful things about Stan.'

'Yeah, well, Stan's Stan and Stan can be a bit cuckoo too. But let's get on. First, because I got Barkus to teach me cataloguing, like I said, I've managed to con him into giving me a reference for a job. A real job. Using my brains. How's that?'

'Rosa,' he gasped, 'that's really good. I'm happy for you, honest.'

'I am too. So I'm going to get him to take us back to Ipswich and I'll try to get a job in the library there. He reckons that place is run by a mob of old dragons and they could use somebody smart and fresh.'

'But Rosa, if you go back there, and then drop him, he'll see you whenever he comes in to change the books in his wagon. He won't be very pleased about that.'

'Too bad,' she shrugged. 'I already told you, I'm doing this for me. There's other girls he can fall for. He went for me quick enough. I don't reckon he's choosy.'

'But you let him think that you loved him?'

'I never said that.'

'You never told him?'

'He never asked. He's stupid like that.'

'So he's got no idea?'

'I guess.'

'And you're going to give him the brush-off just like that?'

'Not until he drives us back. I'm not crazy.'

'And if you get this job — if, remember — you're going to get paid?'

"Course I'll get paid.'

'And you won't have to be with men anymore? Not even librarians?'

'That's the plan,' she laughed. 'No more men. Ever!'

'And us? Me and Stan? What will happen to us?'

'Don't worry about it. Let me get this job, and after I've sorted Barkus out, I'll find a place for you. Yes, Augustus, both of you. Sooner or later Stan will have to find work again. He hasn't had a pay packet since I left the whorehouse and he stopped working down the mine. This holiday can't last forever. I'm okay. I've still got money left from Miss la Vie's. That should see you — us — set up. Don't worry, the redhead's on top of this. You wait and see ...' She sipped her cold tea, wincing.

After their return to Ipswich, Barkus Hardacre seemed to vanish. He was neither visible nor mentioned in despatches.

'I don't feel too good about Rosa dumping that Barkus,' Stan muttered.

Augustus made a face. 'Me neither,' he admitted. But I'm sure not mentioning his name to her again. I don't want another earbashing.'

But Barkus or no Barkus, Rosa did get a library job. And a good job it was too; front desk.

'Must have been some reference he wrote,' Stan observed.

'I reckon he loved her,' Augustus agreed. 'Although that would now be past tense, I reckon.'

'Yeah,' Stan chuckled. 'She's a tough sheila, that one.'

Tough as she might be, Rosa did not forget her promise to set them up. She rented a furnished cottage in Booval, a couple of miles out of Ipswich. She caught the 8.05 train every morning to return every evening on the 5.07.

Stan went back down the pit, working double shifts so he could take three or four days off to be home.

Augustus liked this little house, of the type known as 'workers dwellings' since they were built especially for the miners and their families. Made of timber and clad with weatherboards, the cottage was raised on three-foot timber stumps to allow a cooling breeze under. The interior walls were vertical tongue-and-groove timber with huntsman spiders lurking in the grooves, cockroaches too, in the kitchen; the roof was corrugated iron. Once there had been an open verandah along the front, the roof extending over, but as the previous owner's family had evidently expanded, the verandah had been half enclosed (from the central front steps, and across to the left), to form what was known as the 'sleep-out'; this space serving as Augustus's room, while Rosa and Stan had a proper bedroom each.

Having no memory of where he slept in his mother's big white house (under the piano, was it?), this was the first room of his own that Augustus could remember, and he was happy. He liked sitting up in his narrow cast-iron bed to look out over the front yard and down the street, watching the miners and their families come and go. He liked the belonging; but he also liked the secrecy, that nobody knew he was there, watching. He liked the little front yard behind the unpainted picket fence, the crazy paved path (just bits of rock set into the earth, some amateur gardener's idea of design), leading from the front gate to the front steps, and the narrow garden running along the front with its sandpapery red and yellow and orange zinnias in summer and buttery freesias in spring. But he especially liked to sit and wait for Stan to come home, and then Rosa, walking up from the train, and throwing open the creaky gate to walk that crazy path before coming in to drop down on the faded Genoa lounge, redolent with the aroma of pipe tobacco, before a slab of fruit cake and cup of tea.

One thing that Augustus didn't like was the casement windows. The rest of the house had clear glass sash windows (raised or lowered straight up or down), but those on the sleep-out, being 'an extension' — the added bonus of all timber houses — were casement windows, fixed with panes of frosted glass and purportedly opening at an angle to 'catch the breeze', which was not so in this case. Whoever fitted Augustus's sleep-out casements hinged them in the wrong direction so the cool afternoon breeze struck the exterior glass, deflecting it along the outer wall of the house, leaving Augustus in a lather of Boovalonian sweat. Worse, because the glass was frosted, he could not see out if the window was shut, and even when it was open he could only look out if he sat forward, leaning on the sill. So he piled up his pillows and tucked his legs under and did just that.

Augustus liked this house. It felt like home.

* * *

Because adults stared and children laughed, Augustus rarely went out, his books his constant companions. Having exhausted King Tut and read his way through Egypt, he moved on to other civilisations, selecting them according to their architecture. He did not, however, equate this interest with monumentality, being equally fascinated by the modest Zulu kraal as he was by the spires and towers of the Gothic cathedral. So he thought on the significance of size, and how he was both constructed, and constructed himself.

I am not so much a building, he thought, as a space that might be filled. And when he had given that notion due consideration, he modified it. I am not so much a space that might be filled, he thought, as a space that, being filled, whether with ideas or emotions, then fills others. As a flute perhaps, being filled with the sweet composer's breath, yields yet sweeter music to fill the hearts of those who hear.

So Augustus grew.

One morning, as the boy sat on the front steps of the cottage, Rosa stopped at the wooden gate and turned.

'Augustus,' she said. 'Do you sit there all day?'

'Sometimes,' he said, shading his eyes with his book.

'Wouldn't you like to come to the library with me one day? You could, you know. On the train.'

'People would look at me,' he said.

'People look at me too.'

'I've got nothing to wear,' he said.

'Would it make any difference?'

'I'm reading a book,' he said.

'We're going to a library.'

She's getting smarter, he thought.

Rosa bought Augustus a pair of lederhosen, with accompanying frilly shirt and red felt Tyrolean cap, in the bargain basement at Cribb and Foote's, and next day they caught the 8.05 to the library.

'I look stupid,' the boy complained. 'I hate this outfit.'

'Next time buy your own,' Rosa growled, shoving him into a carriage.

Among other horrors encountered on that visit, Augustus recalled struggling up a flight of sandstone stairs with Rosa half dragging, half lifting him by his left elbow, muttering: 'You're going on thirteen now, so try to act like an adult, okay? This is good clean work, using my brains for once, so I want to keep it. You got that?'

For all Rosa's loving kindness, Augustus was struck by the words graven above the entrance:

LIBRARY
SILENCE

His heart fell. Where there is silence, he thought, there is no song. And where there is no song, I die, but struggle as he might, Rosa dragged him in.

Confronted by the precipitous oak accessions desk rising sheer before him, he gazed up, wondering if boiling oil might momentarily cascade from that battlement, or a bottomless moat might burst, yawning, beneath his feet. Nor could he see any end to this fortification, neither to the right nor the left, and he gripped Rosa's hand, reduced.

'Big, eh?' she whispered, reaching up, and lo, a secret door opened, disguised in that self-same wall, and he wondered at the trickery, as to who was trying to deceive, and why.

'Isn't this a public library?' he asked, mystified by the barrier.

She pushed him through.

Beyond was worse. What were these monoliths cluttering the interior, these timbered stations rearing, island-like, from the bare wood floor; the temporary dwellings of those who manned the wall?

He stumbled between them as through canyons, expecting a hail of arrows or, had they been from an earlier age, a pterodactyl swooping, jaws agape. Nor did the black lianas (telephone cords, were they?) spiralling from these towering walls encourage him as they writhed and clung at his touch, his flesh creeping as he slunk, shoulders hunched, in the shadow of his leader.

'There are three Assistant Librarians,' Rosa whispered. 'These are their desks,' and without further warning Augustus was unceremoniously whooshed to land on a slab of oak the size of a battlefield.

'This,' observed Rosa, stepping back to reveal, 'is Miss Blotting, one of the three. She is in charge of the Fiction catalogue.'

Miss Blotting was indeed a librarian, her hair a grey and marbled coronet plaited and pinned above her head; her face a papery triangle, likewise grey and marbled, stretched, racklike, over her cheek bones; and her teeth, grey and marbled, grinning headstones.

'This,' whispered Rosa, whooshing him again to span the canyon between, 'is Miss Blank. She is in charge of Nonfiction. And this,' whooshing again, equally unceremoniously, though not without some expectation, 'Miss Bland. She looks after newspapers and magazines.'

'And poetry? Who looks after poetry?' Augustus wondered aloud.

Rosa's eyes narrowed. 'I warn you,' she whispered. 'Don't you dare bring up the subject of song, or lyrics, or anything even vaguely to do with the poetic. This is a mining town. People hate that stuff.'

'Hate it,' the Misses B responded as one.

'Ah ...' Augustus.

'Sissy stuff.'

'But ...'

'Got rid of it, we did.'

'You banned it?'

'Chucked it out,' they chorused.

The boy could not believe it.

'Shut up, Augustus ...' Rosa warned.

'But the destruction of poetry spells the death of song.'

'I want this job,' Rosa hissed. 'Shut up now.'

Augustus obeyed, wondering what might happen if he should pluck a pin (or three, or more), from those grey, marbled plaits; would the serpents so released rear and strike from these Gorgon skulls?

'Augustus was asking if he could sing for you,' Rosa lied. 'But don't worry, he won't,' and she glared, as if daring him.

'What a dear little boy,' Miss Blotting wheezed, peering down; then Miss Blank, 'What a delightful child'; then Miss Bland, 'What a perfect treasure.'

They are treating me like an infant, Augustus thought. Yet there is no womblike cave here, no piano to curl up under or emerge from, renewed. This place is as dead as a tomb. Ah, Absalom ... and, leaping from desk to chair to floor, he ran between the canyons hoping to find a door or a window or a keyhole whereby he might escape.

Pausing, breathless, to check, he saw that he had corralled himself in an office of frosted glass where three people (men, were they?) sat at a circular table, each on a wooden stool, each bending forward, evidently busy.

The first was huge, his bum overhanging the stool top (had it melted, like cheese on an unsupervised grill?), his gut overhanging his knees, his chin overhanging his chest, yet this body, for all its enormity had somehow been packed, poured or moulded into a suit of grey flannel, the trousers elephantine, the coat a marquee. Had his black felt bow tie been undone and drawn from the folds of his neck, it could serve as carpet runner in a mortuary.

Augustus stood, too saddened to laugh.

But oh, that hair, that head!

A woolly mammoth might trumpet in envy at the sight of the grey, greasy mass tumbling from the pachyderm's forehead, over his skull and around his ears to fall about his red, cratered neck. And from the head the nose: a mountain of warts, some pink, some purple, all moist and fleshy, erupting in sequence (as do geysers from a rock).

While Augustus watched agog, from the huge one's lips

oozed a rope of spittle, long and languid, almost reaching the desk top and, upon inhalation, drawing back, vanishing within those fleshy lips only to reappear, drooping, then drawing up, drooping, then drawing up, an aqueous ebb and flow well worthy of a boy's attention.

The second person appeared much the same, only slighter.

The third also, skinnier still (a skeleton, was it?).

Yet all three were dressed alike, coiffured alike, dribbled alike. Then Augustus saw what united them, and possibly why he had stopped to stare in the first place. All three — huge, medium and cadaverous — were stamping. Not furiously, not violently, but slowly, rhythmically, the right hand reaching to stamp upon a red-inked pad, then crossing the body to the left to stamp again, in concert; a musical concept which, muted though it was, in breaking the silence pleased him with its soft padded puff. But what were they stamping?

He climbed on a chair to see.

Loan cards, he observed, to verify the borrowing of poetry books!

Augustus steadied himself for a better look, standing on a chair as he was, and noted that these cards were all the same — the very same three — one stamper stamping before sliding the card to his left where his partner did the same. So the cards — the very same three — went round and round the table as the stampers stamped, a hand reaching, a hand stamping, as had been done for years, judging by the cards all red with ink and the unoiled creaking of the skeletal one, and the bodily diminution of the thinner one, and the well-rounded blubber of the leviathan, who was evidently new. Which made Augustus think, Do they stamp until they are dead, I wonder? And his hand went to his mouth as he realised, This is all to add to a lie. There are no poetry books in this library yet they stamp the cards to pretend that there are ... Looking this way and that he saw no person, no borrower, no reader of any kind, and he wondered again at this lifeless place: this library without poetry, this library without readers, this building without sound, save for the Gorgon's hiss or a soft stamped puff. Looking up directly, searching for a book or a poem or a song, he wondered at the shafts of light beaming from above, not bright, never celestial, but grey as flannel, ribboning down, unravelled bolts crisscrossing in space, flecked about with drifting dust. He stood quite still to look again, steady ...

And so he saw: beyond these murky shafts a balcony protruded; a gallery with a railing — much like one he had seen in a photographic work on the architecture of Victorian railway stations — appearing and disappearing out of that miasma of dust motes and grey flannel bolts and shafts of smoggy light, and he wondered if a library book might lurk there; if a poetry collection might be filed there, a manuscript even — a word, he would accept — secret on a shelf in that forbidding place; too distant, too high, too dim for human presence.

Leaping from his chair, he ran towards a flight of iron steps, leading up, he hoped, towards that gallery and the possibilities so promised.

The metal handrail was cold to his touch, and he withdrew his hand, fearful. He had little experience of metal, none at all of its steely cold. He touched again, assessing, sensing no life, no warmth. The legs of his mother's piano were wood, handcrafted from an organic being — a living thing — a tree. The keys of the piano were ivory, crafted from organic matter — a tusk — part of the body of an animal: a living thing. But this metal, this mass of mineral — this tube so cold — what life had it known? What pleasures? What joys? What poetry of wind, of sea, of sun; what pleasant language had brought it to be? He gripped the rail tight, deliberately subjugating its careless form to the human heart, declaring, 'Void of life though you are, you will help me,' and so he climbed, the stair treads, webs of iron, rising ever higher, ever assuring him (each footstep clattering), that if he went on he would find that gallery, but each staircase opened on to a landing and each landing opened on to a staircase and so he climbed, clattering and puffing, ever upward until at the seventh staircase (perhaps the ninth or the eleventh — who could count in that confusion?) the landing expanded to become that distant gallery he had seen from his chair below. Setting foot upon it, he gripped the railing to look down.

I have no feeling for steel, he realised. It's too cold for the poetic, too hard. Even the splinters of Miss la Vie's verandah yielded more romance than this. Yet surely there is a poem, a song — if sung right, if sung to perfection — that would recreate this place?

Looking down through the miasma of dust and fog, he could make out nothing of substance; not the Gorgons, nor their battlements, nor Rosa, nor the Stampers Three, nor the staircase that had bought him here, and gripping the railing tighter, he sighed and stood tall. This is a clerestory level, he told himself. A clear story level. I am safe here. I am clear. I will find that poem, that recreative song...

Until the thought struck him:

LIBRARY
SILENCE.

Even as he sighed, hopeless, he noticed a protrusion from the wall (an eyrie, could it be?) and in that steely pod, a human shape; some mean-fleshed body clad in a sexless cardigan, grey hair knotted in the obligatory plait, the nose severe, the chin lowered, the lips pursed, the eyes small, peering through pince-nez into the morass below. Stamped in grey plate (tin, was it? Or poisonous lead?) upon this creature's desk, the chilling word:

LIBRARIAN

'I have seen stony Gorgons,' Augustus sobbed. 'I have met ghastly stampers. Surely this is the very Murderess of Song!'

Yet as he wept, the circus came to mind, the sorrow he had known there: that time at the willow down by the dribbly creek, and the song he had sung that day; he remembered that awful house, the bitter mango, the jewelled hand, sad Absalom, the lonely death of the Blue Butterfly, and the songs he had sung for them.

I will sing, he thought, wiping his cheeks. I will bring the life-creating joy of song to this deathly place. That is what I do. On pain of destroying my own life, I must not forget that. I am an instrument which, being filled with the sweet composer's breath, yields yet sweeter music to fill the hearts of those who hear. I must remember that, for my own sake, for my own future, if I am to have one, as I will when I have sung myself to grow.

And wiping his eyes, he looked up.

Through a coal-streaked window he saw outside. That is the rear of the building, he understood. And what appears to be a pile of mullock … But such was the murk and grime streaking the pane, he could see no more. Climbing down, tread after weary tread, he understood. I need to explore this place, as I shuffled through that sawdust, trod in that dung, back beneath that big top; as I crawled in that dirt, back there, beneath that whorehouse …

So he did, until Rosa called him home.

When Stan came in from the pit they sat together on the front steps, staring down at the crazy path.

'Stan,' Augustus said, 'I went to the library today. I hated the place. I thought I was going to die.'

'But you didn't, eh?' Stan said.

'No,' Augustus replied. 'I'm sitting here next to you.'

'So?'

'So I might have.'

'Hmmm?'

'It was horrible. I couldn't find a song.'

Stan rested his elbows on the stair above. 'Augie,' he said, 'you aren't s'posed to sing in a library.'

'I know that. But the place was so cold. They reckoned their poetry books had been chucked out because no-one wanted to read them. Not in a mining town, anyway.'

'Dunno 'bout that,' Stan grunted.

'What?'

'Them miners in Wales sing in choirs, hey?'

'Maybe ...'

'Never sung a song meself,' Stan admitted. 'But didn't you tell me you just know the right song for the right place. No matter where?'

'This place was dead.'

'So you was scared, eh?'

'I saw a skeleton.'

'Go on ...'

'And Gorgons, made of stone.'

'When I went to school,' Stan reflected, 'if I remember right, Gorgon weren't made of stone. I thought that she turned the ones she looked at inta stone. But I was stupid, eh?'

'No, Stan. No ...'

'Augie,' Stan said, putting his arm around the boy, 'I reckon the place just got to ya. I reckon you lost your nerve. You gotta go back. You gotta find your song. Like before. Remember that mango tree? That Miss la Vie ...'

Within a month (perhaps three, perhaps seven, maybe more), Augustus found the courage to return to the library.

'Is it true that they disposed of the poetry books?' he asked Rosa as she set herself up at Accessions.

'Don't be ridiculous,' she sneered. 'The Misses B were having a go at you. You're such a child.'

'But last time I was here ...' he began, then fell silent. How could he explain the Stamping Men and their weird ritual of forever validating unborrowed books? So he said, 'Sorry to be a pest. I'll have a little wander ...'

Having negotiated the Valley of the Gorgons and the Circle of Stampers and electing not to climb that cast-iron stairway to the grey, misty gallery in the clerestory, he stumbled upon a circle of steel set into the hardwood floor.

'What's under this?' he muttered. 'A secret repository? A hidden cache of poesy?' and stooping, he gripped the ring, wrenching it upwards with all his might.

'Ugh!' he gasped, catching a whiff of foul air. 'Dung! I know it from the circus.'

But what was dung doing beneath that library floor? And why, indeed, was there a trapdoor opening into this morass? Pinching his nostrils, he dropped to his knees and peered in.

There were stairs leading down: steep but negotiable. Ladder-like.

Taking one last look to see that the coast was clear of pterosaurs or other monstrous beings, he turned about to venture in.

The descent was perilous, the stench overpowering, the pit beneath deep and dark. Hand over hand he clambered, tenuous tread after tenuous tread, his fingers stiff with fear.

'There might be something,' he breathed. 'Some repository. Some cache. Some answer.' Finally he made footfall, unnervingly soft. 'Manure, for sure,' he muttered.

And it was.

But not like that circus dung. Not fresh, not gaudy with yellow straw. No. This was old. This was not even elephant dung. Nor tiger. Nor ostrich, nor ape, nor seal, nor bear.

A band of grey light oozed from a casement, thick with grime. He bent to see. Horse! This was horse manure. In heaps. In piles. In mounds. But here? Beneath a library? Why?

As he peered into the gloom, he made out the shape of a glue-factory nag (no …), and a wagon, commodious too (never …) and a voice hailed from the darkness, 'Rosa? Rosa, my darling, is it you?'

Augustus froze.

Out of that dark, out of that murk, that stench, that memory of days gone by, lurched none other than Barkus Hardacre; wasted, thin, too thin, his pale hands outstretched, calling, 'Rosa? Rosa are you come? Are you come at last?'

'Barkus?' Augustus answered. 'Mr Hardacre, Sir?'

'I am Barkus Hardacre,' he replied. 'But what are you?'

'Not Rosa, Sir, but me, Augustus Trump.'

Barkus lurched closer, to grasp him (those hands once so virile, now thin and pale), where he stood at the foot of the ladder, too terrified to move.

'Augustus?' Barkus called. 'Not him who was her friend? Not the dwarf? Not the dwarf who sang? Not that Augustus, surely?'

'Indeed, it is,' came the reply. 'But I am alone,' and reaching up to take the librarian's death-white fingers, he thought, Absalom, my solitary friend, here is the proof of that pain of love. Ah … Though he chose not to vocalise this; to lie was easier. 'Barkus,' he said, his courage quickening, 'it is good to see you. Our parting was sudden, I am sorry.'

'What are you doing here?' Barkus demanded. 'Did she send you?'

'No,' the boy assured him. 'I am alone. I promise. I was looking for poetry books and stumbled upon this place. But what, may I ask, are *you* doing here? And where are we? I am confused…'

'Poetry?' the librarian sneered. 'Here? In this place? You joke, surely ...' and led him through the oozy dung. 'Sit,' he said. 'There is a pallet of clean straw. The library is old, these stables beneath. I hole up here when I bring the wagon in. It's foul, but the odour suits my spirits. She is above us, my Rosa. I helped her find work here. And I see her, sometimes — not often —coming and going. Augustus, I am finished. She enticed me and I followed. And I cannot cease to follow. To dream. To wait. Which is the hopelessness of love ...' Weeping, he buried his head in his hands.

'I am sorry,' Augustus offered. 'She was cruel, I know. I warned her ...'

'Too cruel,' the librarian wailed. 'I was willing to marry her. I would have given my life for her, and now, I fear, I must. I have ...'

'Is there anything I can do?' Augustus asked, doubting.

'Perhaps you could speak to her for me?'

'She would not listen.'

'You could carry a note for me?'

'She would not read it.'

'What then? I am doomed ...'

'I could sing?' Augustus suggested, brightening.

'Sing to her? Yes! The poetry might lead her to me. Might woo her ...'

'No,' Augustus soothed, 'I could sing for *you*. To cheer you.'

'I am tired,' Barkus sighed. 'I am ...'

'Then lie back,' Augustus crooned. 'Lie back. Close your eyes now. Lie back ...'

And exhausted, Barkus did.

When Augustus saw that Barkus slept (dreaming, was he?), he reached for the ladder, and climbing, sang:

As he reached the top, never looking back, the grimy casement below eased open and she appeared: that faery's child, her hair long, her foot light, her eyes wild, that lady full beautiful, that Belle Dame Sans Merci, and, drifting down, she lifted him, that pale lover, and mounting him upon his steed she called him to her elfin grot where he, all smiling and fulfilled, agreed too gladly to repose eternal in that fruitless dream of love.

Augustus was desperate to escape. Spotting what he took to be the back door, he eagerly stepped out. Before him stretched a muddied pathway and, strutting boldly upon it, three massive crows, their coal black feathers (mourning in bombazine, were they?) all glossy in the foggy light.

'And what are you three doing here?' he asked, mocking. 'Shoo! Shoo! Get off the path. I'm looking for books. Shoo! Shoo!' but they did not go; indeed, the largest bird turned, and tilting its head, cast its golden eye upon him.

'Oh!' Augustus declared. 'You are the cheeky one, aren't you? Go on, get ...' at which the bird faced him directly and in a gravelly voice declared, 'Since when have you turned so rude? I remember you as a nice little fellow, who sang!'

Am I mad? Augustus wondered, staring about, Or did that bird just speak?

'Of course she spoke,' the second bird said. 'When have you known her to be silent, other than out of fear of that Rosa?'

Even as Augustus clapped his hands to his temples, his senses reeling, the third waddled over, as bold as you like, and said, loud and clear, 'Would you sing for us, Augustus? Something moving, something sad, something of that "Plaisir d'amour", perhaps?'

And so Augustus knew them: his Moira, his Betty, his Absalom, and he laughed out loud, delighted. 'What can I say?' he cried. 'Why are you here? Tell me, please.'

But with many a golden wink, and many a shiver of those jet-black plumes, they toddled away with here a peck and there a scratch, but never another word among them.

'What?' he cried. 'What have you come to tell me?' but they would not, those tricksters three, although they strutted purposefully, and he in their thrall followed, until the muddy path passed through a gap in the mullock and he saw them pause and look up, croaking.

'What?' he wondered. 'Is this what you have come to show me?' And standing among them, unafraid, he looked to see a leafless tree (*Salix babylonica*, a weeping willow, he knew), the epitome of sorrow; the very metaphor of death. This is the mullock dump that I spotted from the clerestory last I was here, he realised. I wonder, is there a pit? And if there is …?

As Augustus stepped out to see, his feathered guides departed, their voices hushed, their wings a whisper, and confused as he was, what with Gorgons and Silent Stampers and Grey Flannel streaming, and now these three, these

Crows in Mourning, he wondered: Am I crazy, or still, after all, that Augustus Trump who sang?

He had seen mullock heaps all about the town, but as he left the willow to wander that puddly path, side-stepping the black ooze, he saw that the rocky waste was not randomly dumped (by some miner or machine, careless), but stacked neatly, like walls, or rocky hedgerows, uniform. Nor were the rocks rough-edged, having been blasted from the earth, but regular rectangles and squares, though drizzled with the slag and slime he had mistaken for moss. Is this slate, he wondered, stacked slice upon slice, slab upon slab? And hesitant, he reached out to discover that what he had assumed to be stone was soft and porous to his touch.

'Why!' he gasped. 'These are books. Piles of books, stacked one upon the other, yet rank and weathered. Stacked here by those Gorgons, I bet ...' Drawing back, amazed, he heard the sound of tearing, of paper being ripped, of pages being torn, and fearful, he found a space to peer beyond, wondering.

Though he knew her at once, Miss la Vie was not as he had last seen her. She sat straight-backed on a shabby office chair, surrounded by the mouldering books. No longer dressed in pink, she wore a suit of grey flannel, buttoned up and square shouldered, her hair cut ragged and rough. But it was her face that moved him most; what had once appeared pale and cadaverous, caked as it had been with powder and rouge, now glowed red, all rubbed and scrubbed: the skin of a drover, or a bricklayer, red and raw. He watched as she scanned the page of a book open on her knees then, grimacing, she tore that page out, crumpled it in her fist, and cast it into the pit beside her.

The books are being destroyed. And by Madame ... he realised. Either Rosa does not know, or she is a liar.

'Miss la Vie,' he said, stepping up. 'We meet again.'

She looked up, raising her eyebrows, not especially surprised. 'So you have found me,' she said. 'I was half expecting ...' and she lowered her eyes to scan another page.

'I wasn't looking, I promise.'

'Why are you here?' she asked, careless. 'I thought you'd be on the stage. One way or another.'

'I only wanted to make you happy,' he said. 'I hoped to do that with my song.'

She chucked what remained of a book down the pit and turned to him. 'Yes, well,' she said, 'you mucked that up, didn't you?'

'I had no knowledge of your love life. Certainly of the fact — or so I have been led to believe — that the Blue Butterfly shared a similar passion ...'

'How about you get lost,' she said, reaching down for another slime-caked volume.

And he would have, gladly, had he not needed an answer. 'Those books that you are destroying,' he said. 'Are they poetry, by any chance?'

'Naturally!'

'Unnaturally, I would say,' he rallied.

'Didn't I just tell you to get lost?'

'I will, when you tell me.'

'I'm reading, okay? I'm reading every lying love poem ever written. Those dried-out hags in there were chucking them out. Never had a man between them, they haven't, and wouldn't know what to do with him if they did. So when I came to this library looking, trying to find some hope, some love, even in print if I had to, after what happened to me, after him that betrayed me, and her, that Blue Butt, I found all these poetry books out in the slag pile. Culling, they called it; culling. Not by me, okay? By them, in there, so I'm reading these poetry books, see, but I haven't found anything to make me feel better. So I'm getting rid of the rubbish. You done with me now? Go on, get lost …'

'But I sang you a love song,' he protested. 'I sang you a love poem. The very one that you loved yourself. I climbed that mango tree, I sang my heart out. And you ridiculed me. Or tried to …'

'Are you mad?' she demanded. 'Are you loony? What love song? What love poem? I never told you nothing. I never gave you nothing, though you wanted it bad. And for free …'

'You make yourself cheap,' he said. 'And you are wrong. The Blue Butterfly told me that "Goodbye, Little Yellow Bird" was your favourite song so I sang it for you, special.'

'Ah!' she exclaimed, a slimy hand flying to her mouth. 'So it was her who put you up to that. Ah … And you believed! It was *her* favourite song. And *his*. *Theirs*, not *mine*.' She sighed, reconsidering. 'Now I get it. She told you that to spite me. To destroy me. And she did. She did … My house. My heart, what was left of it. Look at me here. Dried up, I am, dried up with looking for love, like them old bags inside. I thought you were having a go at *me* …' Covering her face, she wept.

He came to her, taking her hands in his. 'I am just a kid. Rosa tells me that every day. And I know nothing about love, and maybe never will, not unless I grow. Unless I *will* myself to manhood.'

'Ha!' she sneered. 'Men!'

'I *will* find that perfect song,' he declared. 'I *will* sing that note sublime and I *will* grow. I will!'

'Yeah, yeah …' The Madam had heard enough.

'And there's something that I have to offer you. You know that song, that Little Yellow Bird?'

'No more,' she wailed. 'Never again. Leave it. Leave me, please.'

'I won't leave you,' he said. 'There's something that you need to hear. That song said, "I'd rather brave the cold, in a leafless tree than a prisoner be, in a cage of gold." That was her song, as you say, and his. Who would know? But I have a better one. I have a better one to cheer you and promise you the love you are looking for. No leafless trees, no, quite the opposite. And no, you won't find this poem in those books. It's here, inside me.'

'Augustus,' she pleaded. 'Go, please.'

But he would not and, planting his tiny feet, and lifting his pretty head, he sang:

Where'er you walk,
Cool gales shall fan the glade.
Trees where you sit
Shall crowd into a shade.
Trees where you sit
Shall crowd into a shade …

Looking beyond him she saw the stark, leafless willows begin to green, and in moments, spontaneously as she would remember, they were leaved all over, crowded with summery shade.

Augustus saw nothing, his head back, content to sing.

When he had finished she said, 'Augustus, I heard you. And having heard — and seen — I must speak.'

'I'm listening,' he said, ignorant of her vision.

'I am no Miss la Vie,' she said, taking his hand. 'Neither am I a whore; not by birth, nor by nature. I am Daphne Fooks, from out Goondi way, and the time has come for me to go back. There's people out there who love me. Under the red gums, down by the river, back home. You have reminded me. Thank you, Augustus, I will go ...' and stepping through the mud and mould, she did.

Augustus had never been interested in money, having no need for it, but now, as part of his plan, the power to purchase became a necessity. If he was going to gain the victory, to emancipate that library, to enrich those bare shelves with poetry, he needed to present as a man, a powerful man, a military man. No boyish lederhosen would do; he needed a uniform. He was, after all, only following Rosa's repeated lectures to 'act like an adult', and since he didn't like the clothes she supplied, maybe he should follow her advice and buy his own. But with what?

Though not well off, Rosa and Stan sometimes left change about: the odd sixpence, the occasional shilling, and once — though he waited a day before snaffling it — he spotted a crumpled pound note under the Genoa lounge. Augustus appropriated an Arnott's biscuit tin, the lid sporting a parrot in red, blue and green, to serve as his money box, not daring to ask for a proper one with a slot in the top for fear of raising suspicion. Thus he began to save, little by little, over six months, nine months, maybe even a year, since life had a certain sameness in that cottage.

He also took to observing what was worn by those who passed by as he sat reading, small and secret, on the front steps. He saw miners in pairs swinging tin lunch boxes, sometimes with a canary (all skinny and terrified), but always black and grim in their sooty grey flannels (was that where those flannel shafts had come from, up there on that cast-iron gallery?). Stan was forever boiling his own filthy clothes, pushing them down in the bubbling suds with a broom handle and a blue stick, but all to no avail other than making them so stiff when they dried they might be used to roof a house. But Augustus could never pass himself off as a miner and besides, that was not the martial self-construction he required.

Nor could he present as a housewife, although there were plenty of them who passed by, lank-haired miners' wives in droopy florals, so ordinary he wondered how the population grew if bodily attraction was a factor, as Rosa had told him all that time ago in the shed down the back of Miss la Vie's.

Children came by too, the schoolboys especially interesting to him, particularly those who wore fancy uniforms and went to private schools. Holding his book high to pretend he was reading, Augustus leaned forward to watch.

These uniforms varied. The Catholic schools were usually too awful to consider, being made of materials that looked itchy, and were invariably in colours calculated to repel: brown and yellow, or brown and blue, or brown and mauve (which was the worst). He sometimes wondered if this repellent colouration was intentional, being designed to make the boys less attractive to their teachers. Mary Smokes had warned him about those 'Brothers', down there in the dirt. So he ignored the ugly Catholic uniforms and gave his attention to the others. The Lutheran get up was okay, if somewhat restrictive (the trousers looking very tight), but the Church of England uniform really caught his eye. Being mostly khaki, featuring a smart little coat (with epaulettes of burgundy and gold) and complete with long trousers, the outfit had a certain military air that he liked; that suited his mission to conquer the library, so to speak.

But how could he get such a uniform? And how much would it cost? These questions vexed him greatly, especially when he considered his only option: to catch the train and sit close enough to engage those C. of E. boys in conversation.

That decision being made, one morning he waited until Rosa had left on the 8.05 then dressed himself in his hated lederhosen. To complete his 'otherness' (being already othered by size), he chose a heavy-weave blanket (the obligatory travelling rug) and a piece of mouldy cheese (to pass as goat's), thus completing his construction as Friedrich from the Tyrol, and allowing him with greater alacrity (or less, perhaps?) to ask silly questions, as tourists often do. Next, this Friedrich in lederhosen took himself to the station to catch the 8.32, the train swarming with school kids. He stood at the back of the uniformed horde, watching, and at 8.30, his mark arrived. A boy (possibly a dwarf) in a C. of E. uniform and hardly taller than himself approached, accompanied by his mother. The Tyrolean tourist insinuated himself.

'*Guten Morgen*,' Friedrich said in his very best Tyrolean. 'The son gotten nice uniform. Where you get?'

'What a darling child!' the mother declared. 'Judging by your own outfit — and that cheesy smell — you must be from the Alps. I did so love *Heidi*.'

Friedrich gaped, dumbfounded.

But all was not lost. 'Roger's uniform?' she remembered. 'I do beg your pardon. That was made by a woman in Brisbane Street. Her sign read, "Nice needlework done here". And will you be going to St Sufferings yourself?'

'*Ach, nein*,' Friedrich squeaked before vanishing into the crowd.

Still clad in the hideous lederhosen (since he had nothing else to wear), Augustus found the shop in Brisbane Street with very little trouble, the average passer-by being only too pleased to move him on, having caught a whiff of that rancid cheese on the sultry Ipswich breeze. And when he pushed at the door, heard the bell and saw the woman there, bending over the treadle-operated Singer, her face as thin as a splinter, her teeth long and yellow, he gasped: 'Needly! Needly Phyllis!' and they fell into each other's arms.

'I was wanting a favour,' Augustus began. 'A uniform to be made, if you would …'

'Luv,' she said. 'Luv, I always said if there's anythin' yer wanted me ta make, let me know. Nothin's too good fer yer, kid. Nothin'. Yer made me cry, yer did. Yer lovely voice like. Ow is yer, Hogie?'

'Hogie was the monkey,' Augustus protested. 'I'm Augustus, the dwarf.'

'Awww,' she groaned.

'But I am well, Needly,' Augustus recovered. 'Very well in fact. Um, is it all right if I call you Needly?'

'Course,' she laughed. 'Them circus days all gone now, eh?' Don't care whatcha call me no more. All gone that lot. An' I don't miss 'em neither.'

'I live with Rosa Colleano and Stan the Roustabout,' Augustus admitted.

'Rosa? Her what killed the monkey?'

'*Did* she?' Augustus gasped, being ignorant of the murderer's identity. 'I don't believe you. Never!'

'Humph,' Needly shrugged. 'Then don't believe me. But everybody knows. All except you. And that Stan, a course. Would have been the end of him, eh?'

So Augustus understood. After all these years. The sense of it, he thought. The raw and bloody logic. The cold hard cruelty. And after Barkus, it had to be. It had to be Rosa.

'I'm sorry Needly, I never knew. It had to be Rosa, hey?'

Seeing his surprise, Phyllis backed away. 'So they say,' she fussed, 'so they say. It was that Bertie Sullivan who told me. But who'd believe Bertie Sullivan? So forgit it. Forgit it, eh. That Stan, he's a good man, eh? I liked him.'

'Yes,' Augustus agreed, his head reeling, perhaps from the news about Hogie's murderer or possibly, and equally potent, that goaty cheese, all manky and mouldy in the chest pocket of his lederhosen. 'Stan is a good man. But I was wondering, Needly, could you make me a uniform?'

'Tell me whatcha after and I'll run it up fer ya,' she declared.

'A school uniform,' he admitted, somewhat sheepishly, 'for St Sufferings Church of England Boys School. I'll pay, of course. I've got a tin full of money ...'

'I don't want no money,' Needly declared. 'I said I'd do ya fer nothin'. And I will. Never heard nothin' like the way ya sang that day you popped outta that spittoon. The day ya sang that 'Please Give Me a Penny', *Sir*. I never forgot that. Never. So yer after the uniform fer what school?'

'St Sufferings.'

'Funny that. Made one just the other day. An' fer another little fella too. Much like yaself.' She clamped her hand to her mouth, sorrowful, 'Like yaself and Little Donny. Ya remember Little Donny, do ya?'

'How could I forget?'

'Yairs,' she said, thinking. 'Wants ta go ta Hollywood he does. Wants ta be in a cartoon 'e does. Fer Disney. Aaaah ...'

'Needly ...' Augustus whispered, calling her back.

'Yairs,' she said, focusing. 'Roger his name was, that other little one. I still got the pattern and a bit a the fabric. Enough, I reckon, since yer only small. Yairs. Tell ya what. Let me check ya fer size and we'll see what we can do. Oright?' And pulling her tape measure from her scrawny neck, she set about taking his vitals.

Once the uniform had been collected and the meagre contents of the Arnott's biscuit tin handed over, despite protests, one thing remained in the way of Augustus's assault upon the library: to find a time when Rosa wouldn't be there. The need for her absence had become an issue for a number of reasons. The first was self evident: Rosa didn't want him singing in her place of work. That much had been made perfectly clear back at Miss la Vie's. Needly's faux pas regarding Rosa's involvement in Hogie's death only added to the boy's reluctance to perform in her presence. If she could kill a creature that had done her no harm, what might she do to him, the yodelling dwarf, the bane of her life? This particular horror rattled around in his brain like a marble in a jam tin. Nor could he relieve his angst by telling anyone. Who would I tell? he wondered. Not Stan, that's for sure. Then he got to fretting over why Rosa had murdered the chimp in the first place — if she had, and he hoped she hadn't — and whether maybe he should ask her outright and get it over with but he couldn't. If I did and she said she did it, what would I do? And if I did and she said she didn't, what would I do?

So Augustus hid his St Suffering's uniform under his bed and sat on the steps for another few months — or was it a year?

I'm suffering, he thought. Suffering...

The drab miners passed, and their drabber wives, and the too-tight Lutherans and the itchy brown Catholics, but in time, as he watched, listless, ceasing to hope, a very small C. of E. boy came into view.

Augustus sat up. Why, he thought, That's Little Roger from St Sufferings, and on the instant he was at the gate, calling.

'What?' the child responded, evidently annoyed.

'Your name's Roger, isn't it?' Augustus asked.

'What's it to ya?'

'I talked to your mum a while back. Down at the station.'

'Yeah, so?'

'So how are you going?'

'I'm all right,' Roger replied, suspicious.

'Just wondering. Don't you catch the train with your mother anymore?'

'No.'

'How come?'

'What?'

'How come you don't catch the train with your mother anymore?'

'Because I'm six years old and two foot six inches tall and a man can't hide behind his mother all his life. So how about you grow up?'

That's it! Augustus realised. Little Roger got it in one. I'm acting as if Rosa is my mother, and she isn't. She's not even my manager anymore. Not since the circus. It's time that I stood up for myself. That I let her know. For poetry, for song. If I am to become a man …

Augustus chose the following Monday to return to the library, thinking midmorning would be the best. Stan was down pit and once Rosa had left, taking the 8.05 as usual, he slipped into his smart St Sufferings uniform.

On looking up at the words engraved above the library door he hesitated, remembering: The Accessions desk. How can I get by? Emboldened by his uniform, or St Suffering himself, Augustus stifled a laugh, skirting the building to enter by the rear.

Once inside he spotted the cast-iron gallery that had so daunted him. 'Not this time,' he announced and taking to the stairs, he climbed floor after floor, reaching dizzying heights until, gripping the cold hard railing, he looked down at the murky light seeping from the clerestory windows, not bright (never celestial), but dense, grey as flannel unravelled from the bolt, its grim yardage adrift in that steely space, and planting his military feet, and lifting his military head, he sang:

The Minstrel boy to the war is gone,
In the ranks of death you'll find him;
His father's sword he has girded on,
And his wild harp slung behind him;
'Land of song!' said the warrior bard,
'Tho' all the world betrays thee,
One sword, at least, thy rights shall guard,
One faithful harp shall praise thee!'

The Minstrel fell, but the foeman's chain
Could not bring his proud soul under;
The harp he loved ne'er spoke again,
For he tore its chords asunder;
And said, 'No chains shall sully thee,
Thou soul of love and bravery.
Thy songs were made for the pure and free,
They shall never sound in slavery.'

The effect was miraculous. Rising out of that pit where the Madam had cast them, books appeared — poetry, surely — to swirl and snake, all pages and print, all songs and sighs, and whirling above the mullock — in all the giddy glory of creation — they rose above that heartless building (a library, was it?) to dive downward, all in a rush, piercing the murky glass of the clerestory windows, so striped with grime, so streaked with dust, to flutter, white-winged, dove-like, into the grey, smog-bound void below.

'Ah!' Augustus sighed, gripping the rail. 'I have achieved. My voice. My song ...' And the books, so grateful to return, having plunged downward through the void, rose up, rejoicing, hurling themselves over that cold cast-iron railing, seeking their rightful shelves where they might nestle, patient, fertile, waiting for that lover to borrow, to open, and reading, to laugh, to cry — as lovers do and always have.

And this time, for the first time, Augustus saw.

Beneath him those steely pins (whether three or nine) sprang from the grey, marbled plaits of the stony librarians and (considering the constraints of their binding) the hairy serpents so released reared from those unfettered heads to escape (all hissy and delighted) into the lush green foliage of the freshly leaved willows beyond.

At the round table in the frosted glass room, the Stampers so released ceased their labours, joining hands to dance, squashing their stamp pads (all red and spongy, oozing ink) into that hardwood floor.

And among this confabulation of poetry and dance, especially the white pages, aflutter like doves, the boy saw a coloured paper (a postcard, was it? A brochure? An airline ticket, possibly; a parrot among doves), and this page, so lively and joyous, having a mind of its own, separated itself from those avian others to land, trembling, upon the chilly desk of the grey librarian in her steely nest and she (being distracted by books; white-winged, dove-like), on reaching out to snatch, sensed her pince-nez darken, such was the brightness, the sheer glare of the tropics on that ticket (was it?), and suddenly she smiled, an island romance in her sights.

Augustus was not alone in witnessing his handiwork. Upon hearing his voice (possibly at the word 'men', probably at the word 'free'), Rosa on Accessions lifted her head, peering through the gloom, to catch his thrilling tones. And having both seen and heard — after all this time, after all those years — she was changed. Pushing aside her catalogue, 'Augustus,' she cried, 'I've tried the life of the body; I've tried the life of the mind. Show me the life of the spirit!'

Looking down from the clerestory, the dwarf laughed.

'Rosa,' he called, 'what will you become? A nun?'

THE TEMPLE

IN THE WEEKS FOLLOWING his emancipation of the library, Augustus returned to sitting on the front steps of the cottage in Booval.

Once, Rosa sat beside him. 'Don't let your little miracle go to your head,' she warned. 'Just as the Bodhisattva sat beneath the Bodhi tree, I am also coming into my own. Spiritually, so to speak.'

Having suffered through a variety of Rosa's egocentric incarnations (personal manager, whore, librarian), Augustus gave her little credence. 'Ah,' he said, never batting an eyelid, 'then you will appreciate that I am meditating myself. Would you mind?' And he nodded in the direction of the crazy paving leading to the gate.

Augustus liked to watch the world pass by. He especially liked the door-to-door hawkers, the household wares in their carts and carpetbags, a cornucopia of the useful and otherwise. Certain of these merchants came with children in tow, usually some pitiful wretch elicited from home or convent, haven or hovel, dragged weeping and alone from the shadowy sanctuary of arch or doorway, hollow log or drain, kennel or carton to stand, hang-dog and soulful, while its master rattled off a spiel about 'scratchin' for a feed, if you could spare a penny?'

Sales pitches meant nothing to Augustus since he had not a penny himself; all the same, he was ever so glad when these colourful rogues happened along — especially those with kids.

Dr A C Jones was a Purveyor of Cure-Alls and Elixirs, or so the faded sign on the hand tray he toted declared. Having examined his array of bottles and jars — to the extent of removing them to shake, to hold against the light, and once to open and sniff — Augustus was of the opinion that their primary ingredient was water, with the addition of a certain pinkness; perhaps cochineal, possibly Condy's crystals. He said nothing.

Augustus liked Dr A. He liked his shortness, his corpulence, his face full and cheery, his bald head, his ears broad and red as the leaves of a cabbage he had seen once in a greengrocer's window out Goodna way. He also liked the man's taste in clothes. Dr A was inclined towards the flashy, favouring suit coats in plaid or tartan worn with a bright, wide tie and white leather spats (sometimes clean, most often not). Augustus liked that Dr A was always on for a yarn about one of his 'regulars' who had the pleurisy or the poonemony, once even the plague, curable only by copious doses of the good doctor's personally branded elixir.

One time — and one time only — when Augustus laughed, the doctor betrayed himself. 'Augustus,' he said, 'mate, a man's gotta earn a crust. You of all people ...' and he looked the dwarf up and down — what there was of him — 'will appreciate that one day.'

Augustus laughed no more.

As amusing as the doctor could be, his offsider, the boy Ralph, also appealed. Ralph was 'soft', as the kinder ones said; the less gracious called him 'loony'. It was the meningitis that had done him in; the brain fever. Yet there were those, the kinder ones, who said God did him a favour. His mother, illiterate, took in laundry; his father, a drinker, beat her regularly. Ralph saw and heard but failed to comprehend. Not that he condoned; he simply turned away, smiling his silly smile, to feed the sparrows down the yard or collect the pegs, dropped by his mother when she was struck. The circumstances of his family life, such as it was, made it easier for the doctor to take him. Three quid, the doc offered; the father took five.

If the day was hot, the doctor might sit in the shade beside the steps, at the top of the crazy paving, sorting his cures. Which was when Augustus would step down and take the only-too-willing Ralph by the hand, lead him around the back for a sugary biscuit and a glass of milk. Conversation there was none; happiness of the smiling and nodding kind there was aplenty.

Bill Brown, who sold buttons, and his boy Bob were also favourites, them in their bib-and-brace overalls and Bill so bright, though Bob was a dill. Different-coloured eyes, the kid had; one bright as the southern sky, the other bleak as concrete. His moods also varied: all giggles and dribbles one minute, then he'd sour, cowering behind his minder's back, snarling and spitting, 'Up you!' or 'Bugger orf', sticking his head out just long enough.

'Two bob both ways is me Bob,' Bill would say by way of explanation, though it was not, neither to Augustus nor anybody else, Bill included.

Still, Augustus liked Bill and Bob Brown as he liked all the hawkers and their kids, because they were different, and respected his difference, mostly.

About the time of the hawkers, Augustus's baby teeth fell out. Two, at the front. He ran his tongue over the gummy gap. I am being reconstructed, he thought. And I have not sung. If I don't find the right song soon, I might be too late. New teeth might come, grown-up teeth, men's teeth. Even hair, down there. And I will be too late to sing myself into being the man I want to be. The one in the white uniform. That broad man. That tall man ... He tongued the space again, afraid.

Of all the hawkers, it was the man with the doves and the finches who fascinated the most. And his girl, especially, who wove cages of cane. So different from the others — if hawkers they were. Yet for all his fascination, when they came, which was rarely, Augustus could not speak, sitting mute, staring, so taken was he by their presence.

They have white skin and white hair, both of them, and keep white doves, he observed. They dress as travelling players, their clothes as multicoloured as their finches, yet white as they are, they are not albino.

Augustus had known such a person; a man who did a stint at the circus. Augustus once talked to him outside his caravan. Nice bloke he was, fine boned, with white skin and white hair; his eyes pink. He talked ordinary, this albino, about ordinary stuff. He said that he was twenty-eight years old, that both his mother and father were normal, as was his sister and brother. He said he had been to school and could read and write but could never keep a job. He was just a week with the circus before he moved on. Didn't draw a crowd. For five bob he sat on a box in a tent, dressed in a robe of blood-red silk. When someone came in for a look (from behind a rope), he stood to let the robe fall, turning this way and that, a white towel knotted about his waist. He could have made more if he'd dropped the towel, but he would not.

Augustus accepted this, being different himself.

The man with the doves and the finches and his girl (his daughter, was she) stepped up the crazy paving like dancers: toes first, then heels, light, soundless in patchy hose of red and green, the colours of their choice. Reaching the stairs to find Augustus sitting, staring, mute, they prepared.

Placing their willow-woven baskets at their feet, they stood, red and green motley drifting in the heat, lifting and drifting, so gauzy was the fabric. From their faces they brushed their hair, hanging heavy as it did in silvery ropes. Then bending, his long fingers knuckled and sinewed, he (the man first, always) twisted the woven tie that held the basket lid and skipped away. Doves rose to circle him; white, silvered, shimmering, hovering about his shoulders, about his head (oh, he was tall!) and he smiled his broad smile, his teeth fine and narrow, never yellowed, never ivoried against his pale skin. Then she — the girl, his daughter, was she? — did the same, loosening the willow-woven basket at her feet, freeing finches to rise, glorious in motley themselves, wings whirring, their gaudy brilliance hallowing her silvery hair as she laughed.

What is it about them that silences me? Augustus wondered. Why can't I speak to them? These questions vexed him for days after each visitation, and they were visitations, being spiritual, almost; more than just a foot in the door.

* * *

When next they visited (was it three weeks or three months?)
Augustus determined to speak but again their appearance
arrested him. They are not white, he observed, astonished.
They are silver. Silver as their downy doves. Nor are their eyes
pink, but blue. And he sat, gaping, as always, until the thought
came: It's their beauty that silences me. The loveliness of
their difference. I've never seen anybody like them, not even
in the circus. And momentarily his chest swelled, since he was
different too, but he would have been other; even ordinary, if
he could.

Next time they visited (was it three months or thirteen?),
Augustus mustered the courage to lean down from his step,
asking, 'Are the birds for sale? Does anybody ever buy?'

'Some do,' the man replied. 'If we offer them.'

'To most we would not,' the girl said. 'Birds are precious.'

'And most who ask have no cages,' the man said. 'How
could they keep them?'

'But you have no cages yourself,' Augustus frowned,
looking down at the willow-woven baskets. 'Other than
them ...'

'Oh, we have cages,' the man laughed. 'My girl makes
them, if we choose.'

'Makes them?' Augustus asked.

They looked to each other, this girl and this man.

'You must first choose a bird,' the man said, and holding
out his hand, flat, a dove landed upon it, nestling its breast
against the mound of his thumb. The girl did likewise with a
finch, waiting.

Augustus paled. 'I'm sorry,' he said. 'I have no money. I'm sorry, truly.'

The girl raised her hand to her silver hair, to the rainbowed ropes of raffia knotted there: crimson and emerald, purple and blue, yellow and orange, waving brilliant in the sun.

'You are so beautiful,' Augustus muttered. 'Why are you here? You know I have nothing. I *am* nothing ...'

'Will we show him?' the man asked.

She nodded, smiling.

'I am sorry ...' Augustus protested. 'I am ...'

The man placed a finger to his lips. 'Wait,' he said. 'Watch.' He swept the hovering doves back into their basket and, standing, reached his hand over his shoulder to draw a bundle of willow canes from behind his back as an archer draws arrows from a quiver. The girl took them, dropping to her knees. Her fingers moved in a frenzy.

As Augustus watched, a shape grew — a construction in cane — an airy cylinder first, two hand spans in diameter, rising row after row, her fingers furious until, at six or eight hands high, a dome top appeared, closing over to complete.

'Your cage,' she said, offering it.

The process had taken minutes.

'I never saw anything like that,' Augustus confessed. 'Your fingers. The speed ...'

'She has the dance,' the man said, smiling.

'The dance?' Augustus asked, stupid. 'What dance? She wove. Or plaited. Or something ...'

'She has the Saint Vitus Dance,' the man said. 'Some call it a curse. We call it a gift.'

'She built the cage in minutes. From nothing. From the ground up. From a pile of sticks. I never saw anything like that. Miraculous, really.'

'Not miraculous,' the man said, laughing. 'Just the dance, as I said. You're the miracle-maker. You're the one with the voice.'

'We came to offer you a bird,' she said. 'A white dove, we would suggest, since that is how the pages fell. The books in the library. The poetry. Fluttering down, then beating upwards, like the wings of doves. Miraculous ...'

'I sang,' Augustus groaned.

'We heard,' the man replied.

'You heard?'

The man smiled.

'Some birds told us,' the girl offered. 'Crows, they were. Very big, very bumptious. Full of tricks. And on their way to a funeral too. All very interesting.'

'No!' Augustus gasped

The man laughed. 'How could we forget? And why would we lie? And there was one other. The young man. The thin man ...'

'True!' the girl cut in. 'Too true. The one riding the pale horse. That librarian, tall and thin and ever so pale. Pale as death, you might say ...'

'Or caught in the grip of Lethe, perhaps. In that river of dream, of oblivion.'

'Where lovers drown,' she added, 'dreaming ...'

The man held up his hand. 'No more. That is a sorry tale. We will say no more, but yes, we know. Which is why we came. We want to thank you. For the return of poetry, you understand. And to offer you a gift, but ...'

Augustus looked at him, his elegance. His stature. Then at her, the girl. Her silver beauty. A woman's body that he would never know. Not as he was, *unless…*

'But you didn't speak,' she said, breaking his thought. 'Whenever we visited you said nothing. Not so much as a greeting. Now we are determined. We will leave a white dove.'

'In thanks for *your* gift. Your miracle,' the man said. 'The poetry of your song.'

At that he drew a dove from his basket and, placing it in the cage at Augustus's feet, they turned, stepping out like dancers, toes first, then heels, light, soundless, to leave the dwarf mute, as they always had.

When they had gone, Augustus set the cage in the shade at the side of the stairs. I am going mad, he thought. But they must come back. They must … and he spat on the paving, all crazy as it was.

By the age of seventeen and still minus his front teeth, Augustus had lost his fascination with all things Egyptian, yet Rosa continued to bring home books on architecture from the library. The fact that she still worked there was curious enough, considering that the others had long since left. The three Assistant Librarians, Miss Bland, Miss Blank and Miss Blotting had opened a tea shoppe, reading leaves on the side; of the Stampers Three, the huge one fell for a cooper (or possibly the barrel itself, as was rumoured), the Medium for a potter, the cadaver for a thimble-maker; and the librarian, she of the cardigan, found trembling satisfaction in the Caribbean, her houseboy proving himself a man. Such is the liberating power of Poesy.

'So why are you borrowing books on architecture,' Augustus finally asked, 'especially when none is about Egypt?'

To which Rosa replied, with an arch look, 'I can't see what business it is of yours what I borrow — or what I read, for that matter — other than that I am experiencing a certain affinity with spiritual buildings. Of the less traditional variety, if you can appreciate that.'

Since he could not, Augustus chose to read the books himself in the hope of gaining some insight, however limited that may be, into the spiritual workings of Rosa's mind.

One night as he sat reading in bed, Augustus caught a movement outside his window. Creeping over the covers, he knelt at the sill to see. There was Rosa, sitting on the front steps, staring up, her nightdress silvered by starlight. She had let herself go since her days at the whorehouse. Not so much her body, although she was no sylph, but her hair. No longer was it bobbed to flatter. Being red and wild, it bushed, untamed, in all its Titian glory.

Putting his elbows on the sill, Augustus prepared to watch, but the movement that had first caught his eye came again: a flash — a whirr of white —and leaning out, he saw. Rosa had the willow cage beside her, the white dove fluttering in her hand.

'You got two front teeth missing,' she said when he sat next to her.

'Rosa,' he sighed, 'they've been gone for months. Years maybe. You never take any notice of me. Not since that episode in the library. Not once.'

'"That episode", as you call it, changed my life,' she told him, staring boldly into his eyes. '"That episode" affected me, Augustus. I felt something I have never felt before.'

'Oh?' he said, doubtful. 'Like what?'

'I don't know,' she said. 'Therein lies the irony.'

'What? That you don't know what you felt, or that you don't know how to explain it?'

'I just don't know,' she said. 'And that is the spirituality of it. That is what I am seeking.'

"Well, that's as clear as mud,' he said. 'I'm going back to bed.'

'What?' she demanded, evidently offended. 'You wanted me to enlighten you? Did you?'

'Well ...'

'You'd like me to quote a few lines from the Gita Govinda, would you?'

'No ...'

'I can, you know. I have been reading:

My one Beloved, sitting by the river
Under the thick kadambas with that throng;
Will there not come an end to this earthly madness?
Shall I not, past the sorrow, have the gladness?
Must not the love-light shine for him ere long?

'There. How's that?'

'Rosa ...'

'Or were you wanting a song? A really good, stirring song, to make the poetry books fly?'

'Definitely not ...'

'I know:

Ta rah-rah boom de-eh!
Ta rah-rah boom de-eh!

'How about that?'

'I'm going to bed.'

'Why? Because I can cite poetry, or because I had the temerity to sing? Which is it? Come on, tell me.'

Watching the dove trembling in her palm, he hesitated to reply.

'I'm waiting,' she said. 'Come on …'

'You're laughing at me,' he said. 'And I won't be laughed at.'

Silence.

'Laughed?' she whispered, finally. 'Laughed at?' Softer. Duller. Flatter. 'I'm not laughing, Augustus. I'm wondering. For the first time, wondering …' And placing her index finger on the dove's head, she drew it downward in one single, silken stroke to the tail, upright, quivering.

'Wondering what?'

'Wondering what is in your voice that can make books fly?' She turned to him again, there on the top step, the crazy paving at their feet, the broken flags silver in the starlight. 'What it is that made Little Donny cry, and that lot in the mess tent the time you popped out of the spittoon, and them in the big top, the night you were Caesar in your chariot, them that were too stupid to appreciate. And maybe a hundred others that I know nothing about, them under lampposts, and in shearing sheds, and wherever the hell else you let fly, except now there's me. Because I finally heard you, Augie, I finally heard you. And I saw you too; I saw what happened when you sang. Something wonderful, something miraculous. Something happened to me too. Something I just can't understand — no, nor express neither. Something spiritual, like I've been trying to tell you, and can't. So don't you say I'm laughing at you, because I'm not. Because I want you to sing for me. Tonight. Out here, under the stars, so something good can happen. For me. Augie, will you?'

'Rosa,' he said, 'I've sung for you before, and you never did understand why. So I'm going to say no. Not forever, just for now. You see, Rosa, I've got a feeling that my front teeth are coming down. My adult teeth. And when that happens, there will probably be other changes, you know, down below ... And if my voice breaks, I'm done, locked into this body: a dwarf forever. So I have to save my songs. Like athletes save their energy before a big race, you know. I have to make every song count. So I can grow. So I can be normal. You understand?'

'No,' she said, honestly enough.

'Well then,' he sighed, getting up, 'let's accept that. Let's accept that we don't understand each other and we probably never will. I'm going back to bed. The dove will be safe here. The cage is solid. We can talk again tomorrow.'

The next morning as Rosa made her way down the crazy path intent on yet another day at the library, who should appear at the front gate but the man with the doves.

He saw her hair, all fiery in the morning sun; she saw his silvery mane. I have imagined my life in silver, he thought, yet here it is in gold. And she, arrested by his appearance wondered, Is this some remnant of starlight?

Augustus saw from his window and hurried out. 'Rosa,' he called. 'This is the man who gave me the dove.'

Loitering, since she hoped — perhaps also expected— Rosa turned to whisper, 'Augustus, could this be instead of your song?'

'Could this be what?' he asked.

'My miracle,' she replied, unabashed.

The dove man heard. He stopped at the head of that crazy paving and, overcome, perched on the stairs beside the caged dove there. The bird flapped and thrashed, hurling itself against the wicker. Reaching out, he released it to soar skyward where it circled against the blue to return, alighting on his shoulder.

'Where is the girl with the finches?' Augustus asked. 'Your daughter, is she?'

'She is not my daughter,' the man replied. 'I found her in the bush out Helidon way. By a spring. I have a hut there.'

'You found her?' Rosa asked, coming closer.

'Yes,' he said. 'Near a spring. In the bush. Years ago.'

'She was lost?' Augustus asked. Having been orphaned himself (well, almost), stories of other children so mislaid appealed to him. 'What? Wandering and alone?'

The man with the dove folded his arms across his chest, the bird to his heart. 'That was years ago,' he said, looking down. 'I was walking near my hut and there she was. In a clearing by a spring. So I took her in. About ten years ago. About five years old, she was. Her hair silver as the water itself. That was out Helidon way. Near a spring bubbling up from the sandstone. From way down. Deep in the earth, they say. Didn't hardly speak, she didn't. I tried to find who owned her. Put a sign on the track out front but nobody came. Been like a daughter to me, she has, but she isn't. I swear ...' He sighed, looking up, first to Augustus, then to Rosa, for approval.

'You swear what?' Rosa asked, frowning.

'I swear that she has been no more. But she does keep the finches. Out of the bush they came, all cheeping and peeping, as finches do. Just arrived, they did. Come down in droves, flocks, as soon as she appeared. All sorts. You saw them, eh? I had the doves, now her the finches.' He turned to Augustus, who nodded. 'You saw her make the cages too. In a fury. In a frenzy. When the dance comes over her.'

'Amazing,' Augustus admitted.

'She dances, this girl?' Rosa asked, confused.

'No,' the man said. 'I explained to the lad here. Augustus, isn't it? I explained to him, she has the Dance, my girl. The St Vitus' Dance. The disease ...'

'Oh,' Rosa muttered, none the wiser.

'But your hair,' Augustus said. 'Your silver hair. It's the same as hers. And yet you say ...'

'She is not my daughter. She is not my blood. Her hair is a gift from the spring. As my name is a gift — or a coincidence.'

'What is your name?' Rosa asked, looking to Augustus who might have known.

'Da Silva,' the dove man said.

Augustus beamed. 'Interesting ...'

'It is a storyteller's name. A black man's name. Yet I am white. As silver-white as my doves.'

Da Silva lifted the dove to his face, pressing its beak to his lips in a kiss.

Rosa came closer. She stroked the hair of this Da Silva. 'Tell me,' she said, her voice silky as her touch. 'Tell me, Sir, about your doves. I have had an experience with doves myself. White doves too. Spiritual, you might say. I want the truth now, not some silver-plated story. Not some black-and-white lie.'

He looked up at her, smiling. 'The truth?' he said, and she nodded, folding her arms across her chest.

'Once upon a time,' he began, cradling the dove, 'there was a king in Haiti ...'

'Oh come on!' Rosa protested. 'You're making that up. You're telling a story. A fairy tale.'

'No,' Da Silva said. 'I am not. All truth takes place in some time, in some place, among some people. So what is wrong with "Once upon a time there was a king in Haiti"?'

'He is right,' Augustus said. 'Isn't that what I sang for, in that library? Isn't poetry what life's all about?'

Silenced, Rosa sat.

'Once upon a time,' Da Silva resumed, 'there was a king in Haiti who fell desperately in love with a woman who kept doves. Although this king wooed her, offering untold riches if she would marry him, she declined. "I have my birds to feed," she said. "I keep silver-white doves which are used by the priests on ceremonial occasions. If I marry you, and take on the responsibilities of the kingdom, who would care for my birds?" Now this king was a mighty man, unused to denial, so he took it upon himself to learn the names of the priests for whom the woman raised the doves and, dressing himself in his robes of office and wearing his golden diadem, he approached the priests saying, "The woman who raises the silver-white doves used in your ceremonies has fallen ill, and cannot care for her birds. Weave me a spell, I pray you, that might allow me, a stranger, to feed them without causing distress." Aware that this was the king, and not used to being denied, the priests wove a spell that changed the monarch into a dove; a silver-white cock bird of such grace and beauty that he might strut among his peers demanding honour and obeisance. In this form, the Dove King returned to the woman. Alighting in a silk cotton tree adjacent to her garden, he waited until the afternoon when she took her leisure among the lilies, and as she reclined, drifting somewhere between waking and sleeping, which is the true realm of fairy tale ...' (here Da Silva paused to wink at Augustus; Rosa having already entered that realm in the first moments of the tale) '... the Dove King approached, thrusting forward his chest, strutting proud as a dancer, and the woman was won. So he eased himself upon her (in his thrall as she was), and took his pleasure. Having satisfied himself, without so much as a bill or coo, he fluttered over the garden wall, whereupon he returned to his rightful body. "Well," he thought, brushing silver-white feathers from his kingly robes, "that didn't amount to much. I might find more ardour in a finch," and satiated, he strutted away.'

'But the woman?' Rosa whispered, barely audible.

Da Silva smiled. 'Ah, the woman,' he sighed. 'Who could forget my mother?'

'Is that the truth?' Augustus asked, already believing.

'Indeed it is,' Da Silva assured him, 'as surely as I have silver-white hair and my father is the black King of Haiti.'

'And the doves live with you, because of your mother?' Rosa wondered, enthralled.

'I suppose,' he replied, avoiding her eye.

'But why did you come here?' Augustus asked. 'To this country. To our place?'

Hearing this, Rosa leaned forward, eager.

'I was called,' Da Silva said, sheepish.

'Called?' Rosa repeated. 'How? Who?'

He lowered his head, murmuring, 'The moan of doves in immemorial elms …'

Augustus shuddered, uneasy. 'Eh?'

'The moan of doves …'

'I heard. But what does that mean? Like, if your father was the King of Haiti — if — how could you hear dove murmuring in Ipswich from way over there?'

'There is no King of Haiti and there never was,' Da Silva laughed.

'What's this all about?' Augustus demanded. 'I mean, why are you doing this? Making this up?'

'Because,' Da Silva replied, 'I am a storyteller, and that is what I do.'

'How about you just tell us the truth,' Augustus suggested. 'Like, where are you from and how come you're here?'

'Once upon a time,' Da Silva began.

'No!' Augustus shouted. 'No! No stories. No tricks. We just want the truth. Man, I'm starting to sound like Stan. Come on. Out with it …'

Da Silva sighed. 'Augustus,' he said, 'can you change the colour of your hair from blond to black because someone demands that you do? Can you make yourself grow into a full-sized man just to make someone else happy? No? I thought not. And nor can I change from being a storyteller because you command me.'

'But I *could* change myself,' Augustus insisted. 'I am sure of it. If I found the right song. The right note. That one pure …'

'Indeed,' Da Silva agreed. 'I too might change myself if I wanted. If my story lent itself to that, but today I am the

King of Haiti's son. And today I came to this country, to you, here, in answer to the moan of doves, which is the truth, being poetry. From Tennyson's "The Princess" if I am not mistaken, and it was the call of poetry that brought me here. The very moan of doves, if I am correct. The doves that your own quest for poesy raised. The very same. In that lovelorn library, I believe. So …'

'And finches?' Augustus whispered. 'The tinkling song of finches? Did you hear that too?'

'Ah,' Da Silva laughed. 'I think, Augustus, the tinkling promise of finches might be your song.'

Augustus blushed, doubting. 'No more,' he said, rubbing his brow. 'I won't bother you anymore. But one thing, now that you are here — and we can see that you are, which is all that matters … and story too, of course. And poetry. And song. But since you are here — do you truly live in a bush hut? By a silver spring, at Helidon?'

'Would I lie to you?' he winked, smiling his smile.

'And is this hut silvered with mist and dappled with moss?'

'No,' he said. 'I have a shed made of corrugated iron. Sheets of tin, you know, galvanised.'

'And is it silver?'

'You might say that — if galvanised iron is silver.' He looked to Augustus, who gaped.

'And would you call this silver shed your temple?' Rosa asked. 'The Temple of the Silver-White Doves?'

'There is rust. And bird droppings,' Da Silva conceded. 'So, to be honest, I wouldn't call it a temple, no. I would call it a tin shed in the bush.'

'But if I saw it, I might call it a temple?' Rosa suggested.

'That is a question I cannot answer,' he said. 'But if you want to see ...'

'Oh, I do!' she cried, leaping up. 'Would you? Will you?'

'I will,' he said. 'I hoped, in fact. Since this morning. From the beginning, you might say, when first I came through that gate and saw you on the crazy path.'

'You are a kidder,' she laughed, slapping him.

'I am a storyteller,' he said. 'There is little difference.'

Had anybody asked, Augustus might have told that Rosa's determination to visit Da Silva's galvanised iron shed (a temple, could it be?) was a turning point in her personal construction; though exactly what she was building, spiritual though that body may be, and why she was building it, was a mystery to him. As were the peculiar dreams he was having of that silver-haired girl with the finches, and her mystical emergence from the sandstone of that Helidon spring. So when Rosa informed him that they were taking a day trip to Da Silva's domain, Augustus did all that he could to bring this excursion to be, not for her benefit (spiritual or otherwise), but hoping that a certain silver-haired girl might be there to greet him.

'Now get this,' the heavenly Rosa declared, appearing at his bedroom door. 'As it happens I have to work right up to the very day that we are going to Helidon, and since Stan seems to be eternally down pit, it looks like you're buying the provisions.'

'I hate shopping,' Augustus complained, sitting up in bed. 'People stare ...'

'Too bad,' she spat. 'You drew the short straw.'

'Was that a joke, or a reminder?'

'You're too thin-skinned,' she growled.

Augustus shrugged. 'Provisions?' he wanted to know, pulling the sheets up to his neck in the hope that he might trap the much-dreamed-of silver girl lurking beneath for just one minute longer. 'How long is it going to take to get there?'

'We're leaving first thing Saturday morning,' she informed him. 'I've hired a pony and trap. Stan will drive us. All taken care of. Da Silva says it will take a few hours. I'd like to leave early and be there for lunch.'

'So Stan knows the way?'

'Probably not,' she admitted, 'but Da Silva says we should head north,' she waved her right hand behind her left shoulder vaguely, 'and I'll just know.'

'Know what?'

'Where to find him.'

'Who?'

'Da Silva, stupid!'

'But how?'

'Don't be childish,' she scowled. 'People in my situation — *our* situation, dare I say — just know these things.'

'Rosa,' Augustus said, throwing back the sheets, his dream-girl evidently evicted, 'I want to go with you, honest, but I don't know what you're talking about. What do you mean by "our situation"?'

'Augustus,' she sighed. 'You're seventeen — and you've finally lost your baby teeth — so surely you can see when two people are in love …'

'Ah!' Augustus declared. He had guessed as much — their lust, at least — when the pair stood gasping and gaping at the front gate. 'So is this the real thing? Not just a matter of convenience like it was with Barkus?'

'That's none of your business,' she sniffed, attempting to flatten her hair in the hallway mirror. 'I'm leaving ten bob on the kitchen table. You'll need to buy something for lunch. Get some ham and a loaf of bread. You can make sandwiches. Stan's got that flask he takes down pit. We can have a cuppa somewhere. A picnic. And since I'm certain that our host is not a meat eater, I'd get him some fruit. Apples are always acceptable.' And off she flounced.

Augustus rarely went to the market. He hated the raucous voices and crowded stalls; he tired of dodging the bulging bags and cane baskets that caught his ears and scratched his cheeks; he could never reach the counters; he was too short to look into display cases. Worst of all were the miners' crotches, vaguely malodorous, should he walk into them; a curse few had the misfortune to suffer.

He bought bread and ham. He liked the promising baker ('You'll be a big boy when you grow up ...'), but not the patronising butcher ('Two front teeth for Christmas, then?'), and hoped that the greengrocer would say nothing. But when he stood before a pile of rosy red apples, he could see nobody.

'Hello?' he called. 'Shop?'

Thinking that the vendor might be asleep behind the counter he dropped to his knees, peering beneath. He saw four paws. Huge. Two pairs of two — one pair black, one pair tan — and catching a whiff of spices, he looked up to see smoke ascending in blue-grey puffs; like that caterpillar in *Alice in Wonderland*. 'A hookah!' he squealed. 'Bozo!

Bonzer. Little Donny!' and in that moment the dwarf appeared, bow-tied and scarlet coated, bawling, 'What? Who? Augustus!'

So they hugged, the past falling about them like a mantle.

'Last time I saw you,' Donny sniffed, 'you and that Rosa Colleano and that Stan the monkey-lover were moochin' across the paddock the night you left the circus. That calliope didn't go down real well, eh?' And having put this provocative remark out there, he gave his attention to rearranging a pyramid of apples.

'No,' Augustus agreed, 'it didn't. A lot of tears have flowed down that dribbly creek, and a lot more fallen from that weeping willow. But I have smartened up since.'

'So you gave up on the singing, eh?' Donny asked with a backward glance.

'Not at all,' Augustus informed him. 'My singing gives me hope. I thought you understood that.'

'What? That you're going to crack the big time?'

'It's more than that. I want to grow through my singing.'

'Eh?'

'Didn't *you* want to find some way?'

'Eh?'

'Being short, you know; didn't you want to grow?'

'Not by singing, that's for sure.'

'But I do. When I sing, I'm another. And if I can sing right, I will become that other. That's what I hope, Donny. That's what I believe. Truly ...'

'Hang on,' Little Donny growled. 'Are you telling me that there's some connection between your singing and your growing?'

'I am.'

'Yeah, what?'

'If I could find the perfect song, and sing it to perfection, I would reconstruct myself.'

Little Donny looked down to tighten the bow in his beard, wondering, 'You still with that pair?'

'What pair?'

'Rosa and Stan Platten.'

'Yes.'

'And they're still filling your head with this bull?'

'What bull?'

'Last time I saw you they had you singing in a chariot. With a calliope and an elephant. Geez ...' He sat himself down on Bozo's back.

'Rosa was my manager then, or going to be. That was a long time ago.'

'And you still haven't accepted what you are?'

'Pardon?'

'What are you?'

'I am not a *What*,' Augustus declared. 'I am a *He*. And I sing.'

'Yeah, and what else?'

'I am Augustus Trump and I'm seventeen years old.'

'You've got no idea, have you? First time I met you, I wondered about that.'

'Wondered about what?'

'If you understood that you were one of us.'

Augustus, shuffled, uncomfortable. 'What do you mean, "one of us"?'

'Geez ...'

'I'm not sure that I understand you,' Augustus protested. 'Do you mean "one of us" being a dwarf, or "one of us'" being a sideshow freak? Depends on how you construct yourself.'

'Hasn't anybody ever told you that the two go together?' Little Donny demanded. 'That since you're a dwarf — and you are, in case you didn't know — then you're a sideshow freak?'

Augustus blanched. 'As I said, that depends on how you construct yourself. Or reconstruct yourself. Depending ...'

Donny thumped his black boots against Bozo's mighty flank. 'You can't *construct* yourself, nor *reconstruct* yourself. You're a dwarf. A freak. And that ain't gonna change, no matter how good you sing. You got that?'

Augustus perched on Bonzer, beside him.

Bonzer wheezed.

'Donny,' Augustus said, 'I've done things that you wouldn't believe ...'

'Every dwarf has,' Donny sneered. 'Some I'm even proud of.'

'Donny,' Augustus said, 'I'm not joking. When I sing the perfect song perfectly, things change. I didn't appreciate that until the other day when something happened in the library. Rosa heard, and saw too ...'

'Enough!' Donny shouted, leaping to his feet. 'I've heard enough! Nobody can make himself grow. And I don't wanna hear about that Rosa Colleano. She's the one who put you in the chariot that night. She's the one who got us sold up. Did you know that?'

'No,' Augustus admitted.

'The big Boss, that Cigar Sullivan, called us into the mess next morning and says he's had a change of heart. Never engaged an artist that was a bigger flop than that Augustus, he says — that's you, mate — and he's handing the business over to his son, that Bertie Sullivan. The first thing Bertie does is sell up and shoot through. With his boyfriend.'

'I'm sorry,' Augustus moaned, fighting back tears. 'I truly am. I didn't know. I *did* see Needly Phyllis once, but she didn't say anything.'

'Yeah, well. Not even Cristo Colleano could bring that Bertie round. And Bertie was keen on him, I reckon. Shot through with some albino, Bertie did. White hair he had. And red eyes. Bertie liked that kind of thing. Anyway, we was sold up. Just days after you left. Hours ... What I'm saying is, why should I care what Rosa Colleano saw or heard after all she did to me? To us. You included. Now do you understand?'

Augustus contained his tears. 'Rosa is Rosa,' he muttered. 'Forget about her. I'm telling you that I can do this. That I can make things happen. But I have to make the change while I'm still young. While my voice is still pure. And when I sing that perfect song, I will grow. I know it. I'll become a normal man. A big man. A broad man. Like that Puccini man in the white uniform. That sea captain, my father ...' Unable to hold back any longer, he wailed, 'Aw, Donny, it's awful, it's awful. I do hope. I do ...' And he began to sob.

Not caring for the tears of men, of dwarves even less, Little Donny got to his feet. 'I understand,' he said. 'I felt the same way once. You remember that song you sang for me, all those years ago?'

Through his tears Augustus mumbled, '"I Dreamt that I Dwelt in Marble Halls". I chose it for you especially.'

Little Donny nodded. 'I know you did, mate. I know. And you chose very well. You see, I wasn't always this sour old man. Grumpy, as they call me. You know, I used to hope too. I hoped that my lousy body was all a nightmare and when I woke up I'd be tall and straight, like those sunflowers that shoot up overnight. Or that fairytale beanstalk and the giant. Everyone that's normal is a giant to us, eh? I mean, when I was your age I wanted to shake hands like other blokes, I so wanted to go out with ordinary girls ...' He stepped away to stand as he had seen Augustus do: his feet planted wide, his hands on his hips, his chin held high. 'Augustus', he said. 'You're young, you're smart and you're classy, so I'm going to let you in on a secret.'

Augustus gulped, uncertain.

'You need to know that Rosa Colleano actually did me a favour. So did Bertie Sullivan. So did you, if it really was your fault the circus closed. Because when I got out, I started going to the movies. The pictures. You been to the pictures? At the circus everyone looks down at us freaks out there in centre ring. At the pictures everyone looks up. They lean back in their canvas seats and look up. They look at the actors on the screen. *Stars*, they call them. They look up at the stars. And every star is a giant. Every one: runts, dwarves, me, you. The pictures are a dream, Augustus. A fairytale come true. So here's my secret: when my dogs are gone, and they're old, believe me, I'm off to movieland — to America — where people like you and me walk tall as giants. And that's how I'm going to grow, Augie, up there on that movie screen — a star, a giant.'

At some point in this revelation — possibly at the mention of fairytale or that more recent *fabula*, the movie — Augustus ceased his snivelling and sat up, dry-eyed.

'Thank you, Donny. I mean it, thanks. After all these years, it's been good to talk. But for all of that, I'm not a child anymore, and you make a mistake if you construct me as one. I am a young man fast approaching adulthood. I have been to the pictures. Rosa has taken me. I've also read books about how movies are made. Rosa brings them home from the library. From such experiences I know that I would rather put my trust in song to bring about change than some moving picture. Poetry isn't about lights and cameras. Poetry springs from the human heart. It always has. I've read poetry written on the walls of pyramids. Poetry that's five thousand years old. And though those poets are long dead, I'd rather grow through their experience — their love, their suffering — than the scripted lines of some celluloid actor on a flickering screen. So Donny, thank you for sharing your secret. You have helped me make up my mind. But there will be no movie dreams for me; no visions of stars or giants. I am going to put my faith in song, in the purer poetry that springs from human suffering.' Slipping from Bonzer's back, he reached for his groceries.

'Wait!' Little Donny called. 'I'm sorry if I hurt you. I meant to help. Honest. Don't leave like that. Not angry, not bitter, not like after the circus. Take this, please.' Polishing a rosy apple on the sleeve of his coat, he held the fruit out, tempting. 'If all else fails,' he suppressed a giggle, 'take a bite. You might even make a wish.'

'No thanks, Donny,' Augustus replied, having no belief, nor the teeth to bite into it. 'Although I hope the movies work out for you. They're a lot of fun, I'm told.'

* * *

In preparation for Saturday's outing, Stan had a shower. His skin turned red. His white flannel shirt was also fresh boiled, as were his duck trousers, stiff as boards. He wore a broadbrimmed straw hat with a feather in the band. Augustus hadn't seen this hat before. It wasn't every day that they ran away.

Stan reined in the trap at the front of the cottage.

'You know where we're goin'?' he greeted Augustus.

'Out Helidon way,' Augustus said, hoisting the picnic basket onto the seat. 'What's the occasion?'

'Rosa's interested in a bloke with a place out there.'

'What bloke?'

'A hawker by the name of Da Silva. Keeps doves and dresses in motley. Got silver hair.'

'What's motley?'

Augustus gave this some thought. 'Like an old-time court jester. His clothes are covered in red and green patches. Says he's a storyteller.'

Stan grunted, suspicious. 'You seen him then?'

'He's been here a few times. And his girl. His daughter maybe, but he says she isn't. She keeps finches in cages made out of sticks.' And remembering, he added, 'Da Silva says she's got "the dance".'

Stan nodded. 'The St Vitus', eh?'

'You know it?'

'Had a mother bring a kid into the circus that had it. Wanted to pass him off as a freak. Always dancin', you know. Crazy like. Young Bertie Sullivan would have hired her there and then, but Cigar seen straight through her. "This kid's sick," he says, and sends her packin'.'

'This girl's pale and silvery, but she's doesn't look sick. She's pretty, I reckon. Like a fairy.' The idea appealed to him. 'Like a fairy child.'

'Umm,' Stan grunted.

Augustus went round to stroke the dozy horse's nose. 'Nice horse,' he said.

'Yeah. Here, give us your hand,' and Stan pulled him up.

The black leather seat was crazed and stiff. If Augustus sat forward, he felt he would tip over and tangle in the harness; if he sat back, his feet stuck out, making the horse look like it had four ears. 'Where will Rosa sit?' he asked. 'I'd feel safer in the middle.'

'Dunno,' Stan grunted, and Rosa appeared on the crazy paving. She wore an ankle-length dress of white muslin, soft and gauzy, the fabric wrapping about her thighs. A sash of silver silk graced her waist. She had whooshed her hair so it flared, fiery and bright, while a picture hat, also of white muslin — possibly starched, probably milliner-wired — framed the fire about her head.

Augustus gasped. 'Just then,' he said, 'in the sun, you looked like an angel.'

'Ha!' Rosa scoffed, loving it.

She handed up a girly little Bo-Peep basket. 'I'm not sitting on the edge,' she said. 'I want the middle. I don't want mud off the wheels dirtying my frock.'

Augustus glared, although he was happy for the outing. Maybe that silver-haired fairy would be there. And the motley finches. So when Rosa was seated and her frock tucked under her thighs, Stan called, 'Git, git!' and they were off.

* * *

Midmorning they crossed a bridge over a dribbly creek. Seeing willows there, Augustus said, 'Can we stop here for our picnic sandwiches and a cup of tea? You did bring your flask, didn't you, Stan?'

'I did,' he said, reining the horse in under a willow. 'It's behind the seat.'

Since Rosa didn't complain or demand that they go on to some other place, they all got down — Stan helping Augustus because Rosa wouldn't — and sat on a rug.

When they were settled, sipping and munching, Augustus looked about and said, 'You remember that dribbly creek and the weeping willow we passed when we left the circus?'

'I do,' Stan grunted.

'I don't,' Rosa chirped.

'Hmm,' Augustus mused. 'I saw Little Donny at the markets. He looked exactly the same. Remember his little red coats? And his dogs, Bozo and Bonzer?'

Rosa shrugged, raising a teacup to her lips. 'That was all so long ago ...' and she attempted to look wistful, lifting her eyes to the weeping leaves.

So they sipped and munched a little longer until Augustus grew bored, teasing, 'Rosa, why are we going to see this Da Silva today?' And he winked at Stan, who didn't get it.

'I am hoping,' Rosa began, alert to Augustus's games, 'that "this Da Silva", as you call him, will put my past even further behind me. That he might offer me a future. A furthering of my spiritual quest, you might say.'

'He might,' Stan offered, 'if we knew where he lived.'

'We never will if we sit here all day,' Rosa huffed, chucking her cup into the picnic basket. And giving her hat a correctional tweak, she waited for a hand up.

Augustus thought Helidon was nice, the town having retained a certain romance in its colonial facades, sandstone churches and lolloping camphor laurels; a mile after, the road turned to dust that billowed.

'Do ya know where this Da Silva lives?' Stan whinged. 'I gotta get this trap back by dusk. And the horse here will want feedin' and waterin'.'

'Shush!' Rosa ordered. 'Have faith.'

'Faith?' Augustus asked, considering this a fair question.

'Faith,' she assured him, though in what, she declined to say.

So a silence fell, the scabby bush and the hush of the dust contributing until, all of a sudden, figures appeared between the gums.

They were dressed in black, as if in mourning, but since the dust obscured, whether they were men or women, or two or three, and whether they wore black frocks or black frockcoats, will remain forever unknown. Augustus claimed to have seen one — Absalom, was it? — with long blond hair. Stan reckoned another was 'a sheila with a beard', while Rosa refused to be drawn at all, fearing that any detailed articulation of the vision might lessen her chances of its fulfilment. Whatever they were, those hirsute tricksters, they pointed, as one, in the direction of a galvanised shed not a hundred yards from where they stood.

'We are there!' Rosa crowed, and in moments Da Silva appeared, stepping lightly as a dancer onto the roadway, toes first, then heels, all dressed in patchy hose of red and green, the colours of his choice. 'You have found me!' he cried and so saying he reached for the harness to lead his visitors, all ogling and agog, to his shed, or temple, in the bush.

'Extraordinary!' Augustus gasped on spotting the place, because it was so ordinary as to be otherwise.

'Oh!' Rosa moaned because, although warned, she had more than hoped. Stan said nothing. He'd seen sheds before.

Approached via a sandy path brittle with sticks (snapping and popping), the shed reared square from the coarse brown grass; a box made of tin, no less. So ordinary was it, so drab: a rectangular prism, twenty feet by thirty feet with a red-and-green door on the narrow end facing the approach. Without eaves or guttering, the roof pitched at thirty degrees, the whole — walls and roof, since that was the lot — clad in sullen silver with three hessian-hung holes (windows, were they?) measuring three feet by three feet along each of the longer sides. This was Da Silva's shed.

'A temple,' Rosa breathed, since she wanted it to be.

Stepping along the path, avoiding the sticks, Da Silva opened the door.

Inside was as ordinary.

A three-dimensional void, twenty by thirty feet with three hessian-hung holes of three feet by three feet along each of the longer sides and an unlined roof of corrugated iron, pitched at thirty degrees.

Inside was the same as out, except for the doves, perched on the rafters.

'Erk!' Augustus groaned, spotting their chalky dribble. 'There's rivers of it!'

Da Silva laughed.

'Will they come down?' Rosa wondered, straightening her hat.

'If I tell a story,' Da Silva said. 'Often they are my only audience.'

Augustus shot him a sly glance. 'What about that finch girl?' he wanted to know.

'Now there's a song for you,' Da Silva chortled. 'Where *is* Sylvie, and *what* is she?' silencing Augustus good and proper.

But not Stan, who was too silly to know. 'Yeah,' he said, looking. 'Where *is* she? And them finches you was talkin' about?'

Da Silva declined to play. 'Shall we have a story?' he asked. 'Who knows who will come?'

'Maybe even those ones in black that I seen beside the road?' Stan suggested, hopeful for a better look, but Da Silva ignored him.

'Over here,' he said, indicating a circle of sandstone blocks on the floor. 'Sit, and I will begin. Water anyone?' He held out a calabash, brimming.

When they had sipped, and were seated, he took the centre and began: 'Once upon a time ...'

Down came the doves, resplendent in white, to settle among them but Stan leapt to his feet. 'No!' he wailed. 'None of that "once upon a time" stuff! None of that kids stuff! I'm outta here.' From the door he cried, 'And I seen them doves afore. Come outta magicians' hats, they do. All trickery, hey! Well, they're not trickin' me. I'm gunna find that spring ...'

When he left, Da Silva began again.

Augustus and Rosa sat in that sandstone circle, transfixed. The sullen afternoon sun struck the silvery walls, the heat absorbed by the low-pitched roof until, almost swooning, Augustus looked up, easing his collar. There in the darkness beneath the tin above, he saw golden eyes staring. Possums, were they? And when he looked deeper, blinking, he saw others, not possums this time, but lizards — skinks, yes — and when he blinked again, he saw others; not possums, not lizards but there, lying flat upon the rafters, as one with the architecture — ants or termites or wasps — yes, mud wasps surely, listening.

The heat eased its heaviness upon him, and he dozed, drifting.

Augustus woke to the slamming of a door, shouting and a turmoil of doves. 'I can't find no silver spring,' Stan roared. 'I can't hear no finches. I can't see no motley girl.'

Da Silva hushed him, his finger to his lips. 'Stan, Stan,' he cooed. 'She hides, my Sylvie. She returns to the earth. To the fallen leaves. To the silvered web. Without her there is no sandstone spring. No finches. Shush now, hush, and I will look with you.'

'Yeah, well,' Stan blustered, 'it's too late now. The day's near over. The sun. See how low it is behind that hessian? Rosa, we gotta go. There's the horse. The cart. Unless you're payin' the extra?'

'No,' she said, standing and wiping her eyes. Had she slept too, had she dreamt, there in that temple of doves? 'We should go. I'm sorry, Da Silva. The heat, the story, the billing and cooing. How quickly time passes,' and she looked to Augustus, who blinked.

'Next time,' Da Silva cheered. 'Next week, shall we say?'

'Yes, please,' Augustus croaked, his voice hoarse, his throat dry. 'Yes, please, Rosa. Can we?'

'Of course we can,' she beamed, one consenting glance from Da Silva being enough. 'We might, if allowed — if invited, should I say? — even stay the night. Can we?'

'Of course you may, you might, you can, you will!' Da Silva laughed. 'I will make you a bed of leaves. A nest, if you prefer. And I will find my Sylvie. I'll call. I'll capture her, if I can, if I might, if I may — although I can't say I will, since she is not my own.'

'Then whose?' Augustus asked.

Da Silva stooped to hug him. 'Like yourself,' he said, 'she is a child of miracle. A child of finches, of stone, of the spring beneath. Who knows where she hides herself? Who knows where she springs from, if she springs at all? Some days, so many days, I see and hear nothing of her.'

The next time they hired the trap for the weekend. This was a special occasion, being Augustus's eighteenth birthday.

Da Silva greeted them with cake and sweet tea and later, after the candles were blown out, Augustus asked, being special, 'Can we go look for Sylvie?'

Da Silva smiled. 'Are you keen on her, eh?'

'Fascinated would be a better word,' Augustus replied, determined not to play childish games.

'Rosa?' Da Silva asked. 'Do you mind?'

'I won't come,' she said, fussing with the remnants of the cake. 'I'd rather stay here. I like the place.'

'I'll come!' Stan declared, jamming on his straw hat. 'I want to see that spring. And those motley finches.'

So they left, eager to find what they might.

Da Silva brought three doves that fluttered about his head and settled on his shoulders. The men walked up front, pushing aside branches, bending and releasing saplings, causing Augustus to sometimes lose sight of the doves.

The scrub reminded him of that patch of straggly gums down the back of Miss la Vie's: that place where Rosa hung the washing. The trees were thin and starved, like people in pain, their foliage grey, silver, as no doubt Rosa would claim, though they were not. Drab would be a better word. He looked at the ground. This was not soil beneath his feet but gritty sand. Remembering what Da Silva had said about the sandstone and the spring, he looked about, hopeful.

Now and then Da Silva called, 'Sylvie? Sylvie?' but though they walked for almost an hour, no answer came; neither voice nor finch.

'Tell me,' Augustus said when they took a breather. 'Where does she live? Really?'

'I have told you,' Da Silva replied.

'You said "without her there is no sandstone spring". Surely she lives by that spring?'

'Perhaps.'

'Then take us there.'

'You don't understand,' Da Silva sighed. 'I said, "Without her there is no sandstone spring", and that is what I meant. Exactly. Insofar as anything can be exact about Sylvie. I am saying that the spring appears when she does.'

'So where is this spring?' Augustus wanted to know.

'Anywhere, or not at all. It comes when she comes, it goes when she goes,' Da Silva artfully explained.

Stan caught Augustus's eye. Evidently he did not believe. 'This is all more a that "Once-upon-a-time" stuff,' he whinged. 'This is more of those magician's tricks, eh mate?' He gave Da Silva a wink. 'I don't reckon she's comin'.' And he turned for the shed.

'Why do you think I came to your house alone?' Da Silva asked. 'Why do you think she came so rarely?'

'Wonder she came at all,' Stan mumbled over his shoulder. 'Come on, Augie. I don't like these tricks.'

But Augustus lingered. 'Why didn't she come? Tell.'

'Because I couldn't find her. Because she comes and she goes. Like when she turned up, all those years ago. I am telling you the truth.'

So they searched all day, Augustus and Da Silva, but Stan, who could not believe, stretched out under the trap, his hat over his eyes.

On their next visit Stan set them down at the shed then returned to Helidon. He left the horse in a stable and took a room at the pub. Rosa stayed in while Da Silva and Augustus went out to look. Rosa shifted things in their absence; particularly the circle of sandstone blocks, which she stacked one upon the other at the far end of the shed, opposite the door.

That night, as they sat upon their leafy pallets, Da Silva perched atop this stony altar, resplendent with doves, to tell a story.

Incense was burned. Smoke ascended.

Bodhisattva of the Doves, Rosa thought (worshipping, was she?).

Later, in the dark, the silver girl appeared in the rafters.

Tricks, Augustus mused (dreaming, was he?). Just full of tricks.

Although he knew all about Little Donny's hookah, Augustus had never given much thought to the phenomenon of smoke. True, he had watched smoke; he had smelt smoke; he had even tasted smoke, in that breathing was tasting, but now, in the swirling dark, he turned his mind to the *ascension* of smoke. Smoke rose from that sandstone altar pure and perpendicular and having reached the roofing tin looped, over and under, between the rafters where those creatures lurked — those possums, those lizards, those wasps, possibly even that sylvan girl — attempting further ascension, but the tin prevented. The smoke, he saw, could go no further; and having done with its attempt, it dispersed.

So song ascends, Augustus thought. Yet may also be prevented. And a memory of the underside of his mother's piano came to mind, the ceiling of that keyboard, the canvas roof of the big top, the pressed metal ceiling of that caravan, the crimson confines of Miss La Vie's parlour — limitations all — and just when he had begun to despair, doubting that his song reached anyone, that anyone heard, that anyone appreciated, that anything happened, he called to mind those jacaranda blooms sweeping through that blood-red hallway, and those blue-green butterflies looping up and out; and how those pages fluttered, white, dove-like, clearing the clerestory, their poetry greening the dismal willows of the library, fleshing those stony hearts, and he felt better, thinking, If this shed is indeed a temple, it needs a tower or two, like those of the temple of Karnak; or a spire, like those cathedrals in France; or a steeple, like those little churches in New England, so my song might rise through and beyond that mundane tin, and having ascended that tower or spire or steeple might soar, out there, beyond the stars.

And in this hope he slept.

When next they visited, Stan again stayed at the pub. As usual, Rosa remained in the shed while Augustus and Da Silva looked for the girl, calling and calling. 'I must be careful not to damage my voice,' Augustus observed as they returned unfulfilled. 'And you too, Da Silva, being a storyteller.'

'I will,' Da Silva replied. 'But to tell the truth, there's little chance that she will answer. It's been a long time. I haven't seen her since she made that cage for you. How long ago was that?'

'I was seventeen,' Augustus replied. 'Now I'm eighteen, so I'd say it was six months.'

'She's been gone longer before,' Da Silva informed him. 'Once, for over a year.'

'What brought her back?'

'I don't know. Although she brought new finches with her.'

'New finches?'

'A different species. Firetails, they were. Not from around here. From way out west. In the heat. The desert. They like the seed of desert grasses.'

'How does she get there? How does she travel?'

'I have no idea. Whether she can't tell or won't, it's all the same. She just doesn't.'

'Do you worry about her?'

'I did. But no more. Although this time, with you here, and your interest …' He glanced down at Augustus, who refused to bite. 'That's different.'

'And there's Stan,' Augustus said, 'who doesn't believe. Wherever she is, she might sense that.'

'He's hardly here,' Da Silva pointed out.

Augustus thought about that. 'True,' he agreed. 'Besides, he's never seen her, so it can't be him that's putting her off.'

Da Silva frowned, wondering. He knew what Stan thought of him. 'Then again,' he said, cheering, 'nor has Rosa. But she believes.'

'She believes in *you*,' Augustus corrected. 'That's the difference.'

'Let's not look for reasons,' Da Silva countered. 'I never have before. Sylvie will appear. I know.'

So they fell silent, kicking up sand as they walked.

That night as they lolled on their leafy pallets sipping tea, Rosa said, 'Da Silva, when you first came to our cottage in Booval, how did you get there?'

He laughed. 'Matter of fact, I caught the train.'

'With your doves?'

'Yes …'

'And didn't she …?'

'Sylvie?' he suggested.

'Didn't Sylvie bring her finches?'

'She did. We sat in the guard's van, at the back. My doves nestle under my shirt when I travel. Sylvie keeps her finches caged. It's all right.'

'How do you know who wants these birds?'

'It's a feeling that I have. That Sylvie has too.'

'A feeling?'

'Some communication. Some *knowing*. Like, we knew what Augustus did in the library. When he set the books flying. Like doves. Like white doves, fluttering. When he sang poetry to life. We just knew. So we took him a gift …'

'And made me a cage,' Augustus added, for veracity.

They sat, sipping in silence, until Rosa said, 'So there's a railway station at Helidon?'

'There is.'

'And how long does it take to get to Booval?'

'About an hour.'

'So why have I been hiring a pony and trap?'

'I have no idea.'

'Hmmm,' she mused, making Augustus uncomfortable.

Later, while Da Silva slept, Rosa came to sit on the pallet beside Augustus. 'I can't sleep,' she groaned, stretching.

'Oh?' he said, only half caring.

'Could we talk?' she asked, lying down, her head on his pillow, waiting.

'Why?' he asked the dark, finally.

Satisfied that she had him, she said, 'You are aware, no doubt, of my feelings for Da Silva?'

'I'm aware that you have feelings for him,' Augustus replied. 'I have heard your whisperings, through the hessian, when you sit with him outside. But I have no understanding of their nature. Not exactly, since it isn't any of my business.'

'No one can ever know the exact nature of feelings,' she

said, turning to gaze into the rafters. 'They are experiences of considerable inexactitude.'

'I appreciate that,' he said, mainly to let her know that he was not entirely stupid, or worse, immature.

'But since I have known you most of your life, and you know me better than anyone,' she turned to him, there on the pillow, their faces inches apart, 'then I suppose I can confess to both awe, and lust.'

'Lust?' he spat. 'I thought the concept disgusted you.'

'It does. It did back there, at that house. That lust entrapped. Enslaved. But what I feel for Da Silva is lust in love, which is very different. Liberating, dare I say?'

'I'm glad to hear it,' Augustus muttered. 'Especially that you feel for Da Silva and not for me.'

'Very funny,' she chuckled. 'Although it is interesting, particularly since I never expected to feel anything for a man again. After what I went through at Miss la Vie's, you understand. And with that Barkus person.'

'They were purely business transactions, weren't they?' Augustus offered, rolling away in the hope that this intimacy would end.

'Well said!' she declared. 'You're smarter than I thought.'

For a midget, he might have added. For a dwarf. But considering he wanted her to leave, he did not. Instead, he said, 'Thank you.' The implication terminal.

'Da Silva's body is a wonder to me,' she sighed, not taking the hint.

One day, Augustus thought, a woman will say that to me. I know it. I am certain. When I am grown. When I have become. But he heard himself saying, 'So much for lust; what about awe?' And he was surprised to hear sobs.

'I shouldn't have said that,' she squirmed. 'I'm sorry. Love is so confusing. I talk rubbish sometimes.'

Seeing that she suffered he sank back, not asking for more. And so they lay, side by side, these two, as they had never done, until, with a sniff, she said, 'Augustus, I am sorry. I really came to tell you something else.'

'Oh?' he grunted, careless.

'I wanted to tell you that I have decided to live here. That I'm going to live with Da Silva. Now that I know I can catch the train and still work at the library, and still earn money, and come and go, I would like to do that. Would that be all right with you?'

He was taken by surprise. Surely this was not his Rosa. Surely this was not that girl he had once known, that great lump in that awful red dress, her hair all frizzed and carroty, who had bossed him about in the circus, who had dominated his life (or had she made it?) and doubting, he scrambled up to stand away.

'What about Stan? What will Stan do?' he demanded.

She propped herself up on one elbow, her hair wild, her cheeks teary. 'This has nothing to do with Stan,' she informed him. 'I'm not living my life for Stan. I'm not that monkey. I'm not that Hogarth.'

No, he thought, you're not. You're his murderer, which is a thing to be considered. 'I can't leave Stan,' he said. 'He would never leave me.'

She looked up, shocked. 'What? You'd choose him over me?'

'You left both of us for that librarian.'

'We already talked about that. That was business. You said so yourself.'

'Dirty business,' he said, surprising himself.

'But you did all right out of it, eh,' she snarled. 'Like you did all right out of Miss la Vie's. Out of me, all your life, I reckon.'

He looked down at her, wondering. 'So maybe it's time to end that life,' he said, his mouth taking on a life of its own. 'So maybe it's time we both sorted out who we preferred. Me with Stan and you with Da Silva. How about that? I mean it's not like we're getting a divorce. It's not like we're husband and wife.'

She gaped, astonished. 'When did you get so smart?' she demanded.

'Well, isn't that what you're implying? That we're some sort of pair?'

She sat, silent.

'Rosa?' he encouraged. 'Rosa?'

'Yes,' she yelled. 'And no!'

'What's that supposed to mean? Tell me.'

She rolled onto her back, breathing deeply, composing herself. 'Yes,' she said, 'I am in awe of Da Silva. I'm in awe of his presence. Not just his physical presence, but *who* he is. How he knows things. His intuition. And his stories, of course. His "Once upon a time ..." Ah! But no, I wasn't implying that you and I are some sort of couple, like married. That's horrible. But yes, I'm in awe of you too. There, I've said it. I'm in awe of you too.'

Augustus covered his mouth, stifling a laugh. 'Yeah, sure,' he chuckled. 'Especially my body. That's the horrible part, hey?'

She stood. She went to him. She put one hand on his shoulder and one under his chin, lifting his face to hers. 'I'm in awe of your spirit. How you always bounce back. How you never complain. I'm even in awe of how you think; at least the thoughts that you express, if that makes sense. But most of all I'm in awe of your voice. I always have been, since that very first time. Since we talked about Melba, back there in the circus, and you sang me that song about that ship, a trim white vessel as I remember, appearing on the horizon. I couldn't say so then, I was too stupid, too proud, I reckon, but I knew. I knew even then that I loved the spirit in your voice. And now, believe it or not, since I've seen, there's that episode in the library. The bloody miraculous …' She dropped to her knees to hug him to her. 'Augie,' she sighed. 'Augie, you could stay. You must. For my sake. Like our boy. Like our son. Stay. Please.'

Augustus arched away, fearful. What was this? What was happening? Had she no idea? He was eighteen years old. He was a man. Almost. Or becoming … Gripping her hair, he attempted to drag her up. 'No, Rosa,' he cried. 'Don't say things like that. Don't say things you never said before. You shouldn't talk like that. You really shouldn't.'

She hugged him tighter, weeping.

'Rosa,' he pleaded. 'Rosa …'

She rocked backwards, releasing him. 'I don't want to lose you,' she moaned. 'You've been with me all my life. But I don't want to lose him either. I never loved a man before. Not like that …'

'Rosa,' he said, 'I might be a dwarf, but I'm a man first. Or nearly. I'm not your *boy* and never was. And I'm certainly not your *son*.'

'I'm sorry,' she spluttered. 'Sorry. That slipped out. Sorry.'

'It's okay,' he assured her. 'It's okay. You're all worked up. We say stupid things. But what about Stan? Doesn't he deserve someone? Even a monkey, eh?'

She caught her breath when he said that, and looked up.

'I know about Hogie,' he said. 'I know.'

'You do?'

'I've known for ages. That Needly Phyllis told me. I saw her in Ipswich.'

'Does Stan?'

'Not unless you told him. I sure didn't. And I never will.'

'Stan doesn't like me,' she sniffed. 'He never has, ape or no ape. So it makes no difference, I reckon.'

He accepted that, but added, whispering almost, 'Yet he's been so close. So close. I can't leave him. I just can't.'

'I've been stupid,' she admitted. 'All my life. And selfish. But I never had anything. Never had anyone, except you and Stan. So I wanted to stay with you. Not Stan anymore, because he doesn't care; he doesn't like Da Silva much either. But you could stay with me. With Da Silva. The three of us. That's what I want. In this place. This temple ...'

'Get up,' he said. 'Come on, get up.' And when she did, sniffing and wiping her face, he led her to the pile of rocks that was her altar. 'This is a shed,' he said, indicating. 'A tin shed in the bush. And this is a pile of rocks. No altar, like you make out, with incense and doves, but a pile of rocks. Rocks, see? And I'm a dwarf. Okay? That's how it is and how it always will be unless, as you say, there's a miracle. Unless I can sing myself otherwise. Unless I can reconstruct myself through song.'

'I would have laughed once,' she said. 'I would have said that you were a loony. That you were nuts, but now I'm beginning to believe. And Da Silva would, I know.'

'When Rosa?' he demanded. 'When? I'm sure it has to be before my voice breaks, before I turn into a proper man in a boy's body. Like Little Donny. Before I lose my voice, you understand ...'

'You think that you will?' she asked, betraying a tremor of doubt. 'That you can?'

'Sometimes. Every time I sing, I think will be this be the time? Will the change come, and I worry. I worry ...' And suddenly conscious of his meanderings, he stopped. 'Now *I'm* sorry,' he said. 'That's enough. We've both been talking tommyrot. Here, let me make you a cuppa. All right?'

So, having got her up, he sat her down. And when she was settled he made the tea. And as she sipped there by that pile of rocks, he said, 'Rosa, I know that I should save my voice. I know that I should make every song count, and that I said I wouldn't but I will. After all these years, I will sing for you. I will. Because I know that you believe,' and planting his tiny feet, he sang:

O for the wings, for the wings of a dove,
Far away, far away would I rove.
Oh, for the wings, for the wings of a dove,
Far away, far away would I fly.

In the wilderness build me a nest,
And remain there forever at rest,
In the wilderness build me,

As Augustus sang, in the midnight heat, the rafters warped and cracked, the possums fled, the lizards, the wasps, and the roofing tin, once so limiting, rose up in sheets, pure and perpendicular, to form a tower, a spire, a steeple — a flute, was it? — directing his sweet breath, his glorious song, out there, beyond the stars.

'This is my home,' Rosa sighed, wondering. 'My spiritual home. My temple. Your song my incense, ascending.' So saying, she whooshed him to stand, ascendant, upon that sandstone altar.

And in the morning, when Augustus woke, his adult teeth were down.

THE NECROPOLIS

For most, the descent of adult teeth is not an event to lose sleep over; but when that descent is accompanied by — or possibly provoked by — the miraculous ascent of a tower, a spire or a steeple on the low-pitched roof of a galvanised shed in the bush, and the person whose teeth so descended is more than eighteen years of age, then it is little wonder that the said person should suffer a degree of nocturnal disturbance, if not downright sweaty insomnia, as did Augustus.

While some of this disturbance was attributable to his dreaming of the finch girl, the real cause of Augustus's distress lay deeper. Every morning when he woke, eyeing the jumble and crumple of pillows and sheets, it was not the extent of the washing or bed-making that distressed him but the possibility, drawing closer by the day, that the descent of his teeth might herald the end of his adolescence and the terrifying advent — not to be denied, if Little Donny had it right — of terminal adult dwarfism; the cessation of construction on that singing site, his body. And if anything else happens down there, he thought, furtively checking beneath the sheets, my Big Broad Man, my Captain in White, My Hope, My Future, is doomed.

Yet, when Augustus showered — all sweaty from his dreaming, his night-time fears and horrors — he cheered himself in this: Though my throat feels dry at times, even sore, my voice is not gone, not broken, not yet, so he might sing a bit of Melba or a bar or two of Caruso, to make sure.

It was under that shower, at the back of the cottage at Booval, that the possibility of another change occurred.

Perhaps more than a possibility.

An epiphany, even.

One morning, after another turgid night, having lathered himself all over, Augustus dropped the soap.

In itself, soap-dropping is not an unusual event, and given Augustus's proximity to the ground, would ordinarily be a matter of no consequence, but the design of this shower, which was extraordinary, contributed significantly to his illumination.

Set beneath a four-stumped tankstand draped all round with potato sacks, under a perforated kero tin suspended there, was a slab of concrete, the whole (stumps, sack, kero tin and slab) being called 'the shower', pre-eminently. And if the bar of Sunlight was dropped, as happened to Augustus that morning, it slithered, all greasy and gritty, across that slab, beneath those sacks, ending up in the surrounding garden to sink into that coal-black Boovalonian dirt, among the spotty-leaved caladiums there: the droopy khaki of the alocasia, the weedy coleus, all wan and wilting in the soapy damp.

So Augustus bent to retrieve, sliding his tiny hand beneath the dripping sacking, and as he did, he observed with a certain astonishment the peculiar colour of the concrete slab beneath him. Ordinarily, this was an unremarkable grey although, having a coal miner in the house, the slab was, at times (depending on Stan's shifts down pit), streaked black. But this morning, the slab was red, a curious sandy red, which reminded Augustus of something, somewhere, someplace, that he could not quite recall.

Forgetting the soap, he stood erect, turning around and around, looking down into the red-tinged water.

Who has been here? he wondered. This is not the colour of our black Boovalonan dirt, nor that of the pit. Who has showered here? And seeing Stan's stripy towel on the nail, he took it down to look. Sure enough, the towel was red, the colour on the slab, and he remembered then, in a flash, this was the colour of Helidon, the sandstone red from the bush, since he had walked that path so often.

That evening, as they sat together on the front steps, watching three black ants running the crazy path towards the gate, Augustus said, 'Stan, have you been out to Helidon?'

'That a trick question?' Stan muttered, not being adept at deceit.

Augustus observed the ants appearing and reappearing under and over the rocks in the path and said, 'Not with me and Rosa. I mean alone.'

'I dropped you and Rosa and took meself down the pub,' Stan said, in an attempt.

Augustus turned to look at him, putting all thoughts of those tricky black ants out of his head. 'Stan,' he said, 'I saw red sand in the shower. On the concrete slab. And your towel.

Unless I'm mistaken, you were the last one to use the shower before me. Last night, when you came home. Weren't you?'

Stan shrugged, wearying.

'Stan,' Augustus said, reaching out to take his hand, 'you have always told me the truth. I think ...'

'I have,' Stan said, smarting. 'You don't have to think. I have.'

'Well?' Augustus wondered.

Stan sat, tracking the dodging ants. 'I hired that horse,' he admitted, finally. 'I been out Helidon way a cuppla times. Lookin'...'

'For what?' Augustus wanted to know.

Stan shrugged.

'Not her? Not that silver girl? Not the one with the finches?'

Now Stan turned to him, looking down, frowning, which was rare. 'Me?' he asked, wide-eyed. 'Me lookin' for the finch girl? Why?'

'So why did you go?'

Stan looked for the ants. They were nowhere to be seen, those tricksters. 'To be near you, eh,' he grunted.

'But I'm here, Stan!' Augustus scoffed. 'I'm right here beside you.'

'Yeah?' Stan demanded. 'Fer how long?'

Augustus paled. 'Where would I go?' he whispered. 'Where else would I be?'

Stan stood, his arms wrapped about his chest, to walk down the path. He reached the gate, stopped, looked out, and turned back. He looked towards the steps, raising his eyes to Augustus, crouched there, miserable. 'You'd be out there,' he said, pointing. 'In that shed. With her. With Rosa, and him.'

Augustus hung his head.

'You think I'm stupid?' Stan demanded. 'You think I'm some idiot? You and your tricky friends. You and your silver sheds and incense. I know. I seen. Worse, I feel,' and he sighed, looking down, grinding his heel into the paving, crazy as it was. 'I left the mine, okay? I quit. I hired that horse. I been goin' out there, out Helidon, lookin' for work, for a place. Cause I know you're goin'. You and her. Movin' in with him. So I want me own place out there. Near you. Always. Okay?' And he turned to the gate, to stare over again, since he could not look back for tears.

'Stan,' Augustus called from the stairs, his voice low.

Stan refused, at first, then turned.

'Stan,' Augustus said, standing. 'You are right, but you are wrong. She did ask, yes. But I said no. I would rather be with you. I told her that.'

The man looked at him, shaking his head, overcome. He stumbled forward to fall to his knees. 'I got no-one,' he mumbled through his tears. 'I got no-one. Some mongrel took my Hogie, and I thought I lost you. I got no-one, see?'

'But you have,' Augustus assured. 'But you have. I said no, I promise.' And he gave Stan a kiss, because that was right.

When they had settled, wiped their faces, blown their noses and made some silly remarks about being so silly, then contradicted themselves, they sat.

'So what's she doin'?' Stan wanted to know. 'She is goin', ain't she?'

'So she told me, when she asked me.'

'Yeah? When?'

Augustus shrugged. 'I don't know. She never said.'

'You seen her packin'?'

'No.'

'Maybe he said no.'

'Maybe, but I doubt it. Not after the whispering and love talk I heard through the hessian at the shed.'

'Hmmm ...'

'And you?' Augustus asked. 'Did you really chuck your job down pit?'

'I did,' Stan nodded. 'I had enough, anyway. That dirt and them canaries. I want a job outside. In the wind, the sun, the rain even. I been in the dark too long.'

'And you've really been looking? Out Helidon way?'

'I told ya that.'

'And?'

'I seen some blokes on the land like. Some stone cutters too. That sandstone. But ...' he shrugged, 'I'm seein' a certain Father Brown on Wensdy.'

'*Farmer* Brown?'

'No, Father. Least that's what the ad said. Wants a labourer, he does.'

'Got land, has he?'

'Dunno. I'll have a look. I got the horse booked for the day.'

'And the trap,' Augustus chirped, 'since I'm coming too.'

So they laughed, and went in.

* * *

The horse trotted passed the Helidon pub and the colonial shops and the camphor laurels until Stan said, 'Call me stupid, but I reckon we missed that Father Brown's place. Here, have a look ...' He took off his straw hat and from inside produced a newspaper clipping. 'Read that,' he said, thrusting it at Augustus.

'"Labourer wanted",' Augustus read. '"Apply Father Brown, The Hedges, Helidon".' Hardly had he finished when he cried, 'There's the sign, Stan. Turn left!'

When Stan did, they knew they had arrived.

To their right, a six-foot privet hedge ran the length of the road, thick and impenetrable. The horse trotted alongside it for a good three-quarters of a mile until, abruptly, the green stopped and a wrought-iron gate (all gorgeously got up in ecclesiastical brass) made an appearance bearing a sign: 'The Hedges'.

Augustus slipped from the trap to push.

The gate yawned.

Before them burst a rejoicing of hollyhocks; of lavender and lupin, of pink and purple, of lattice and trellis and dovecote and fountain and somewhere a bird trilled — was it a nightingale? Surely no bush bird — and there, nestled snug as a teapot on a doily, a delightful stone cottage.

'The Hedges,' Augustus informed Stan, since it had to be.

So the front door, as blue as heaven, opened and a crooked man appeared, calling 'Hello. Hello. I am Father Brown,' extending his right hand to greet.

'Stan Platten,' Stan muttered, threatened. 'This here's me mate, Augustus.'

Father Brown was spindly all over, Augustus could tell, his stovepipe trousers being no disguise, but his eyes were bright (blue as his front door), and for all of his miserable body, he lacked no well-being. 'Come in,' he encouraged, 'do come in. I will make tea. Hello. Hello. Do come in.'

Stan hesitated, distrusting enthusiasm overly demonstrated. 'Aw,' he said, acting dopey. 'All right.'

But once in the parlour, he changed. Once in the parlour, amid the chintz, gawping, he beamed big and broad. 'This is the same as me mum's place,' he declared. 'Just like hers.'

'Really?' the Father wondered. 'How lovely. Really? Lovely.'

'Yairs,' Stan confirmed. 'Yairs. All second-hand, y'know. All of it. We had nothin'. Nothin'. All of it second-hand. But clean.'

'Lovely. Just lovely,' Father Brown nodded, boiling the kettle. 'Lovely and clean, I'm sure.'

'But all gone now,' Stan assured him, lapsing into a sudden melancholy. 'All gone, yairs ...'

'Oh dear,' the Father worried, pouring. 'All gone? All? A fire was there? A flood? Dear me. Oh dear ...' He wrapped his skinny fingers about the pot, mothering.

'Nope,' Stan declared. 'The booze, eh.'

'And this is your cottage?' Augustus asked, anxious to distract.

'Yes,' the Father replied, 'and no. It is the property of the church, you understand. It belongs to the church. I serve as vicar. In Helidon. Or did. Yes, the church. Milk for you both? And sugar? Hmmm?'

'Did?' Augustus asked. 'Surely you are ... Your title. Your collar?'

'Sit,' the Father invited. 'Please. Sit.'

They sat, the pot steaming, the crockery clinking, the cutlery clattering and Stan despondent.

But Augustus would have none of it. '*Did?*' he said. 'Surely …?'

'Ah,' the Father sighed, stirring. 'This place is too much for me. And since I've lost Patrick …'

'Patrick?' Augustus asked, sipping.

'My helper. My man. Patrick. Gone. Passed on. So I must too. I am off to see the Holy Father. In Rome. Personally, you understand. If the church allows. Or asks. This has become too much. So I advertised. The church will pay. Indeed. The church will pay.'

'You have lost your helper?'

'Patrick. Yes. So I will go. But the cottage will be free. If you want it, Mr Platting …'

'Platten,' Augustus corrected.

The Father hurried on. 'If you want the job, I mean. And the cottage. And you, young man. You too? Do you?'

Stan said nothing, but Augustus gaped. This cottage? This garden? This paradise? 'All this?' he said. 'We could have all of this?'

'Not have,' the Father corrected, 'since it is the church's. But to live in. To maintain. To labour. Yes …'

Which is when Augustus saw the piano (his mother's, was it?). An ancient upright, open, revealing sheet music scattered on the yellowing keyboard, and turning he said, 'Do you play, Father?'

'No, no,' the Father chuckled. 'Miss Bloomfield does, you understand.'

'Who is Miss Bloomfield?'

'Oh, Miss Bloomfield cleans the house. Miss Bloomfield cooks. Miss Bloomfield washes. Miss Bloomfield *does,* you understand.'

'Ah,' Augustus paused beside the piano, his fingers straying over the keys. 'You are saying that Miss Bloomfield is the housekeeper?'

'Yes. The housekeeper.'

'Does she live here?'

'Oh no. Miss Bloomfield lives in Helidon. In the town. By the stables.'

'But you pay her to look after this cottage?'

'No. The church pays Miss Bloomfield to look after the place.'

'And she comes in daily to cook for you?'

'No, no. You misunderstand. No. No. I don't live here. I live in the vicarage. In the glebe. In the grounds of the church. In the town. Behind the laurels. The glebe. You must have missed it. Patrick Bloomfield lived here. Miss Bloomfield's brother. He was my worker. But he is gone. Passed on. Out there, you see?' and he swung a spidery hand in the direction of the back garden, glimpsed beyond the windows.

'Out there?' Stan asked, waking as from a sleep.

'Behind the hedge,' the Father declared. 'The Hedges is private, you know. For the faithful only. Consecrated ground, you understand. I do hope that you will respect that if you labour here, Mr Plodding.'

'Platten,' Augustus corrected.

The Father ignored him. 'If you dig, so to speak,' and he opened the kitchen door to reveal the back garden — the lavender and lupin, the pink and purple — and the cemetery beyond.

'Would you?' Augustus asked as they trotted by the Helidon pub and the colonial shops and the laurels and the vicarage. 'Would you be a gravedigger?'

'It's a good job,' Stan conceded. 'With the house and the housekeeper, and it's workin' outside, and that garden. Never had a garden. Never grew a flower. Nice, eh? And you can stay; there's a bedroom for you, the Father said. So there's you. Yeah, when a bloke thinks about it, it's a real good job.'

'But once Rosa goes, we could stay where we are at Booval,' Augustus suggested. 'We don't have to live at Helidon. We could stay at Booval.'

Stan reined the horse in. 'No,' he said, determined. 'I ain't goin' down pit agin. Not ever. I ain't gunna die down there, all black and bloody like that Blue Butterfly's man. This gravedigger job will be good, I reckon.'

In the days (or weeks or months) that followed, Rosa left to be with Da Silva, so Stan bought the horse and trap, naming the animal 'Useful' because it was, and having loaded the little that they owned, he and Augustus set out.

Miss Bloomfield was at the sky-blue door when they arrived. 'Tea?' she called. 'I've just put it on.'

'Yes, please,' Augustus replied, and leaving Stan to unload (being next to useless himself), he went inside to perch on a floral chair, ready to chat; but first, to look, since Miss Bloomfield appeared interesting.

She was gaunt, Miss Bloomfield, her body a breadstick, her limbs pretzels, though why he configured her in pastry, he could not imagine, considering her lack of bulk. Is it the graveyard? Augustus wondered, recalling the Father being the same. She is a pretzel, yes, that could snap … Is it the proximity of the dead that makes them so thin? So he watched, wondering.

'And what is your name?' she enquired, pouring.

'My name is Augustus Trump,' he replied.

'And how old are you, Augustus?'

'I am eighteen, going on nineteen. Although sometimes I forget. My life has been so strange.' And he steeled himself for the inevitable.

'You are small for nineteen,' she said, on cue.

Having expected this, he answered fully. 'But I will grow. Through song. The perfection of which will reconstruct me. My attainment of the sublime. Then I will become a tall man. A broad man. A normal man. Of that I am certain. Or hope …' Having said a mouthful, he stared into his tea, which was served.

'Well, well,' she sighed, perching on the chair opposite, her teacup precarious on those pointy knees. 'Just goes to show, doesn't it? My brother, Patrick, rest his soul, didn't grow either. Much like yourself, at first, I imagine. Tiny he was, although maybe a *bit* taller, even considerable, now I look at you …' Augustus took this as fair comment, considering his sustained observations of herself. 'But Mother put him on to liquorice. Thick as razor strops. And black! Black! And he grew. Like mad. Shot straight up. Must have been six foot at your age. A veritable beanstalk, I'd say. He did all right too. Being a gravedigger and all. For the parish. Rest his soul. For the Father …'

'Interesting,' Augustus responded, sotto-voiced. Yet he was struck by her allusion to vegetables; beans being appropriate, no doubt, but celery also, and other stalky stuff. Yes, he thought, she is right. The vegetable is more suited to her physical construction than any reference to bread; dough, especially, and drawing himself back into the conversation he said, 'Remarkable, even. But speaking of the Father, he mentioned that you play. *Do* you play the pianoforte, Miss Bloomfield?'

'Indeed I do,' she chortled. 'All the old favourites,' and having placed her teacup on the occasional table beside her, casually, even graciously, she held out her hands.

'Oh!' he gasped. 'Oh!'

Her fingers conjured images of a label he had seen years ago on a skinny tin down the back of the grocer's at Goodna. Strange, he thought, how that memory remained, and he recalled the stalks of yellow asparagus pictured there. Was there such a thing as yellow asparagus, or was it just that ancient label, fading? But now, as he stared, he noted that her fingers were not yellow, and certainly not asparagus, but ivory, and a dreadful fear came over him. These were the fingers of a pianist, not his mother's exactly, but fearfully similar, itching to play, and he sank back, anticipating. 'I'm sorry,' he mumbled. 'I didn't mean ... It's just that ... I thought ... if you were to play, then I might sing — I *would* sing, I know — and if I sang, I wonder, am I ready?'

'Ready?' she asked. 'For what?'

'To grow,' he muttered. 'Ah! Here is Stan, with my things ...' And he leapt up, grateful.

* * *

That evening, when Miss Bloomfield had left for the day and Stan unpacked, Augustus sat on his bed, alone.

What is happening to me? he wondered. Why have I so constructed her? Why vegetables, I wonder. How mad is that? And how can I bear her, every day, with those long thin fingers, itching to play? And if she does, which she will, and I sing, then the change will come, the reconstruction of myself. And what if I'm not ready? What if I give too much and sing myself hoarse and fail to grow. Because she will play, I know that she will, as my mother did, and I will sing. I will sing myself stupid, and the sublime, who knows? What if I sing myself out? What if I break my voice? Oh dear. Oh dear. Stan or no Stan, I should have gone with Rosa. Oh dear ...

So he sighed and fretted, yet placing his palm against the wall to steady himself, a certain security came over him, a certain solidarity, a certain sense of safety. He turned to look. This house is built of stone, he realised. I had not thought. And he touched again, moving his palm, sensing, caressing. I have never lived in a stone house. Even that big white house, my mother's house, was timber. And Miss la Vie's ... He raised his other hand, to place it beside the first, moving them freely, savouring the strength. And catching himself smiling, he leaned forward to press his pale forehead against the stone, then his mouth, and soon he kissed, his lips brushing, and drew back to see. 'Sandstone,' he whispered. 'I am certain. Perhaps I should stay, since she comes from sandstone, with her spring, with her finches ...' So he sank onto the pillow to sleep.

When he woke, and bathed, he walked in the garden relieved, having no desire for Melba or Caruso, not so much as a bar, vowing that he would be wary of Miss Bloomfield and her ivory hands.

In the days that followed, the weeks, the months (or was it a year?), Augustus fell silent, choosing to wander in the cemetery with Stan. He rarely saw Miss Bloomfield, nor did he choose to sit, sipping tea, which was her favourite pastime, and soon she slipped from his mind, if not his memory, entirely.

Being outside with Stan, he came to love the sandy red of the slab, of the headstone cast down, of the cenotaph fallen, sometimes even the columns, because they toppled too, in storms, washouts and frost, cracking sharp in winter; the sandstone so brittle.

He especially liked walking among the graven images of angels and cherubs, of saints and sinners, of sheep and lambs and dogs and birds and flowers and columns and crosses (Christian, crooked, leaning, wreathed); and the sculptures that dotted this deathly landscape that had once been something, but were no more, being eroded, chipped, amputated or otherwise vandalised.

All of sandstone they were. And sometimes — not often — should Stan look away, or disappear into a pit, digging, six feet down, Augustus might stoop to feel that stone upon his lips, bending to kiss, and he began to wonder, Why am I doing this? What is it about this sandstone that attracts me?

Though Augustus denied that it might be Sylvie, the finch girl — born of the sandstone spring — who caused him to pine, he could not stop thinking of her. These thoughts were worst when Rosa and Da Silva visited, which they often did, but every time he saw them — especially Da Silva with his silvery hair — he was reminded of her and, try as he might, he could not put her from his mind, wondering what might have been. Had he not been made like this, had he been built like any other man, might she come back? To him, for him? But to hive up such feelings was ridiculous, he being a dwarf and she being so lovely, and he closed them down, thinking of other things.

There was a lamb that he particularly liked. A little sandstone lamb, its feet tucked under, its head raised, its eyes staring heavenwards, and the lines, graven beneath,

Roger Owens.

3 years.

Lent to us for a while.

As he passed, Augustus might stroke the lamb's nose, since it was low and Roger was little too, he knew.

A truncated column also appealed to him, and he stopped every time he passed. This column stood on a rectangular plinth, perhaps three feet high, so it was harder to inspect, let alone touch, but if Stan had taken a bucket, Augustus would upturn it and standing on tiptoe, take a better look, even touch. He liked this column because it had a photograph set into the plinth, under glass, although the glass was cracked and the image beneath ruined. This was a war grave, though not really, since it said that the boy whose life it celebrated had died 'over there', and Stan said there was no chance his body would have been brought back. 'Buried over there, he'd be,' Stan said. 'Under the mud, I reckon, like the rest of 'em. Just kids, eh. Kids ...' and he would leave Augustus to wonder and stroke the stony wreath. I bet he was tall, Augustus thought. Gangly, like Stan. Which set him wondering, Why didn't Stan go; though he never dared ask.

Outside the back gate of The Hedges stood the Mancini family mausoleum, a massive block of sandstone ('Not like the Ities; they like their marble,' Stan said), its sides measuring thirty feet. The interior of this stone was accessed by tunnel-like transepts, cut midway along the length of each of the four sides, and intersecting in the centre. Access to these transepts was not sealed, allowing Augustus to walk in, fingertips brushing, savouring the stone. There are no ghosts here, no phantoms, he mused, stroking the rock as he wandered. The stone is too solid.

There was provision for twelve bodies inside, each allocated a rectangular niche, opening off a transept. Once filled, these niches were sealed in perpetuity, no name being carved on the sealing stone, only that one Mancini, outside. So they are no more individuals, Augustus thought. The stone encompasses all ...

One niche remained empty.

Approaching this unfilled space one solitary day, Augustus upturned his bucket and clambered in. 'Ach!' he grunted, wriggling, headfirst. 'This isn't right. But I can't turn myself around in midair, and Stan would never lift me up,' so he crawled on his stomach, his head facing the blind wall at the rear. Once in, he lay still as a corpse, pretending. But his was a sentient body. I need to move. I need to see, to touch, to taste, to smell, to hear ... So he focused on the dark, the dark at the end, and presently, as in a dream, he saw shapes: the swirls and sediments within the stone, and after, Dust motes, or planets, are they? he wondered, moving one about the other, as stars in the Milky Way, and he sighed, watching. If this is death, he thought, it is alive, then he laughed, since he knew that he was not dead, but pretending, so he drew his arm up, freeing his hand, and touched. The surface of the stone was colder inside the tomb, rougher too, less well finished, less well dressed. Intended for the dead, who wouldn't know, he thought. As for taste, he licked, he kissed the stone, as he had done before (in his bedroom, and elsewhere, secret), but now, being private — private as the dead — he gave this more thought. Do I taste salt? he wondered. Was this stone once the bed of a mighty sea? Or is there salt spread, in readiness for the body to come? To preserve, possibly? For salt he tasted, he knew. As for smell, he pressed his nose flat, and sniffed. At first there was nothing other than cold. Cold is not a smell, but a feeling, he thought, and he was about to lift his head, chastising himself for expecting too much; for expecting to alert all his senses in this dead place, then reconsidered. But I can smell the cold, I can, and it isn't a smell, not really, but then again it is. It is the smell of this cold, inanimate stone. And he sighed, eager to hear, to know if there was sound there, but what he heard came from outside, the sighs and whispers of the sunlight; the life out there. Those are borrowed sounds, he thought, borrowed from life. In here there is no sound, other than myself breathing, which does not count. He worried then about the silence when he cast off his sweet voice, his song, his poetry; when he cast off this dwarfish body to become a man. A tall man. A broad man. A normal man. A man who might not sing — which was possible, wasn't it? A real man yes, but silent as this stone.

And he wriggled out to stand in the sunshine, afraid.

The circumstances of a day at The Hedges might be called routine; then again, they might not, unless death is routine, which it is.

In the circumstance of a death, the hearse would arrive at those wrought-iron gates (ecclesiastical, in bronze), and Augustus, in order to make himself useful, would open them. Miss Bloomfield had made him a smart black suit, a smart black tie and a smart black hat that he wore each morning except Sunday, when no-one was buried. But when the hearse arrived, drawn by a fine pair of greys festooned in black ostrich, and the dread-black entourage, on foot, following behind, he was always there, the pretty dwarf, all done up in his mourning suit, to let them in.

'Follow me,' he would say, tucking his hat under his arm much as he had done in the mess tent at the circus, all those years ago, and he would lead the entourage, horses snuffling and blowing, heads bent, mourners shuffling, tears streaking, noses blowing, along the raked gravel path around the stone cottage to the rear garden, where he would throw open the back gate (not near as grand as the front), to allow entry to the cemetery itself.

Once they were in, Augustus would direct them to the pit that Stan had dug the day before, because afternoons were cooler, generally, and the pile of red dirt heaped there, then stand away and Father Brown would take over (since the Holy Father had not called him away, as he had so desired). He would say what he had to say, tell the lies, the platitudes or the truth, sometimes, though rarely, because either he didn't know it or couldn't tell it, or wouldn't, above the weeping, until it was over, and the coffin lowered, and one ceremonial silver shovel of dirt cast down. Then everyone would leave except Augustus, and Stan of course, who had lurked behind a headstone or a tree stump, or otherwise rendered himself invisible until it was his time. Then he would fill the pit while Augustus watched, perched on a headstone, a stray rock or a pile of dirt, keeping company.

There might be days when it rained or blew, which was not routine, and the mourners grumbled rather then wept, or froze, swore or once or twice fought, since here were feuds, this being the scrub. Sometimes there were dead children and sometimes those who died before their time, the good, often; like Doctor Forster, who was kind, and Mrs Armitage, who gave up her home when there was a fire, out there in the scrub, and the lot that she gave it to disrespected her and abused her place something savage ('Because they was savages themselves,' Stan said). Once or twice they saw Rosa and her Da Silva because they knew people who had died, though they were of no set faith themselves, especially not Catholics. That went all right, because there was no bad blood between Rosa and Stan and Da Silva, just distance, which was probably best, considering. It is obvious they are in love, Augustus thought, the way they stand so close and whisper.

And sometimes Da Silva's doves came in, even out there in the graveyard, landing on them both, Da Silva's head and Rosa's slender shoulders, nor were they shooed away. Because they had become the stuff of story themselves, that pair, dressed all in motley as they were, his hair silver as the celestial moon, hers all fierce and bold in fiery gold. To rival the sun, Augustus wondered, in ever living glory, as another poet had said, and as story should be.

Ever living. Ever giving. Ever new.

Some days were just strange, such as was the day of the staring man.

A poet, was he?

Augustus had gone out to the big gate, as he did, and the hearse came through, and the mourners, straggling, but one man stood out, stepping from the mob to stare at Augustus, and stare and stare, right through the graveside service and the shovelling with the single shovel (and the deceased a woman too, as Augustus knew, having listened to the Father for once; an older woman at that, perhaps even the starer's mother). Yet still he stared. He was a well-presented man. All done up in a three-piece suit in worsted, with a waistcoat and a fob in gold and a smart hat and very fine tan leather boots (not country wear, but city styled, clean and polished) and under his arm a book, bound in red leather, so he might have been a teacher or a poet. Whatever he was, when the crowd left, he remained to stare, even when Augustus and Stan were the only ones left and the pit needed to be covered, since there was rain coming in. He kept it up, the starer, so Augustus went over and said, 'Sir, have I offended you in some way? Did I do something wrong, back there at the gate?'

The man sighed and looked down, then looking up, he said, 'My name is Oliver Dogson. I owe you my sight.'

'I beg your pardon?' Augustus replied, since the situation was formal. 'You mistake me for somebody else. We have never met, I am certain.'

'No, we have not,' the gentleman agreed. 'But that does not alter the truth of my statement. You were dressed, I remember, in a toga, and stood upon a silver chariot drawn by a zebra. And you sang 'Rule Britannia' to the uproar of a calliope. There was an elephant too, draped in marigolds. All this in a circus tent, the canvas firmament patched blue above.'

Augustus stood still. 'The big top,' he breathed.

'That song gave me my sight,' he said. 'Your voice gave me my poetry, my life …'

That night, alone in his room, Augustus could not sleep. That night his finger traced the grain of his life, embedded in the pale sandstone there, beside his bed. It is coming, he thought. My time is coming. My end, my beginning, I know.

Then there was the day of the silken crows. The afternoon was hot, the sun a ball of fire, the red earth baking.

'I should go in,' Augustus called to Stan, who dug. 'I am too fair for this heat. The sun.'

So he left.

In the stone house, in the parlour, he found Miss Bloomfield, whom he rarely saw. She left their meals, true, she washed their clothes (and ironed them, which was unnecessary), and she swept.

'Oh!' she exclaimed, seeing him enter through the back door. 'Augustus! What a nice surprise,' but she made no attempt to get up, having a rectangular embroidery frame before her, and silken thread trailing.

'Hello, Miss Bloomfield,' he muttered, and not wanting to engage, he headed directly for the water jug in the kitchen. 'I didn't expect you. I have come in out of the heat. I'll go to my room and lie down. I'm feeling faint. I won't disturb you.'

'You won't disturb me,' she declared, as he knew she would. 'I can't get up. Not with all of this, you see ...' She waved a long, lean hand in the air. 'I have just put on some scones, and need to sit for half an hour, while they rise.'

'I'll get a glass of water and be off,' he said, hurrying.

'Look,' she said (or *ordered*, did she?). 'See what I am doing.'

He poured the water first and sipped, then warning, declared, 'Just for a minute. I am faint. Woozy, even ...' But he went and stood behind her.

So he saw the work on the frame: a length of stretched white linen, and on that, within that, embroidered in silk, a view of the cemetery: The Hedges no doubt, the sandstone cottage, the hollyhocks, the lupins and the great ecclesiastical gate in bronze. But beyond (or should he say 'without'?), peering through, their hands clutching the iron, stood three people (women, were they?), all dressed in black.

'What are they?' Augustus asked, shaken.

'Ah,' she sighed, 'visitants. Mourners who stop by occasionally. Heralds, you might say. It is strange, I must say: they come before the date of the funeral has even been announced.'

'What?' he asked, dry-mouthed and groggy.

'Especially before an auspicious death. Like before that Dr Forster passed away, who was kind, and Mrs Armitage, who gave up her home, and my Patrick, of course, who was a saint. But they don't come in. They wait at the gate, shoving sometimes, as if they want to, but if I went out, they would leave. Pffft … Like a zephyr. A breath …'

'Excuse me,' Augustus muttered, 'I must lie down. My head …' So he went to his room, sipping his water, giddy as he was.

Later, when he heard the oven open and smelled the scones come out, then heard the front door click, he went into the parlour. The scones were on a tray in the kitchen, covered with a tea towel, and all was in order, but the embroidery was gone, that vision of those three dressed in black.

My old friends, he thought. Warning me of something. But what?

Confused — since they were strange days; strange messengers — he went out to sit with Stan in the cemetery, because he, at least, made sense.

As he sat on a slab, dreaming, drifting, he began to hum, the tune carrying over the red dirt, over the pit in which Stan laboured. The gravedigger lifted his head and, from that hole six feet down, shouted, 'What's that you're humming? What's that called? Its name?'

'*Plaisir d'amour*, the joy of love …'

Stan laughed. 'Nice,' he said, 'but silly, hey, that joy of love. It's gone in a minute, I reckon. Hogie, you remember? Just a few years, and he was gone. My boy …'

'Ah, Hogie,' Augustus sighed. 'And his suit, you remember, the one that Needly made?'

'What?' Stan yelled from the pit.

'That Hogie suit I wore,' Augustus called, leaning into the

abyss. 'You know, back then. You ever think it's the same as the one that I wear now? The one Miss Bloomfield made? The black one I wear to lead the mourners?'

'Yeah,' Stan called, 'I do. But you ain't Hogie, eh? He's gone. He's dead, mate.'

'Dead,' Augustus sighed, woozy again, and three crows flew over, crying, 'Caw! Caw!', leaving Hogie to loom large in Augie's heart.

Those were strange days, before the end.

Stan was serious about Augustus's twenty-first birthday celebrations. Or what they said was his twenty-first birthday, since no-one knew for sure. Augustus himself considered the day to be the last of boyhood, the first of manhood — a death, a birth — a proper rite of passage.

'While I want to celebrate,' Stan said, 'I'm not real keen on parties. I only want a cuppla people over. Who do you reckon?'

Sitting atop a pile of red dirt, graveside, Augustus cringed. Nobody, would have been his answer. I want nobody because there's nothing to celebrate. But knowing he couldn't admit to that, he said, 'Well ... Rosa and Da Silva, I guess. And ...' he shook his head, defeated. 'Nobody else. We haven't exactly kept up with people, have we? Besides, there's a few from back then that I really wouldn't want to see again. So, just Rosa and Da Silva. Okay?'

'And the finch girl?' Stan asked from the pit.

'Ha!' Augustus scoffed. 'Ha, ha! So you know where she is, do you?'

'By that sandstone spring, wherever that is,' came the reply. 'You reckon you could find her?'

I would like to, Augustus thought, I would like to very much, if I make it. If I become ... though he said nothing.

When the evening came, Stan gave Augustus a present: a dear little walnut cane with a silver handle in the shape of a dove, so Augustus did himself up in his suit, looking very smart, though he did not wear the hat, which would have been ostentatious, and Rosa and Da Silva arrived, decked out in silver and white, and Father Brown and Miss Bloomfield, because 'They had to be asked,' Stan said, 'To be civil.'

Augustus wasn't so pleased, feeling threatened: those hands, that piano, that repertoire of old favourites, as yet unheard. Worse, unsung.

But if the truth were told, Miss Bloomfield was an asset, since she could cook, and the Father proved a bonus too, being adept at organising parlour games: charades, forfeits, blind man's bluff and Chinese whispers, all of which Augustus enjoyed, since they were diversions. As midnight approached Miss Bloomfield produced a jelly and custard trifle while the priest discovered a bottle of sherry (very dusty, very old), and when they had partaken — Augustus included, though not Stan, who declined — Rosa suggested a song.

For Augustus, any attempt at good cheer was lost.

'Give me a minute,' he said. 'It's been a big night,' and leaving them to the sherry, he slipped away to his room.

What will become of me? he wondered, perching on his bed. What will happen if this is the last? If I open my mouth and a croak comes out? Like a crow's call? Like the death of poetry? Or nothing? What is nothing comes? Ah ...

He reached out to touch the wall, the reassuring sandstone, fearful. Will I be like Little Donny, a man in a boy's body? Or will I wheeze and choke and finally admit that I am a freak and be done with it, like some cartoon character in a Hollywood movie? Or will my voice break, leaving me forever as I am: a boy in a boy's body, though mute; useless — worse, loveless — and incapable of being loved. So he struck the stone, crying, 'Now is my end, or my beginning...' Upon which Rosa came barging in, demanding, and he went out.

'Augustus is ready,' she declared, as of old. 'Miss Bloomfield has agreed to play. Right, Miss B?'

'Indeed,' the woman nodded. 'All the old favourites.'

Augustus stood in the parlour doorway, trembling. This is it, he thought. I am come of age. I am knackered, am I? Or becoming?

Yet as he raised his head, and planted his feet in readiness, there behind the chintz lounge he saw Stan, hunched and miserable, his roustabout eyes downcast (was he sobbing?), and Augustus paused, suddenly aware that this was Hogie's night, not his; that though Stan loved him, would give his life for him, and sure as hell had chosen to live with him, Augustus knew he was thinking of Hogie, pining for him, who should have been here, all suited out as he never had been in life.

So when Rosa gripped Augustus from behind to unceremoniously whoosh him onto the very lid of the piano, he declared, 'Stan, this is for you. This is for Hogie.' Glancing down into that shadowy space between the keyboard and the floor, he planted his feet, lifted his pretty chin and sang:

Just a-wearyin' for you,
All the time a-feelin' blue,
Wishin' for you, wond'rin' when
You'll be comin' home again.
Restless, don't know what to do,
Just a-wearyin' for you …

And as he sang (his voice sublime), he called upon Sylvie, the finch girl, wherever she was, to come weaving there, to come dancing, and a cage grew, a dome of supple willow, rising up in that parlour, covering that chintz, the piano even, and within, chattering, leaping and laughing, a chimp: Hogie come back, come home — that first love, returned — and Stan Platten, grinning like an ape himself, stood upright to applaud.

THE SANDSTONE
SPRING

WHEN THE GUESTS HAD left and Stan romped unbridled with his love come home, Augustus walked in the moonlight, hoping, if he could, to greet the dawn. 'This will be the first day of my adult life,' he declared to the scattered tombs. 'I would make myself a man, a normal man, my future constructed in the architecture of song ...'

There was a willow in the graveyard, down by a dribbly creek (a spring, was it? Beneath the sandstone?) where he stopped to think.

'Here,' he decided. 'Now,' and readying himself, he sang.

So Augustus Trump became tall, broad, clad white by moonlight.

Yet as he turned, admiring, he glimpsed the full extent of the cemetery, that liminal space between heaven and hell, and realised for the first time how many poets had come into his life — Stan in his love, Miss la Vie in her agony, Barkus with his Belle Dame, Da Silva with his stories; even Rosa, finally, even Rosa, that blooming spirit — and how many would pass? How many — mortals all — would sleep, mute, in some shadowy vault?

Planting his feet, Augustus raised his eyes to the fading stars, crying, 'I was mistaken! I should have remained a child

— a dwarf even — since now I am reconstructed, now I am made tall, I see, and seeing, know …

So he waited, silent (his poetry, his song), until dawn and the promise of finches, there by that sandstone spring.